"It was an addicting journey th[at had me guessing where] my next clue would come from and [when in time] would I get it. A classic whodunit t[hriller.]" **Rowland, Voice of the Sooners**

"*The Day She Died* is a mind-bending, page-turning mystery that showcases Bill Garrison's ability to weave a complex plot line into an unforgettable story. Highly recommended!"-- **Rene Gutteridge, best-selling author** of *Misery Loves Company*

"Writing a mystery requires skill. Telling a tale of time-travel is rank with pitfalls. Throwing in twists of plot can confound the reader. However, Bill Garrison in *The Day She Died* delivers an interesting and well-paced story with all these elements. Not only is the reader captivated by characters, the reader is right with them, not only on the same page, but also at the right time. A fascinating book that will delight lovers of mystery and fantasy." --**Donita K. Paul, best-selling author** of *Dragon Keeper Chronicles* and *The Realm Walkers*.

"Bill Garrison paints a believable, easily followed story line that will immerse even the most seasoned of mystery readers and time travel enthusiasts, to surprise and delight right up to the end." -- **D. Donovan, eBook Reviewer, Midwest Book Review**

"Very early in my reading I found myself saying, 'This book was written just for me!' An entertaining mystery that taps into the fantasy of what it could be like to go back and redo parts of life." --**Jason Gunter, Ph.D.** licensed psychologist

"In the mood for a time-travel mystery? Then this is the book for you. ... Debut author Bill Garrison pens an intriguing story of mystery, love, and danger." – **Michelle Griep, author** of *Brentwood's Ward* and *A Heart Deceived*.

"*The Day She Died* is an exciting, fast-paced read! It's part time travel and part mystery with a little romance thrown in. I literally didn't want to put the book down. All I can say is, you won't be disappointed!" -- **Terri Weldon, author** of *Mistletoe Magic*

For Mandy, Parker, Reagan, and Tucker.
I wouldn't change a thing.

For financial support for this project, I would also like to
thank RC and Joyce Salmons.

THE DAY SHE DIED

A NOVEL

BILL GARRISON

I hope you enjoy! God Bless,

Castle Gate Press

The Day She Died by Bill Garrison
Published by Castle Gate Press
244 E Glendale Rd
Saint Louis, Missouri 63119
www.CastleGatePress.com

Copyright © 2014 by Bill Garrison
All rights reserved

This book or parts thereof may not be reproduced in any form, stored in a retrieval system, or transmitted in any form by any means—electronic, mechanical, photocopy, recording, or otherwise—without prior written permission of the publisher, except as provided by United States of America copyright law.

This is a work of fiction. Any similarity to actual people, organizations, and/or events is purely coincidental.

Cover Designer: Jeff Gerke

Library of Congress Cataloging-in-Publication Data
An application to register this book for cataloging has been filed with the Library of Congress.

ISBN 978-0-9904399-0-5
ISBN 978-0-9904399-1-2 (electronic)

Library of Congress Control Number: 2014942009

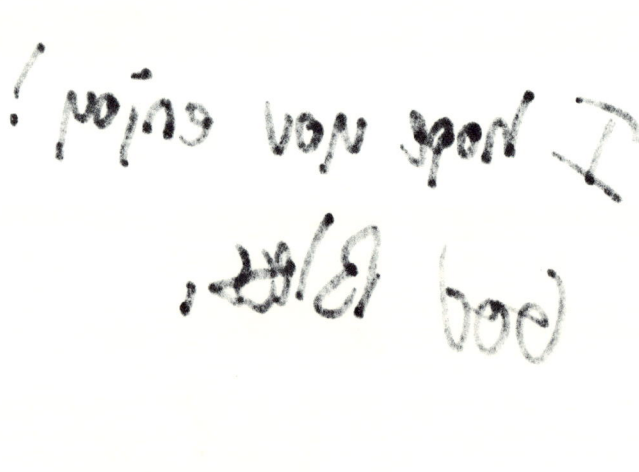

Part One

Chapter 1

Darkness pulled at John Michaels. It weighed him down like an anchor. Tendrils of memories and light penetrated his subconscious and lifted him toward the noise hammering against his mind.

Buzz, buzz, buzz, followed by heavy silence, not the usual "Dora the Explorer" from the living room television.

Would today be any better, or would Renee still not look him in the eyes?

The musty smell of dirty laundry wafted to his nose. Twisted covers. Brightness.

Brightness! Why hadn't Renee or the kids awakened him?

He threw the covers aside and swung his feet to the floor. He sat at the edge of the bed and looked around in stunned silence.

Heart pounding, he tried to make sense of the sight before him. This had to be a dream. But dreams were never this real, the smells never this strong, the colors never this bright. He squeezed his eyes shut, but he knew nothing would change. This was real.

Buzz, buzz, buzz.

He shut off the alarm.

He sat on a twin bed in a small apartment. Not just any apartment. His old Village Square efficiency, the place he lived during the fall of 1992.

Could it be an elaborate prank? Would Dennis do something like this? Would Renee let him?

John stepped to the window. Overgrown weeds shot up through cracked asphalt. His dark-gray 1988 Grand Am with the racing pinstripe, a car he'd relegated to the junk pile many years ago, sat in perfect condition to left of the front door.

He turned back to the room and took it all in. The bed with its sagging mattress also served as chair and couch. The ironing board, a permanent fixture along the wall, doubled as more shelf space.

The dirty laundry formed a pile in the corner between the bed and the wall. His pride and joy during college, a Compaq 386 computer, sat on top of a rickety computer desk that had taken him hours to put together. A TV rested on a milk crate with a VCR perched on top. It had been luxury . . . twenty-two years ago.

Clicking at the window made him jump.

The window air conditioning unit powered up and began delivering ice cold air.

This wasn't a joke. It was his old apartment.

The phone sitting on the dresser rang.

John stared at it. Four rings. Five. Six. No answering machine. No Caller ID.

Should he answer it? He shrugged. Why not? "Hello."

"Are you coming over or what?" He recognized the voice right away. Dennis Vance. Music pounded in the background, the Fresh Prince's "Summertime."

"Um, sure. What time?"

"Now would be good. Don't forget the money. I have the tickets." Dennis hung up.

Tickets?

A memory slammed into his mind. *The Red River Rivalry.* The Oklahoma Sooners vs. Texas Longhorns football game at the Texas State Fair. Dennis had gotten him seats on the forty-five yard line. His hand tightened around the phone.

No! It couldn't be.

He swallowed, and his gaze darted around the room for anything that would tell him the date. He dropped the receiver on the dresser. His trembling fingers grabbed the *Oklahoma Daily*, the college newspaper, off the kitchen counter. A cockroach scurried away.

His heart pounded as he focused on the date.

October 9, 1992.

The day Kim disappeared.

The worst day of his life, and he was living it again.

He slammed his fist into the refrigerator. The appliance shook, and a framed picture of his parents and siblings fell from the wall onto the vinyl kitchenette floor. The glass shattered. He shook the pain out of his hand. You didn't feel pain in dreams.

He grabbed a pair of Levi's off the floor and pulled them on. They fastened easily, a sensation he hadn't experienced in a while. After putting on a Sooners sweatshirt, he stepped into the tiny bathroom.

He leaned toward the mirror and stopped cold. A smooth face with thick, dark hair stared back at him. No wrinkles and no gray. Somehow, someone or something had reached into the life of John Michaels, forty-five-year-old coffee shop owner, and transported him back into the life and body of a twenty-three-year-old college student.

How had this happened? And why? Fear stole into his heart, but he pushed it away. He had a chance to make a difference, to change the past.

He grabbed his watch off the ironing board. Two-fifteen. The tickets could wait. He still had time. He took his wallet and keys from the ironing board but couldn't find his phone. He threw clothes and papers across the room looking for it. He'd lost the stupid thing again.

No, wait. He halted his frenzied search. He didn't have a cell phone in 1992. No one did. He picked up the cordless phone again. His fingers clenched the receiver as he dialed Kim's number from memory, even after so many years.

The phone rang. And rang again. No answer.

"I can do this. I can do this." Where would Kim be? Another memory hit him. The police had talked to all of her acquaintances, but never figured out her exact movements that day. Except for one thing . . . she had last been seen going to Gittinger Hall on the South Oval of the University of Oklahoma campus.

Chapter 2

As John drove across campus, the craziness of his situation hit him. A forty-five-year old stuck in a twenty-three-year old body. He couldn't hold back a laugh, but he shook it off. Nothing funny about this. Tragic, maybe. Desperate.

He sped onto Boyd Street. The trees overhead towered above the old, ornate houses like they always had and probably always would. Turning south on Elm, he entered the heart of the west side of the campus and pulled into the lot closest to Gittinger Hall.

Why so many empty parking places? A memory surfaced. Classes were always cancelled the Friday before the OU-Texas game to give the students more time to get to Dallas.

John entered the three-story brick building and tried to get his bearings. The English Department was on the third floor, wasn't it? As he rode the elevator, he braced himself to spot Kim rounding a corner or talking to a professor. What would it be like to see her again?

He only found deserted offices, and classrooms with nothing but empty chairs and cleared tables. A young girl smiled at him as she walked past, but he encountered no familiar faces.

On the second floor, two guys huddled at a table, going over a stack of papers. John cleared his throat. "Excuse me. I'm looking for Kim Addison. She works in the English department."

Both students looked up. "Try the office," suggested the one with a shaggy haircut.

"Where is it?"

"First floor, northeast hallway."

"Thanks." John hurled himself down the stairs rather than wait for the elevator, thankful for his twenty-three-year-old legs but cursing because he hadn't remembered where Kim's office was.

* * *

Her desk was in a small, cramped waiting area with musty carpet and cheap paneling that had been present for generations of students.

John scanned the area. He didn't recall Kim's desk exactly, but she had at least a few personal effects. This desk had only a stapler and tape dispenser tucked neatly next to a typewriter.

Maybe he'd gone to the wrong office.

No, this had to be it. He recognized the Native American painting on the south wall.

He reached for the top desk drawer, but stopped when he spotted a copy-paper box pushed beneath the desk. Why was it hidden? He pulled it out and took off the lid. Kim's personal effects filled the bottom.

Why were they under the desk? Did she quit? Was she fired? Was she already dead?

Old memories flooded his mind. He set the box on top of the desk and rifled through it. He thought he'd forgotten, but Kim had never really left him.

A snapshot of their spring break outing to Silver Dollar City. Not his first choice as a destination, but they'd had a great time with all their friends.

He picked up the cassette case for Whitney Houston's *Bodyguard* soundtrack, his Christmas present to her the year before. The weight of the cool plastic indicated the cassette wasn't in the case.

"May I help you?"

John jumped. The cassette case popped out of his hands, bounced on the desk, and clattered to the floor. He looked up and faced a fit man about his own age in a tweed jacket, with a denim shirt tucked too tightly into a pair of blue jeans. John paused. Okay, not close to his age anymore. "I'm looking for Kim Addison."

"I'm sorry. She quit yesterday." The man ran his hands through his dark hair.

Quit? Kim never told him she'd quit. "What was your name?"

The man flashed him a smug smile. "Professor Hazelton."

Kim told him once that Hazelton was one of the profs in the suite of offices where she worked. He flinched. He'd heard that name one other time. "Why did she quit?"

The professor's eyes bored into John for several seconds, and then he smirked. "You should ask her about it."

"I will." John backed away as Hazelton sauntered out the door.

As the owner of a coffee shop, John welcomed and served all types, even those he didn't care for. Professor Hazelton fit into that category. *Smarmy* would be a good word for the man.

He pushed those thoughts away. He had to find Kim. He hurried out the door but waited until he rounded the corner before sprinting to his car. He gunned the accelerator and pulled out onto Elm. Where should he go now? Where could Kim be?

He cruised down Lindsay, south of the cathedral of football, Memorial Stadium. Could he really keep Kim from disappearing from the face of the earth in this surreal repetition? Her body had never been found. Her parents had spent years searching for her, and probably still held out hope she was alive, but he'd given up within days. The possibilities of what happened to her constantly tormented his soul. Kidnapping? Rape? Murder?

He could go days without thinking of her. Then something, anything, would trigger a burst of memories that crushed him. A spirited song, a softly spoken word, the scent of roses, a smile. The memory of his first true love would rip open his wounds of loss and regret.

Enough. He shook the cobwebs of memory out of his mind.

Since he didn't know where to look for Kim, he turned at Garfield into a neighborhood of homes built long before the era of cookie-cutter suburban subdivisions. Some were beautiful, some decrepit, all unique.

Dennis lived in the best house on the block, a square two-story of the darkest red brick with two white, Ionic columns on the porch that supported a small deck on the second floor. He rented it along with a few other people of suspicious character. Although John and Dennis remained friends two decades later, part of Dennis always bothered him.

Cars littered the driveway and front yard like a puzzle with too many pieces. An old pickup truck filled the carport, a Fiero and a Trans Am parked behind it. John pulled onto the grass next to a Ford Probe.

Heavy-metal music, guaranteed to induce a headache, pounded from the house.

A young girl in a Ford Escort pulled in next to John. She waved as if she knew him and ran into the house.

He's almost forgotten that he looked like a college student, not an out-of-place adult. He checked his reflection in the rear-view mirror. Amazing!

He bounded up the front steps, found the door cracked open, and stepped inside. The television and stereo in the living room sat silent. The music receded as he moved into the living area. Dennis must have set up speakers in the back yard.

The 1950s-era house had hardwood floors and décor befitting Dennis Vance: a blue love seat and gold sofa, a card table in the small kitchen, and movie posters from *The Godfather* and *Goodfellas* on the wall. Cigarette smoke fouled the air.

A tall guy with a buzz cut filled a cup from a keg in the middle of the living room. A shorter guy with glasses waited his turn.

"Hey, Travis. Hey, Joe." Their names came easily, in spite of the years since he'd last seen them.

"Hey, John," said Travis.

Loud bass kicked in as another song began.

"Dennis has your tickets." Joe jerked his thumb toward the back of the house.

"His room," Travis added.

A young Dennis, with a full head of wavy brown hair, sat on the corner of his bed. He was talking to a girl in blue jeans with dark hair tied into a pony tail. He looked up and nodded to John as the girl continued to talk.

John shook his head. How crazy to see a person he knew so well look so young again.

Dennis's expression emphasized his square jaw and the strong lines of his face. It compressed into a look of concentration, probably just for show. The girl talked in serious, muted tones that John strained to hear. ". . . I might have to leave school. I don't know what I should do."

"Dennis glanced at him and then back to the girl, who twisted around to look at John.

His heart expanded and then popped like a balloon. So far, everything happened as it had the first time he'd lived his life.

Except this.

He wasn't supposed to meet Renee Templin for four years. His wife, who had slept in the guest bedroom for the past week. She wouldn't tell him why. All she said was "Trust me." Now, years before, she talked to Dennis in his bedroom on the day Kim disappeared. Had she and Dennis known each other before he met her?

"I wish I could go with you, dude," Dennis said as he pulled an envelope from a back pocket.

John couldn't answer. He stared at Renee—at her dark brown eyes rimmed with red and the freckles on the bridge of her nose. Had she been crying? He curbed the urge to hug the eighteen-year-old version of his wife. Seeing this incredibly young, innocent, full-life-ahead-of-her version of his wife made him forget the all the problems they faced. The money problems, the fears, the questions all swept away by seeing a Renee who had yet to say yes when he proposed . . . and who had yet to withdraw from him into her own little world of secrets.

Confusion disabled him. Kim and Renee had never interacted in his real life. He met Kim. She died. He grieved. He met Renee. But now, Renee had been dropped into the middle of the worst day of his life. Why?

"Dude, snap out of it." Dennis stood and waved the tickets in front of John's eyes. "I've got your tickets right here. Willy already paid me, so you're good."

John snatched the small brown envelope from Dennis, but his gaze stayed locked on Renee. "You, um . . ." He couldn't finish.

"Sorry." Dennis said, "John Michaels, this is Renee Templin."

She stood and put her right hand on her hip. "Hi."

"We met—?"

"We've never met. I'd remember."

"Maybe you were drunk," Dennis said.

"Shut up." Renee backhanded his arm. "I don't drink, and I don't forget a face."

John knew his wife. She put on a show, but beneath the tough surface lurked a joking, playful spirit. He'd love to spend the rest of the day talking to her, using his knowledge of the woman she would become to mess with her. All in good fun, of course.

If none of this was real—and none of this could be—why not spend time with Renee? Why not do whatever he wanted?

But what about Kim? What if he somehow had a chance to save her?

"I'm sorry," John said, "I guess you looked familiar. So, how do you know Dennis?"

"We took a class over the summer at OCC."

Oklahoma Community College. She hadn't lasted a semester at Oklahoma University. But if she knew Dennis then, why hadn't she ever told him?

The phone on the nightstand rang. Dennis picked it up and stepped into the corner to talk.

"What are you doing out here?" John stepped closer to Renee.

"I have some friends."

"Dennis?"

"Sure. He's a good guy." She shrugged.

"You don't know him that well then."

"He just told me a lot about you." Her sparkling eyes made him smile. "Dennis thinks you're the greatest. He talks about you all the time."

"That's funny; he's never mentioned you before."

He broke through and got a smile. The dimpled cheeks, the flushed skin. His future wife. How did he want to play this? He could hit on her or—

"Dude, it's for you." Dennis held out the phone.

He took it and answered. "Hello."

"John. I need your help," Kim's voice said. "I'm scared."

Chapter 3

John never got to say goodbye to Kim, never got to tell her how much he loved her. The regret had eaten at his soul every moment since that day. The words not spoken would sneak up on him without notice. The gut-twisting, needle-sharp pain he could never escape knifed him with renewed strength.

Now he held a phone with her on the other end of the line.

"K-Kim, where are you?"

"Is everything all right?" Dennis asked.

John waved him off and turned his back.

"I'm at the Texaco by the Baileys' house. My car died, and I thought I saw someone in the trees behind the house. So I ran here."

The Baileys? That rang a bell, but this time his memory failed him. "Where's the Texaco?"

"It's on Highway 9 and 108th Street, I think."

"I'll be right there."

"Okay. Hurry."

"Bye." He should say more, but how could he possibly tell her over the phone how the thoughts of what happened to her had consumed days and months—no, years—of his life? It tortured him to let her sweet, precious voice go, but he had a chance to see her, maybe to save her.

Rushing out the door, he looked back, but Renee had left the room. That made it easier for him to leave his heart for the moment. "See you later, Dennis."

"What's going on?

"It's Kim. Car trouble."

"I can go get her, so you can get going." Dennis took his keys off the dresser.

"No, I'm fine."

"Come on, man. Let me go. She is so hot."

John stared into Dennis's eyes.

Dennis smiled mischievously. "Hey, relax. I was just joking."

John grunted, left the small room, and threaded his way through the people hovering near the keg. He kept an eye out for Renee as he hurried to his car.

As John pulled out, Dennis lumbered down the front steps.

John rolled down his window. "What?"

Dennis waved at him. "Nothing. Beer run."

"One keg isn't enough?"

"Actually, we have plenty of beer. I'm going to get hard stuff for later tonight, when this place will be really rocking."

* * *

After a few wrong turns, John ended up on Jenkins, took it straight south, and went east on Highway 9. The city of Norman quickly gave way to farmland and open prairies.

When he saw the Texaco ahead, he slowed and turned on his blinker. A pickup blew by him with an angry honk.

He shouldn't pull in, he should just keep going, drive to Shawnee, then to Fort Smith, and off the face of the earth. That could happen just as easily as seeing Kim again. Hearing her voice and talking to Dennis and Renee had made it seem real. But it couldn't be. Things like this didn't happen. Life didn't give second chances.

But what if it did? What if he saved Kim today? Would it change his life? Would he still marry Renee? Would he still have his children?

"I'm not going to play this game." His voice sounded weak as he waited for a delivery truck to pass. He was a forty-five-year-old man with two great kids, a wonderful wife, and a business he loved. None of them perfect, but he would never choose to give them up. Yet here he was, driving to save Kim.

He thought of the movie *Bill and Ted's Excellent Adventure*. If only he could hop in a phone booth and travel back home. Or speed up to eighty-five miles per hour and disappear in a blaze of fire and lightning, like in *Back to the Future*.

He'd taken the last few hours with a grain of salt. Seeing Dennis had amused him; seeing Renee had given him a jolt. But what if he just stopped? Didn't look for Kim? Just did his best to try and get back to the future?

Traffic cleared, and he answered his own question by pulling into the Texaco. He parked to the right of the gas station entrance and took a deep breath. Kim would be here. Could he handle seeing a ghost?

Bang!

He jumped at the sound of someone pounding on his passenger window. Kim!

She pulled at the door handle. "Open up."

His fingers searched for the power locks, but the car didn't have any. Instead, he reached across the seat and flipped the lock.

Kim swung the door open and plopped into the seat, bringing with her a whiff of flowery perfume.

A burst of sunlight replaced the shadow of her memory. Shoulder-length, honey-blond hair. Freckles dotting her creamy skin. Smooth, flushed cheeks. The beautiful woman he could never forget, yet found too painful to remember, now sat next to him. The impossibility boggled his mind.

"Oh my goodness, what a day." She blew out a long breath.

John looked out his window at the old pickup parked next to him. His heart ricocheted around his chest, and his hands felt clammy.

"Thanks for coming." She cleared her throat. "My car broke down back at the Baileys'. When I tried to leave, I didn't make it ten feet before the engine shuddered, and smoke poured out the radiator."

The Baileys? She said that name on the phone. Why did he feel like it should it mean something to him?

"I'm glad I caught you. I was going to ask Dennis to come and help me. Why haven't you left for the game yet?"

He opened his mouth, but nothing came out. He swallowed hard and tried again. "I was just leaving when you called."

"Let's hurry so you can go. I don't want you to miss out on anything."

Her words pierced his heart. So unselfish, so kind. He held back the urge to hold her and never let go. He put the Grand Am in reverse. "Tell me where to go. I have no idea."

At her direction, he turned south onto an unnamed road. The crumbling asphalt quickly turned into gravel and crunched beneath the tires. "How far did you walk? Couldn't you have called from the house?"

"Slow down or you'll miss it. There it is." She pointed to a ranch-style house on the left, surrounded by trees. "No one was home, even though I'm supposed to meet them today. I don't know if they forgot or were running late or what."

"Why were you supposed to meet them?"

She laughed. A short, joyful sound. "I'm going to work for them."

"Doing what?"

"Seriously?"

"Yes. I forgot." John tried not to look at her. Instead, he focused on the worn tire tracks in the dirt driveway. The grass strip down the middle reminded him of the concrete strip down the middle of those car rides at amusement parks. Did the police know Kim had gone out here the day she died?

"A nanny, silly."

The driveway curved to the right before opening up into a large yard adorned with giant oaks. He followed the circular drive and parked behind Kim's Civic. They climbed out of the car, and Kim popped the hood.

John did what any man should and looked under the hood. He didn't see anything.

"What do you think?" Kim sidled next to him.

An electric current buzzed through his body. He reached out for her hand, and she took it. "I don't know." Always the car expert.

"This has happened before," Kim said. "I think the radiator needs water."

"Okay. I can do that." He looked at the sprawling house. "Is there an outside faucet?"

"I started looking for one, but then I heard something and thought I saw someone moving in the forest."

John's gaze drifted across the recently mowed yard. Beyond were thick trees and bushes, with no close neighbors. Did someone still lurk in the woods? Should he find a tire iron to protect them? "So you ran to the gas station?"

"Yep."

"And called Dennis."

Her eyebrows arched. "I thought you were gone. I would have called you."

Why did he say that? He didn't care about Dennis. Kim was alive and by his side. He gave her a swift hug and a peck on the cheek.

"Maybe we should call the police."

"And say that someone was in the woods a half an hour ago? Doesn't sound very compelling."

"Let's hurry and get that water. You need to get going to Dallas, and Leslee and I are going to go see *Far and Away*." She dragged him across the yard to the corner of the house.

"What are we going to use to hold the water?"

"I saw a bucket in the back."

Toys littered the backyard. Big wheels, bikes, a swing set, a sand box. Whiffleballs and bats, footballs, Nerf toys. Everything a kid would need. John slowed as they passed the air conditioning unit. "There it is." He pointed to the faucet hidden behind the charcoal grill. "Where's the bucket?"

"Over there." Kim waved a hand toward the swing set at the edge of the property near the tree line.

"You say you saw someone in the trees?"

"I don't know." She shrugged and smiled sheepishly. "Maybe I didn't."

John jogged through the maze of toys, stepped over a bat, and almost tripped over a tricycle. He grabbed a yellow sand bucket that sat upside-down just past the swing and held it up. "This one has a hole in it."

It hit him just as he saw another bucket at the edge of the tree line. The Baileys. He finally remembered where he had heard that name. He inspected the new bucket for holes, found none, and turned back to the house. "Hey Kim, who told you about the Baileys needing a nanny?"

"I, um . . ." Kim let out a piercing scream. "John, look out!"

He saw a flash of movement before blinding pain shattered his thoughts to blackness.

Chapter 4

His senses told him he wasn't dead, but his head ached as if it had been used as a bowling ball.

Kim! Was she here? Where was the attacker? He tried to open his eyes but somehow could not. He'd been with her. He had a chance to save her. Had he failed, or did his presence allow her enough warning to escape from the attacker?

Not knowing what happened ate at him. He'd spent years erasing memories of Kim because he couldn't face the pain. Now he'd relived her last day in the worst way imaginable. If only he could wake up. Maybe Kim was sitting next to him, as worried about his welfare as he was about hers. *Wake up!* He tried, but an incredible sleep weighed him down as if his limbs were made of lead, and he faded away again.

* * *

"John. John, wake up."

Renee? Had she come back to their bed?

No. Something wasn't right. The noise of opening doors and clanking dishes filtered through the wall behind the headboard. Muffled cartoon voices came from the TV in the living room. A familiar smell wafted to him.

This was another dream. It had to be. He swung his legs onto the floor, took in his surroundings, and buried his head in his hands. He clenched his fists and gritted his teeth, allowing the hot fire of anger to run its course. Who was doing this to him? And why? When would he return to his real life, to Renee, Mark, and Sara? A rising fear grew in his chest. Would he never see them again?

He stood slowly, keeping his hand on the bed for balance.

His shiny bookshelf-desk combo unit contained a cluttered array of papers, textbooks, and pens. A set of impressive-looking but never-used *Encyclopaedia Britannica* lined one of the shelves.

He wore only a T-shirt and underwear, so he grabbed a pair of shorts from the floor and stared at the door. Was he ready to see his family almost thirty years younger?

Wait a minute. If he'd returned to his twenty-three-year old body in 1992, did that mean. . . ? John darted to the mirror above his dresser.

A few pimples dotting an unlined face confirmed his suspicion. Yep, he was a teenager again. He took a deep breath. He survived a few hours of college. Surely he could interact with his family as a teenager for a few more.

He'd grown up in this house. In his real life, his parents still lived here. He knew where everything was and where everything would be. He stepped into the kitchen, and although he knew what he'd see, his mouth dropped open.

Dad sat at the dining room table, reading the paper over a bowl of Cheerios. He had a full head of thick, brown hair and wore a bushy mustache that didn't make it out of the eighties. Mom stood at the sink. She looked so young and thin. And probably about his own age . . . well, his real age. Becky watched cartoons in the living room, and the door to Sam's bedroom was closed, so he was probably still getting ready. It was all just as he remembered.

"Hurry and eat, John. We'll be late for church." Mom spoke without looking at him. She put the last of the dishes into the dishwasher.

"I've got the paper here for you." Dad flipped through classifieds as he sipped coffee. The gray suit and fresh smell of Old Spice indicated he was ready to leave.

John exhaled loudly. He'd forgotten to breathe.

The newspaper pulled at him like a magnet. He pushed aside the carton of milk and grabbed the sports section. The bold headline sent chills down his spine.

"Royals rally in 9th to force Game Seven."

The Royals were in the World Series? He stopped reading and found the date on the paper.

Sunday, October 27, 1985.

That meant he was sixteen again. "Great game last night," Dad said. "I like the Royals' chances tonight."

The Royals, of course, would win Game Seven 11-0 behind the pitching of Bret Saberhagen. John always had been a Royals fan—still was—and he remembered the game as if it were yesterday. "The Royals will roll tonight." His voice cracked as he spoke.

"I hope you're right."

He smirked. Of course he was right. "I'm going to get ready for church."

After washing his face, brushing his teeth, and shaving, John sculpted his unruly hair into something presentable. In the closet, he found blue slacks and a freshly ironed Generra shirt set apart from the rest of the clothes. Ugly! He sifted through the rest of the clothes, and then searched through drawers, but found no better options. Oh well, he'd look just as bad as everyone else at church, or just as good. Mom always made sure of that.

He faced the door again. He could do this. Pretend. Play. Then go home to Renee, Mark, and Sara. Yet something tugged at him. The Baileys'. He'd been attacked. What happened to Kim? And why was he now trapped in a teenage body, when just minutes ago he'd been reliving the worst day of his life?

He put on the navy slacks and a cream, short-sleeved, dress shirt with a tacky cursive "G" sewn onto one of the sleeves. As he stepped out into the hall, giggles came from the living room.

Becky sat Indian style—or criss-cross applesauce as his own kids called it— in front of the television. She sat transfixed by a cartoon episode, of all things, *Mr. T.*

John smiled. Mr. T. would still be doing commercials twenty years later, living off his *A-Team* and *Rocky III* fame. "Hey, Becky."

Sam's door was closed, so he was probably still getting ready.

"We need to leave," Mom called from the hallway. "John, you haven't had any breakfast."

"I'll grab something."

"Hurry. We need to go now. Come on, Becky." She knocked on Sam's door. "It's time to go, Sam."

"It's not over," Becky whined.

"Now!"

She jumped up as Dad switched off the television.

John hurried to the kitchen and grabbed a banana. After locking the front door, he paused to look at his own car, a 1980 gray Ford Mustang, and then joined his family in their station wagon.

* * *

John's dad parked the car behind Nichols Park Community Church, a mid-sized church with an average attendance of five hundred for a Sunday morning service. John trudged towards the building with the rest of his family.

A gust of wind rattled the trees that lined the east lawn of the church.

John rubbed his palms on his pants. He breathed slowly and deeply in a struggle to look calm, but inside, his nerves sizzled. He'd see people he hadn't seen since high school. Or there'd be people here he saw last week, but they'd be almost thirty years younger.

He didn't want to interact with anyone. He wanted to be home in the future. But he couldn't control that. Or could he? After all, he'd changed some things during his redo of the day Kim died. Could he make himself go back to his wife and kids? Maybe just lie down and take a nap. Then he'd wake up at home. Could it be that easy?

Inside, his family went their separate ways. They'd arrived a few minutes late, so they walked through halls that were mostly empty. What should he do? Easy, flee. He looked over his shoulder to make sure no one saw him and headed for the door. He stepped outside and then stopped.

Wait a minute. First, he'd relived the day Kim disappeared and had a chance to save her. Could he be reliving this day for a reason, too? Should he should dive into this world and see what happened? Perhaps he should show a little faith and trust that this day *did* matter. Maybe *everything* mattered. Every word, every person, every action.

He retraced his steps and made his way to his Sunday School class. Naomi Coley, the teacher, spoke in her nasal, monotonous, eternally boring voice. John made his way to the back row and sat down in a metal folding chair next to his friend, Willy Carpenter.

Willy looked up at him. "What's up?"

John snickered at the white slacks, sky-blue shirt, and navy string tie Willy wore, but it was good to see a young Willy with the full head of hair and the goofy smile he remembered.

"What?" Willy whispered.

"Nothing," John mouthed. As he studied the kids in front of him, sadness trickled through his body. In his real life, their fates had already been determined. After graduation, Nathan would join the army, Darrell would die from cancer, and Lance would sell medical equipment.

At the end of class, Naomi held up a flyer. "Before we take prayer requests, I want to remind everyone about the district-wide Fall Festival coming up at the Mission Acres Church in Moore. There will be food, Bible quizzing, talent competitions, volleyball, and basketball. It'll be a lot of fun."

Good memories of the annual Fall Festival warmed John's heart. It gave everyone a chance to play sports, eat pizza, and see friends from across the state. If he was still living the fantasy life of a sixteen-year-old that weekend, he would go.

* * *

In the crowded sanctuary, stained glass windows filtered the outside sun into an array of colors. John sat in the back with Willy and the youth group because it was expected of him. The bulletin proclaimed a special day with a revival speaker, which explained the packed pews.

Reverend Washington spoke with a booming voice that contrasted with his diminutive stature, but the kids didn't seem to notice. They whispered and passed notes. At first, John had to bite his lip to keep from telling them to pay attention, but eventually found himself struggling to listen. After years of hearing his own pastor's excellent sermons, it was hard to listen to anyone else. Instead, he watched the people in the congregation. Men wore argyle sweaters, Izod polos, and Members Only jackets. The women had lots of hair and shoulder pads in their power suits.

When Willy nudged him and set a sheet of paper on top of his Bible, John finally gave up. They spent the rest of the hour-long sermon playing that connect-the-dot squares game.

At the end of the service, John followed Willy and mingled with the rest of the teens at the back of the sanctuary. Willy talked to a bubbly blonde named Ashley. They'd date their senior year, and it would end badly. He considered warning him, but didn't. What difference would it make, since this world couldn't be real?

John wandered away from the teens. Back by the sound booth, a kid with mousy hair and a boyish face peppered the man behind the console with questions. "What does that do?" "Are the microphones on?"

John stopped. "Brad?"

The kid looked up but didn't say a word.

John looked away. Incredible. Brad Mullins. Now Reverend Brad Mullins, the pastor of John's church, and a far better speaker than Reverend Washington.

Brad still looked at him. His eyebrows arched in confusion.

"I'm sorry. I'm John Michaels. I haven't seen you here before."

"Yeah, I came with my mom and dad," Brad said in a high-pitched voice that hadn't come close to puberty.

"There you are!" A girl whizzed by, and Brad took off running. He ran circles in and around pews, giggling and laughing as the older girl gave chase. Her fluffy hair bounced, and her poufy dress swished around her legs.

John studied her blond hair, worn in pigtails, the freckled, unblemished face, and the thin body in middle adolescence. For the second time in a few hours, he had encountered Kim Addison.

In real life, he hadn't met her until college. Seeing her in this teenager life confirmed that it must be happening for a reason. But what was that reason? If it was to save her, he could have done that at the Baileys' house.

Kim caught up to Brad, grabbed an arm, and gave him a big squeeze.

"Let go of me. Let me go," Brad cried in mock despair.

John stepped forward. "Hey, let go of him."

In sync, their eyes grew wide, and their jaws fell open.

Why did he say that? He was sixteen-year old kid, not a forty-five-year-old parent telling youngsters to quit roughhousing.

"She was joking," Brad said.

"Is she your sister?" John tried to move on.

"No. Why?" Brad's eyes narrowed.

"Hey, lighten up. I was kidding." Kim put both hands on her hips. The regal tilt of her head told him he should feel privileged to be a part of her world.

John leaned against the back edge of the nearest pew. "I'm John."

"My name is Kim." Her eyes challenged him.

"Have you ever been here before?"

She sighed and looked around. "No, my parents are around here somewhere. We're looking for a new church."

"How do you know each other?"

"We're friends." Brad eyed him suspiciously.

"Our parents have been best friends forever. I've known him since he was a baby."

"How cute." John rubbed Brad's head, and Brad swiped his hand away.

Kim chuckled.

"I hope your family will come back, Kim," John said. "Our services aren't always this long."

"Maybe."

"You could hang out with the youth group. They're a lot of fun. Buzz Baker is a great youth pastor."

"Maybe."

"Can you say anything besides 'maybe'?"

Her eyes sparkled. "Maybe. What do you want me to say?"

John wanted to ask her on a date or joke with her about the boyfriends she would have in high school. In the ocean-blue eyes of this fourteen-year-old girl, he saw the woman he would grow to love, then lose.

"What do you want to be when you grow up?" She'd never get the chance to fulfill the wondrous hopes and dreams he'd wanted to share. Did this Kim have the same dreams?

"Are you serious?" Again she put her hands on her hips.

"Sure."

She opened her mouth as if to speak and then stopped. "You first."

"Kim, let's go."

They all turned to the door leading out of the sanctuary, where a broad-shouldered man in a three-piece navy suit stood. Kim's dad. Her mom stood next to him, a tiny woman with feathered hair that flowed over her shoulders.

John nodded at them. Her dad ignored him, but her mom smiled.

"I've got to go. Come on, Brad." Kim tugged Brad's arm and pulled him away.

John's heart started pounding. He might never see her again. When she disappeared out the door, he hurried after her.

She walked next to her mom, and Brad walked behind his parents with his two sisters.

"Hey, Kim."

All seven heads turned to look at him.

"Umm." John stammered. Now what? "I hope you guys can come back. It was nice to meet you." Lame.

Kim's mom looked at her husband. "Thank you, young man. We enjoyed the service. We may come back again." Her dad guided her toward the front door.

As Kim reached the drinking fountain next to the men's restroom, she looked back at him.

John gave her two thumbs up.

Her eyes widened, and then she flashed him a big smile.

That smile made his day. It melted his heart.

Two thumbs up, a simple gesture. Also a big family tradition in the Addison household. A joke they would share in the future.

His heart told him to chase after her, not to let her out of his sight until he returned to his life with Renee and the kids. He took a step forward and stopped. He had to let go. He had to trust there was a reason he became sixteen again.

Chapter 5

John wolfed down a Super Roast Beef at Arby's, the kind with tons of sauce, shredded lettuce, and tomatoes. He kept quiet and enjoyed his family's conversation, which centered around church, work, and school. The same kind of conversations he led with his wife and kids. Needles pricked his heart. He missed them.

After they got home, Sam went outside to help the kid next door practice his pitching. Becky went to her room, and Mom sorted laundry. Dad watched NFL football, and John took a closer look at the Sunday paper.

The front page of the *Sunday Oklahoman* ran the headline "AIDS Strikes, Kills—All Vulnerable." AIDS didn't receive many headlines in America anymore.

Now, for the good stuff. The sports section detailed the Oklahoma Sooners 59-14 victory over the Iowa State Cyclones. It was the first game played after the Sooners lost to the Miami Hurricanes, a game in which quarterback Troy Aikman broke his leg. John could create a lot of waves by revealing that Oklahoma's team would go on to win the national championship.

In comparison to what he was used to, the new cars in the classifieds were cheap and looked like garbage. The auto industry lamented losing sales to the Japanese, and the Koreans were preparing to enter the US auto market. *Was the US ready for the Yugo?* He shook his head. He'd forgotten about that piece of junk.

There wasn't much on at the movies. Freddy was back in *Nightmare on Elm Street 2*. Arnold rescued his daughter in *Commando*. *Rambo II* and *Teen Wolf* were also in theaters. Had movies gotten any better over the years? He wasn't so sure.

Sam barged in from outside, the front door banging into the wall. "Dad, when are we going to the batting cages?"

"Ten minutes. Did you hear me, John? Batting cages in ten minutes," Dad called from the sofa in the living room.

John scratched his head. He had planned to call Kim, if he could find her number. But the batting cages sounded fun. He returned to his room and stripped to his underwear. His lean body had no muscle on it. He'd never considered weight training at this age. Maybe it would have made a difference in his athletic career if he had. He rummaged for clothes and came up with a pair of gray sweats and a T-shirt. After grabbing a jacket, he joined Sam and Dad outside.

* * *

The pinging of balls against bats echoed loudly off the metal walls of the warehouse that contained four batting cages side by side, a snack bar, and some arcade games. Dad bought some tokens, and Sam pulled his bat out of his bag. He tightened his batting gloves and stepped into the first cage.

John leaned against the railing next to Dad. The light glowed red, and the conveyer belt began moving.

A yellow ball settled into the notch in the belt, and *wham*! A metal arm flung a pitch toward them.

Sam's bat connected, and he crushed the ball into the net above the machine. A solid, long drive. He connected with every pitch and sprayed hits right and left.

His brother looked like every other normal-sized kid, except when you got him on an athletic field. His blazing speed allowed him to steal bases, get to balls in the gaps, blow by defenders, and outrun tacklers. It didn't matter what sport it was, Sam excelled.

John's claim to fame was that he could shoot in the low 80s on the golf course.

Sam burned through another bucket of balls and then left the cage. "Your turn."

John picked a bat from the rack in front of the cage, one that hadn't had the grip torn to shreds. He hefted the 25-oz bat. It felt good. "Okay, I'm ready." He stepped into the cage and fed a token into the machine.

The first pitch blew by before he got the bat off his shoulder. The second time, he swung for the fences and got nothing but air.

Sam chuckled.

"Watch it," John warned. Little brothers were a pain.

"Keep your eye on the ball, John," Dad said.

This time, John followed the yellow dimpled ball from the moment it left the machine until it met his bat. He grounded the ball back toward the machine, where it crashed into the protective netting.

That was fun.

He hit the next few back up the middle. With soft, easy swings, he made solid contact. He pulled a few to the right and then pushed some to the left. Every hit solid. Line drives into the net on the wall. How was this happening? He never hit like this in his real life.

Time to swing harder. *Bam*, he crushed one. The sound told him he got all of it. The ball ricocheted around the netting before rolling back to his feet. He kicked it away and got ready for the next one.

Only no more balls came. John stepped out of the cage, with a broad smile. His hands hurt, and sweat trickled down his face, but he didn't care. He'd never been able to hit the ball like that.

Sam gave him a strange look as they traded places but said nothing. His session went by in a blur, and then it was John's turn again.

"How fast does this one go?" John stood in front of the next cage.

"There's a sign right there." Sam pointed above the cage door.

Cage 2: 55 mph.

John looked down the line. Cage 3: 70 mph. Cage 4: 85 mph. "I'm going to try Cage 4." "Seriously?" Sam grabbed his bag and followed.

John shrugged. "Why not?" Eighty-five miles per hour. Could he hit that? If he could relive Kim's final day and then skip through time back to high school, maybe he could hit a major-league fastball. "Could I borrow your batting gloves?"

"Sure." Sam handed them to him. "Good luck."

John fastened the Velcro straps of the warm, sweaty gloves.

The first pitch flew by.

Just make contact. He brought the bat forward, and with the next pitch, guided the bat to the ball. The impact of the pitch almost knocked the bat out of his hands.

He settled back into his true stance but missed the next pitch. And the next. Then something seemed to shift. He focused on the ball. His eyes tracked it, and his hands moved the bat towards it. He made solid contact and hit a line drive into the netting.

"Nice one," Sam said.

Smiling, John relaxed a bit and swung late on the next pitch. He quickly regained focus and pounded the last ten pitches into the netting just as he had in the 55-mph cage. After the last pitch, he twirled the bat in the air like a baton and caught it.

"When did you learn to hit like that?" Sam stared at him, wide-eyed. His little brother's admiring eyes sent a rush of love through him. Growing up, he never fathomed how much his brother and sister had looked up to him. "Watching you, of course."

"I can't hit like that."

"You will someday."

"Looks as if you shouldn't have given up baseball." Dad shook his head with stunned amusement.

John shrugged. He'd played baseball until he was thirteen. The practices became a grind and the games methodical. By the time he graduated high school and became a big Royals fan, he regretted quitting. But leagues didn't exist for slow-footed, nearsighted teenagers.

Wait a minute. His hands flew to his face. He wasn't wearing glasses, yet he could see! He'd worn glasses and then contacts until his thirties, when he had laser corrective surgery. Now, in this sixteen-year-old body, he could see perfectly. But perfect vision couldn't completely explain his hitting. Now he also had the coordination to catch up with an 85-mph fastball.

Why? If his reason for being here had to do with Kim, the ability to hit a baseball had to fit in somehow.

They gathered their things and left. During the ride home, John sat in the front of Dad's Town Car. The cloth-covered red seats, more plush than his bed at home, threatened to swallow him into dreamland.

Without warning, Dad announced, "You know John, it's not too late."

John's eyes popped open. "What do you mean?"

"Not too late to play baseball."

"I think it is." John pressed the eject button on the cassette player, but it was empty.

"I know you haven't played in a few years, but not many kids your age can hit like that. If you want to play, you should give it a shot. I could call the coach tomorrow and see what he suggests."

"Sure, Dad." Dad's voice had held so much hope, John couldn't brush off his dreams. While it would be fun to play baseball again, tomorrow he'd wake up at home. Wouldn't he?

Dad turned the radio dial to the Dallas Cowboys game.

John looked out the window at the old cars, the old houses, the old stores. What was Kim doing right now? Was she thinking about him?

The park they passed on Rockwell, where children ran and played, reminded him of his own family. He missed Mark. He missed Sara. He missed Renee. He missed his life. Wrestling on the floor, baking cookies, swinging at the park, watching a DVR'd episode of "Parenthood" after the kids went to bed. Greeting customers. Experimenting with coffee blends. Life. Even an imperfect life with a failing business and a wife with secrets.

Hopefully, tomorrow he'd be home. Instead of worrying about how to hit a fastball, he'd have to worry about meeting payroll . . . and saving his marriage.

Chapter 6

John spent the afternoon in his room, sifting through his textbooks and looking at the homework due tomorrow. He'd brought home algebra, history, and literature textbooks. The notes in his spiral notebooks were a different language. He flipped through the algebra book. The finances at The Coffee Beast continually gave him headaches. How had he ever passed algebra? He shoved the text into his backpack. No way he'd even try working on any assignments. Ridiculous!

A bird chirped outside his bedroom window, reminding him of the reality of his situation. Whatever this was, it wasn't a dream. But surely he'd wake up in his own bed, so why even begin?

Before dinner, he'd snuck the phone book into his room. He turned to the As. Edward and Gayle Addison. That was easy enough.

He dialed, but no one answered. No answering machine.

He hung up and tried again. Nothing.

He turned to the Ts. Templin. Randy and Suzanne. And their cute little daughter Renee. He pressed the first three digits and then stopped.

She'd only be eleven. Way too young.

* * *

After a supper of chicken and rice, John settled on the couch with Dad and Sam to watch Game Seven of the World Series.

"The Cardinals are going to win," Sam said. "I bet they're really mad after last night."

"That call at first base created quite a controversy," Dad said, "but it's a part of the game. They're professionals; they understand that."

John's fingers itched to try Kim's number again. But leaving before the game started would be out of place. He waited until the end of the first inning and hurried to his room.

After the third ring, Kim's mom answered.

"May I speak to Kim, please?"

At fourteen, would Kim be allowed to talk to boys on the phone? His own daughter would probably not only have a phone when she reached that age, but access to texting, chatting, Facetime, and Facebook. Ugh! How times had changed.

The pause stretched unpleasantly long before she said, "May I ask who's calling?"

Oh, boy. "I'm John Michaels. I met Kim at church today."

"Okay, John. How did you get this number?"

Gayle was a sweet, good humored person. He could handle this. "I looked it up in the phone book."

"How did you know our names?"

"Kim told me." John sat on his bed. His insides squirmed at the half-truth. She *had* told him, just in the future.

"She told you her last name."

"Yes." That was the truth.

"Did she tell you my name, or my husband's name?"

"Um, no ma'am, she did not. I asked around at church." He rubbed his hand through his hair.

"You're an enterprising young man. May I ask you how old you are?"

"I'm sixteen," he said, shaking his head at the thought.

"Well, John, Kim's only fourteen. Her father and I don't let her talk to boys on the phone. Perhaps she'll see you at church again sometime."

"Mrs. Addison, let me be honest with you. I'm not going to ask her out on a date. I'm not going to call her every day. I'm the most trustworthy guy she's ever met. I just want to talk to her for a minute. I had something to ask her. We didn't get to finish our conversation today. It'll only take a minute."

Gayle paused again. "Okay, John. You're quite persuasive. I'll give Kim five minutes."

"Great. Thanks." He slowly exhaled.

After a few moments, Kim answered. "What did you say to her, anyway? She doesn't let me talk to boys on the phone."

"I was honest and promised I only wanted to ask you a question."

She giggled. "Okay."

"I was glad to meet you today."

"Me too."

What should he say next? He knew everything about her, and she knew nothing about him. What could he possibly say now that would save her life six years from now? Don't go to the Baileys. Don't work for the English Department. Don't ever go out with me.

No, he couldn't say any of that. But he had to start somewhere. "I guess I called because we never got to finish our conversation at church. I asked you what you wanted to be when you grew up."

"And I asked you to answer first," she answered firmly.

"Okay. I'd like to be a writer. And you might think I'm crazy, but being a pastor always appealed to me. I've always wanted to help people, especially when times are tough."

"You want to be a preacher?"

"Sure. I think it would be fun." Such silly dreams. The pastor dream had fallen by the wayside, but he still harbored hopes of being a writer. But it would never happen. Running The Coffee Beast took up way too much of his time.

"Fun?" she asked. "I don't think you decide to become a pastor because it's fun."

John thought of Brad Mullins, the adult Brad Mullins, his pastor. The real Kim had never mentioned knowing him. "No, probably not. Your turn. What do you want to do?"

"Why would you ask me what I want to do when I grow up? Why not my favorite movie? Or if I like Madonna?"

"Okay. What's your favorite movie? Do you like Madonna?" He scooted against the wall and crossed his legs.

"I saw *Goonies* with my friend Leslee. My parents don't let me listen to Madonna."

"Your parents know what they're talking about." Were his five minutes almost up? If he was only here for a day, he might not get another chance to warn her. But how could he talk to her about her future without freaking her out? "Enough side-stepping. Tell me about your future. What do you want to be?"

"I want to be a mom, have kids."

His soul constricted in a flash of pain. She'd never have that chance. "Okay. While you're a mom . . ."

"Just a second."

Kim and her mom talked in muffled voices. "I have to go."

He weighed his options. He jumped off the bed and walked to the window. This could be his last chance to talk to Kim. He had to say something. He had to make a difference.

She said, "Maybe you could call tomorrow."

He couldn't help it. "What about later tonight?"

A door closed in the background. "Mom," Kim said. "Can you give me just a second?"

After some muffled talking, Kim said, "I'll try and call you back after my parents go to bed. It'll be around ten-thirty. What's your number?"

He told her and then sighed. It was the best he could hope for.

"Good night."

"I . . ." He almost said, "I love you." Wouldn't that have shocked her? At one time, the phrase had flowed so easily between them, and then he'd suppressed it for years, had trouble saying it even to Renee. Now it came back so easily. And so did the pain. "I'll talk to you later."

He held the phone in his hand. He'd been sixteen for a day. He'd been twenty-three for a few hours. Both times, he'd been thrown into a life with Kim. Why? It had only ripped open old wounds and thrown salt on them. His chest tightened, and he struggled to take a deep breath. He was so close to her, yet so powerless.

"John, get back in here," Dad called from the living room. "The Royals have a rally going."

He got up out of duty and put on his game face. The Royals were about to win the World Series. He should be excited.

As he passed Becky in the hallway, he rubbed her head and said, "Hey, sweetie." His automatic response to call her the same thing he called Sara opened another wound. He missed his kids' laughter, their unconditional love.

Oh God. Please let me be back home when I wake up tomorrow.

* * *

When Darryl Motley caught the fly ball for the final out of Game Seven, John jumped for joy and whooped and hollered with Dad and Sam. He laughed at the silly craziness of doing all of this again.

"Be quiet. Becky's asleep," Mom implored from her room.

Later, John waited by the phone in his room. By ten thirty, the lights were off elsewhere in the house, and everything was quiet. Still no phone call. He quickly brushed his teeth and washed his face. A shower could wait. He climbed into bed and stretched the phone cord to reach to his side. He lay in his bed and stared at the ceiling.

Come on, Kim. Call back.

The silence illuminated his desperation. He pushed the covers away and turned on his side. He had to save her. That had to be the reason he was here. But how? Could he just tell her to never go to the Bailey's house? How stupid would that sound? But if it saved her, he didn't care what she thought of him.

He picked up the phone. He started to dial her number and then put it back. She said she'd call if she could. If he called, he'd be talking to angry parents. He'd have to trust that if he was supposed to warn her somehow, she'd call again. Each tick of the clock took him further away from her. His eyelids drooped in spite of his best efforts. He snapped awake and began pacing. As much as he wanted to wake up in his own bed, he couldn't go to sleep yet; he might lose his last chance to talk to Kim.

His eyelids grew heavy, and his mind floated to more comforting thoughts. Although it seemed far away, it was only last night that he'd gone to sleep in his own home after putting his own kids to bed.

* * *

"Why is Mom sleeping in the extra room?" Mark asked.

"She's . . ." John searched for an adequate answer. "She's sleeping in there because I've been snoring, and it's been hard for her to rest." He swallowed hard at the outright lie.

"Hmm." Mark pulled his blanket up to his chin. "Dad, what's heaven like?"

"We talked about this last night."

"Tell me again." They went through the same questions again.

Sara yelled from down the hallway. "Daddy!"

John hugged his son. "Good night, Mark. I love you."

"Love you, too." Mark squeezed back as hard as he could, let go, and snuggled up to his stuffed bulldog, Flip Flop. He turned to face the wall.

The fan in Sara's room whirled overhead. The closet light made the room seem too bright for sleep, but she demanded it always be on. The two kids couldn't be more different, especially at bedtime. Mark would be asleep in seconds, his left arm draped over Flip Flop and his right under his pillow. Sara fought sleep in an epic battle.

She lay on her back without covers.

John pulled the sheet up.

"No." She pushed the sheet away. "I'm hot."

He caught her legs and pulled the sheet over them. "You at least need a sheet."

"Okay."

"Has Mommy prayed with you?"

"Yes."

"Good." Had Sara noticed the problems between him and Renee yet?

John knelt and ran a hand through his daughter's still-wet-from-the-bath hair. "Love you, princess. Close your eyes and try to go to sleep. I'll be right here."

"Okay." She tossed and turned for an eternity before settling down.

When her movement stopped and her breathing became slow and steady, John eased away from the bed.

Taking one last walk through the house, he turned off all the lights and adjusted the thermostat. He walked by the fourth bedroom. He stepped toward the door, hesitated, stopped. Not tonight.

After brushing his teeth and flossing—he hated flossing—John climbed into bed alone. Renee hadn't slept in their bed for a week now. There hadn't been a fight. No arguments or disagreements. One night, after she talked with Dennis Vance, she moved into the spare room.

She'd said there was nothing he could do, that she wasn't mad at him. She promised to tell him when she got it worked out. She'd never been like this before, and he didn't understand it. He could only trust. He didn't want to lose her. He didn't want to lose her as he'd lost Kim.

His brain latched on to his next-biggest worry: how long could The Coffee Beast survive with its cash flow problems? Coffee. Why didn't more people buy it? From his shop, specifically?

The pressures from home and work pushed aside sleep. They pounded against gate of his castle like battering rams, threatening to crumble the structure at any time. Still, he had a life blessed by God. He held on to that life with a death grip and would do anything to defend it.

If only he knew what to do.

He drifted towards sleep. Wisps of fantasy curled through his mind like early morning fog. He was an army of one, ridding the world of terrorism. Secret X-ray vision allowed him to make a fortune at the poker tables. Charisma and charm earned him the votes of millions as he was swept into the office of the presidency in a landslide.

Then sleep came.

Chapter 7

The buzzing alarm startled John out of deep sleep. His eyes opened to posters of Larry Bird, George Brett, and Joe Montana instead of sky-blue walls decorated with pictures of a happy family and a large flat-screen TV.

He wasn't home.

He hurried through the morning ritual mechanically. Renee would have to get the kids ready for school by herself. Did she miss him? Did she even know he was gone?

Dressed in jeans and a polo shirt, he looked at himself in the mirror. He was going back to high school. Stupid, but he actually looked forward to it. So far, many moments he'd relived tied to Kim. Would today be any different?

When he walked into the kitchen, Becky sat at the table while Mom poured milk into her Fruit Loops. "Would you like a bowl of cereal, John?"

"No, thanks. I'll eat a Pop Tart in the car."

In his real life, his parents were still alive and in great health. He and Sam went golfing six times a year. He and Becky spent hours debating politics, religion, movies, and pop culture. He loved being around the younger version of his family, seeing in them the people they would become, but he didn't need it like he needed to talk with Kim.

John hugged Mom and patted Becky on the head. He found Sam in his room. "See you, Sam."

"You're leaving early." He slipped on his shoes.

"I have stuff to do."

"Are you going to talk to the baseball coach?"

"Oh man, I don't know." No, he wouldn't talk to the coach. He'd be back home before the season even started. Yet something had obviously changed. He had baseball talent now. Like meeting Kim and Brad, it was different than in his real life. Could all changes be happening for the same reason?

Sam stood. "You should. That was nice hitting. Let's go back to the cages tonight. I want to see if you can do it again."

"You're on." John stuck out his fist.

Sam looked puzzled.

"Here, make a fist and hit mine." He grabbed Sam's wrist and lifted his arm until his hand was even with John's fist. "It's a fist bump. It's what guys do to look cool."

Sam lips turned up in a smile. "Cool."

John laughed as he turned away. A fist bump. What else could he tell his brother about the future without making him think he was crazy?

He was going back to high school. They made movies about this. *Big* with Tom Hanks. The one with Fred Savage and Judge Reinhold. Oscar material for sure. But how well could he play the part of a teenager?

* * *

At seven-thirty, John pulled up to the stoplight at 50th and McArthur. He turned left and took his place in the long line of cars proceeding through the school zone. His stomach fluttered. High school again. His nerves of steel would be severely tested today. What if the teachers called on him? He wouldn't know the answers. What if he'd forgotten someone's name?

He didn't know his class schedule. How could he remember that? He had English first. He thought harder.

It came to him, just like the routine of the last day. Just like he'd known where his clothes were and that there were potato chips in the pantry. Somehow, details of his school day filled the gaps in his memory. After English came economics, Spanish, algebra, then lunch. Debate and history in the afternoon, and he finished with a bang: chemistry.

John cruised through the last stoplight before the turn into the student parking lot. He squeezed his eyes shut briefly. He was ready.

He passed Camaros, Firebirds, Sunfires, pickups, and Citations. All clunkers. He crossed the faded blacktop with his backpack flung across his shoulder. The brisk late-October morning had already warmed up. He squinted as he walked into the sun. At the third row of cars, a brunette he didn't recognize exited a Honda Civic. He looked down to avoid any possible conversation

"Hi, John."

At the sound of her voice, a name came to him. He glanced up. "Hi, April."

More names came back to him when two more people greeted him. By the time he reached the sidewalk, he felt confident enough to wave at someone he recognized. But he'd still better find Willy soon. They had four classes together, so Willy could be his security blanket in case his memory failed.

When he reached the row of hedges lining the sidewalk, swift movement caught his attention. A tall kid in red flannel and jeans jumped out from the shadows.

Dennis?

The younger version of John's long-time friend cocked his arm back.

John stepped to the side, and the blow glanced off his jaw.

Dennis swung again. His eyes were glazed. His long bangs flowed from side to side as he moved.

John raised his arms to block it. "What's your problem, Dennis?"

A crowd gathered to watch the fight.

Dennis cursed and charged him. He drove his shoulder into John's gut.

The blow knocked the wind out of him and drove him back.

Dennis tackled him and they hit the ground.

Nearby students clapped and hollered encouragement.

Dennis threw soft, ineffective punches as they rolled on the ground.

John blocked them with his arms, rolled to his left, and jumped to his feet. He braced for another attack.

Dennis pulled himself up and spit out saliva.

Two guys stepped out of the crowd and grabbed Dennis's arms from behind. Devon and Phil.

"Let go of me." Dennis squirmed against the arms holding him and cursed. "This is none of your business, Devon." He addressed the kid with the flattop haircut and the number 32 etched into the hair on one side of his head.

Devon Washington. The other kid was Phil Prince. He hadn't thought of those guys in years.

Mr. Walker, the baseball coach, burst through the doors. His red face looked as if it could pop. "What's going on?" His face compressed in anger at the sight of Dennis. "Dennis! You knew not to come back."

"I had some unfinished business," he seethed.

Unfinished business? What? This never happened in his real life.

"Not on school property, you don't. Come with me." Coach Walker dragged Dennis by an arm into the building.

As soon as the door slammed shut, everyone turned to John.

"Are you okay?" April asked.

"I'm fine." He touched his face for signs of blood. "I sure didn't expect my Monday to start that way."

April grinned. "I'll see you in Spanish."

"Hey, Devon, Phil, thanks for helping me out."

"Looked as if you needed it."

"Well, he ambushed me. I don't know why. We're friends." Why was he defending himself to these jocks? John picked up his backpack and brushed the grass off. As he slid it over his shoulders, he almost collided with Lanie Simpson.

Face to face, he stared straight into her cobalt-blue eyes. He could smell her citrusy perfume, even her makeup. He stepped back out of her space. "Sorry, I didn't see you there."

"That's okay." Her brown hair rested softly on her shoulders.

He'd known Lanie in high school but never had the guts to talk to her. Never had the guts to tell her she was by far the prettiest girl in school. But after years of dealing with customers at the Coffee Beast, he could talk to anyone.

"Your cheek is a little red."

Heat rushed up his face under her scrutiny.

"Why was Dennis mad at you?"

"I don't know." He looped his thumbs around his backpack straps.

"He's a jerk. Don't worry about it."

"I won't. Thanks."

"See you later." She smiled and disappeared into the building.

Okay, what just happened? Why had Dennis attacked him?

A new memory filled his mind. In real life, John had been ready to tell the principal about Dennis selling cigarettes to the students. But he'd been sick for several days, and someone else turned him in. In this life, John had followed through and betrayed his friend. He now had the memory of talking to the principal. Weird!

He'd relived the day Kim disappeared, and Dennis stood right in the middle of it. In his real life, John hadn't been there to take Kim's call. Had she talked to Dennis instead? Did Dennis go to the Baileys' to help her? Or kill her?

Now, in this life, Dennis attacked him at school. If reliving his sixteen-year-old life was happening for a reason, this new attack had to mean something.

Chapter 8

John met up with Willy outside their English class, and they cruised through their classes together. John had a blast seeing old friends and going through each class with the knowledge that none of the schoolwork mattered. He wrote an essay in English on why the Soviet Union would fail, learned all about the Taft-Harley Act in history, and failed a test on the periodic table in chemistry. Algebraic thinking seeped back into his memory as the teacher explained the quadratic formula, and he floundered through the first half of Spanish until words and phrases began to pop into his mind.

On his way home, his thoughts returned to Dennis and Kim. Maybe he could talk to Kim later and tell her about his day. What if something different happened to her today too? Or would she even know?

He pulled into a driveway full of cars. Odd. Why would Dad be home from work this early? John hesitated. He had a feeling it wasn't a good reason. He put his backpack in his room and went into the kitchen.

Dad leaned against the stove, a cup of coffee in hand, his eyes bleary. Mom stood by the sink and looked down when he looked at her.

"I talked to Coach Walker today," Dad said.

Uh-oh, the fight.

"He said he'd love to see you hit, if you want. He's not making any promises, but it doesn't matter that you didn't play JV last year."

John nodded. A small battle waged in his mind. He didn't want to mess with baseball. He wanted to go home to Renee, Mark, and Sara. But how long would he be here? A day? A week? A month? If he had to relive high school, he might as well use this curious new ability to play baseball, whatever the reason for it.

Dad continued. "If you're free Thursday after school, Coach told me you should come out to the field."

"Okay. I might do that."

"I guess that's the good news," Dad said.

"Your father got laid off today." Seeing his mother with red eyes and tear-streaked mascara broke his heart.

"What?"

"They gave me a nice severance, so we'll be okay for a while. I'd appreciate it if you didn't talk to Sam or Becky about it."

"Yeah, sure." John ran a shaky hand through his hair. Dad had worked with Kerr-McGee his entire career in real life. The company's move to Houston coincided perfectly with his retirement age.

What changed? Did it have anything to do with this time-traveling or alternate universe or whatever he was experiencing? He dropped onto a chair at the kitchen table. "What are you going to do?"

Dad shrugged. "It'll be nice to have a few weeks off. Maybe I can repair the shed and dig up the pine tree in the back yard that your mom has been bugging me about. Then I'll start looking for another job. Don't worry, John. We'll be fine. We have savings, and they gave me three months' pay."

"That's good." He nodded as he considered the situation. "That'll take you through the year."

"Sure. We'll be fine financially. It was just a rough day. They let four of us go. We were blindsided. It was a . . . a shock." He started to say more but closed his mouth and looked away.

It killed John to see Dad like this. This couldn't be real. John's life had already happened. But those were real tears in Mom's eyes. Fear crept into his soul. Was he reliving his life, or redoing his life? If this was a do-over, Dad's life just took a turn for the worse.

* * *

They returned to the batting cages that night, as planned, and settled on Cage 3. John held his own against Sam. In the first round, they competed to see who could hit more line drives into the netting. In the second, they hit for the opposite field. They alternated, and both hit well. Even Dad took a turn.

John hadn't lost the skill he'd shown yesterday. While growing up, he could never hit better than Sam. Tonight he stayed even with Sam, and only John knew he was hardly trying. Where had this newfound skill come from? And why?

As he continued crushing baseballs, he decided to let this new ability take him wherever it could. He'd try out for the team. He couldn't see how, but it was something different in this life, so it must be related to Kim.

Chapter 9

John moaned in his sleep. He tugged on the blanket and pulled it up over his ears. His feet twisted the bedding into knots. But the dream about the police questioning on the day Kim disappeared didn't go away. He'd repressed the interrogation for more than twenty years, yet tonight it haunted him with detailed clarity.

"Tell us about your relationship with Kim Addison."

John sighed heavily. He rested his hands on top of the metal desk. Beneath it, his foot tapped continually. "We were friends."

"Okay. Go on." Detective Bruner sat across from him with a yellow legal pad in his lap and a red No. 2 pencil in his right hand.

"We met our freshman year in philosophy. We were part of a big group, and we all hung out together, but we never really went out. I'm sorry. I'm rambling. Can you be more specific?"

Detective Bruner smiled sympathetically. "Was she your girlfriend?"

"Yes. We were friends long before we started dating, so we had already established a comfort level. We didn't have to hide anything; we already knew so much about each other. I knew she hates—" He stopped and corrected himself. "She hated horror movies and regretted never joining a sorority. She knew I couldn't stand Mexican food. Things like that."

"When did you start dating?"

"End of August. We saw each other off and on during the summer, but once we arrived back on campus, our group of friends had all either hooked up or dropped out. So it was just the two of us when we went to the movies or dinner—things we'd usually do in the group"

"Tell me about last Friday."

John focused on a picture of a baby girl, which sat on top of a battered metal file cabinet. His stomach churned at the thought of that day.

"No class, of course, because of the game. Kim and I usually go out for breakfast on Saturday, but since I planned to be gone, we went out Friday morning instead. The

Village Inn. Then I went back to my apartment and she went to hers. I watched *The Price is Right* and then took a nap."

"Why?"

"Why did I take a nap?"

The detective nodded.

"I'd been out late on Thursday."

"Okay. What next?"

"I set my alarm for 2:00 p.m. When it went off, I threw on my clothes and put my suitcase in my trunk. I drove to Dennis Vance's house and picked up the tickets for the game. Then I picked up Willy Carpenter, and we left for Dallas."

"Why did Dennis Vance have your tickets?"

"He had connections. He could get seats on the forty-yard line, twenty rows up."

"You didn't talk to Kim again that day?"

"No."

Detective Bruner looked over his notes. "I'll be right back, John. Can I get you anything? Coffee or water?"

"No thanks."

Bruner left the office without shutting the door. John closed his eyes and buried his head in his hands. His muscles ached to the bones, and his eyes burned.

The police hadn't immediately investigated Kim's disappearance. He could see their point. A college girl, the OU-Texas weekend. She could have gone to Dallas; she could have run off with friends.

Could have. That was the point. But she didn't. He knew it. Her friends knew it. All her friends were around, and no one knew anything.

When the police finally took an interest, he purposely kept himself in the dark. He didn't want to face the reality that he might never see Kim again.

A few minutes later, Detective Bruner returned. "John, could you come with me." He took him into a room with drab walls, drab flooring, a table bolted to the floor, and a mirrored window.

His muscles tightened as he took a seat. Was he a suspect? No doubt, the two detectives hadn't ruled anything out. He hoped they wouldn't. Yet everyone had alibis. From what he'd heard, Kim had last been seen around 4:00 p.m.

An older man with a pot belly came in and sat with Detective Bruner. "This is Detective Sanders. He's going ask you a few questions too."

John shook the fleshy hand Sanders offered.

"We came down here because Detective Bruner's office couldn't quite hold the three of us." Sanders smiled.

John realized it was his attempt at self-deprecating humor and gave him a feeble smile. "No problem."

Bruner spoke first. "Can you tell us about Kim's life outside of class? What did she like to do? Who did she hang out with?"

John wiped his sweaty palms on his jeans. "She hung out with me." A tiny laugh, more to himself, escaped. "She lived with Leslee Williams. Look, you guys know who her friends were. You've talked to all of us."

"Tell us about her job," Bruner said.

"She worked as a secretary in the English department. She answered the phones, coordinated student appointments, and ran errands."

Sanders asked his first question. "Did she like the professors she worked for?"

"Sure. She never complained. I take that back, she did complain, but not about the job. She needed more money so, last week, she started looking for another job."

"And she didn't tell you why."

"She did," John said. "She needed more money."

The detectives exchanged looks. Bruner said, "Did she ever mention Professor Hazelton?"

John shook his head. "I'm sure I've heard the name before, but she never talked about him in any fashion that indicated she had a problem with him. I would remember that."

"What about Larkin Connor?" Sanders asked.

"Who's he?"

"It's a she, a freshman."

"No, never."

Bruner glanced at his legal pad. "John, did you ever hear about Chad or Debbie Bailey?"

"No."

"Ray Pope?"

"No." The two detectives stared at him.

A tiny mass of anger began boiling in John's soul. They were talking about his Kim, his future. "Honestly, I've never heard of them. You're looking at me like I should know everything about her life. I didn't, but I know she wasn't hiding anything from me. Kim is—" He paused and swallowed hard. "She was as pure and innocent as they come. Trust me. She didn't hang around the wrong kind of people. She didn't invite trouble. If she found it, it came looking for her."

"Don't be alarmed, John," Bruner said. "These names have come up. We're trying to build a complete picture of Kim, trying to see how it all connects."

"Okay, fine." John leaned back and looked up. The water-stained ceiling tiles provided little comfort.

Bruner continued, "How would you characterize Kim's relationship with Dennis Vance?"

A twinge of fear nipped at him. John knew Dennis Vance well. Too well.

"They're friends."

"Did they ever date?" Bruner asked.

"No," John said quickly.

"Would you have known if they did?"

"So, you're saying they did date," John asked.

"No. I'm saying Dennis said they did."

John scowled. "He's lying."

Sanders cut in. "Is Dennis Vance a violent person?"

"I don't think so." But a flash went off in his mind. They suspected Dennis. They must have a reason. Dennis always had a crush on Kim, always said she was pretty.

"You don't think he's violent? Do you have any doubts?"

"I've never seen him be violent or lose his temper." He looked down at the floor. "But I know he's conniving, charming, witty, and as smart as they come."

The three discussed Dennis Vance's character for a few more minutes. "We have another name to throw at you," Sanders said. "Renee Templin."

"Never heard of her. Is she one of Dennis's friends?"

"You've never heard of her."

"No."

"John, what is the latest you believe you could have been at your apartment last Friday?"

"Two thirty. I know I left by then."

"Okay. We pulled your phone records. You received a call from Kim Addison at 3:25. Do you know of any reason why she would have called?"

"I do not," John barely managed to say. Why couldn't he have been home to take that call?

Sanders said, "You received another call at 4:15 from a gas station east of Norman on Highway 9." He shook his head. "I don't get it."

"That gas station is a quarter mile away from land owned by Chad and Debbie Bailey. Witnesses say a girl matching Kim's description was seen at there around 4:15. We believe she tried to call you from a pay phone there."

Bruner took over. *"We lost track of her after that. No one saw her leave. No trace of her car. Nothing."*

Why couldn't he have been home to take Kim's call? She'd called him *in her last moments, no one else. And he had failed her.*

John burst upright, his covers tossed aside, covered with a sheen of sweat. He was home. Well, not exactly. But in his sixteen-year-old home.

His body heaved with each breath, and his heart burned with the fire of regret. If he hadn't repressed those memories, he would have known where to look for Kim when he relived the day she died. If he'd been there earlier, maybe they would have been gone before the attacker showed up.

He fell back onto the mattress. He'd locked away the information that might have allowed him to save her. He truly had failed.

The glowing digital alarm clock read 3:24 a.m. No way he'd be going back to sleep.

He tried to convince himself that it was just a vivid dream. But in this new life, there were no coincidences.

Suddenly it hit him. He saw Professor Hazelton when he relived the day Kim disappeared. Then he saw Dennis. He'd expected to see him at college—he had to get the tickets from him—but not in high school. Violent Dennis. Angry Dennis. Dennis who had a thing for Kim. Had John's lifelong quasi-friend killed Kim?

And then there was Renee. Why in the world had she been talking with Dennis? John didn't meet her until much later, and she only knew Dennis through him in real life.

He grabbed a notebook off the bookshelf, flicked on the desk lamp, and jotted down each name from the interview.

Hazelton: Kim's boss. Smarmy.

Baileys: Where Kim was last seen. Suspects?

Dennis: Violent. Likes Kim. Always around. Friend of Kim? More than a friend?

Renee: Why? How was she related to Kim?

Chapter 10

By the time chemistry class rolled around on Friday, John had completed letters to Mark, Sara, and Renee. Writing letters they'd probably never read helped fill the need to communicate with them and eased some of his loneliness.

He craved the type of social interaction he got every day with the regulars at The Coffee Beast and his wife and kids at home. Being around his family and high school friends over the last five days had been amusing, but he couldn't be himself with them.

He slumped down into a chair and rubbed his temples to relieve the pressure of a building headache. Pretending to be a teenager and hiding the thoughts and knowledge of his adult experiences wore on him. Loneliness crept up and took root.

If he was going to be stuck in this world, he needed new friends, people who'd be open to the confident person he had become. People who wouldn't notice any difference in his behavior.

Lanie Simpson sat in front of him and to the right. While she turned her head to watch Mrs. Gidley, John watched her. She caught him looking, and he quickly turned away.

The next time she caught him looking, he didn't turn away. When she smiled, he smiled back, as if they'd shared an inside joke.

When class ended, he left the room before her, but waited just outside the door.

When she came out, she swatted him with a rolled-up notebook. "You're crazy. What got into you today?"

"Come on, I'll walk you to your car." Not waiting for her to answer, he started down the hallway.

She followed. "Have you stared at me like that every day this year?"

"No, but I should have. I've turned over a new leaf. I'm trying not to take life so seriously."

"And when did you figure that out?"

"I think on Monday when Dennis Vance beat me senseless." He held the door open for her, and they walked out to a beautiful cloudless day. They merged into a crowd of students heading for their cars.

"I saw the whole fight," Lanie said. "He didn't beat you senseless."

"No, but I didn't put up a very good fight."

"I noticed."

"Dennis and I are good friends. I didn't want to do something I'd regret." They stepped off the sidewalk and onto the parking lot.

"That's awfully nice of you."

"I don't want you to think I'm crazy. I promise not to stare at you in class anymore." He shrugged. "Of course, you'll always have doubts. You'll always wonder if I have my eyes on you."

They walked around a pickup as it pulled out. Two rows over, horns honked, and someone rolled down his window to curse.

"Here's my car." Lanie unlocked the door to her navy Ford Granada. It was polished and clean, but not exactly the mid-eighties luxury car he'd expected her to drive. "Well . . ."

"I'll see you tomorrow."

"Sounds good." She sat in her seat and started the engine but didn't close the door. "Where did you park? Do you need a ride to your car?"

"Thanks, but I'm meeting Coach Walker in fifteen minutes."

"Really?" She leaned out of the car to look up at him.

"Yeah, I'm thinking about playing baseball. He's going to give me a tryout, I guess. I don't know exactly what I'll be doing."

"Cool. Tell me how it goes."

"I will." She closed her door and backed up. As she drove by, she waved.

He grinned at the hint of puzzlement on her face. He'd surprised her in class, and again with the baseball. As he trudged back to his car to get his gear, he thought about Renee, Kim, and the fantasy he was now living. Had his real life stopped in a freeze frame, with time suspended until he returned? Or had Renee spent the last few days in misery, trying to figure out what happened to him?

Somewhere in the city, Kim went about her day, having no clue her life would end in a few short years.

* * *

After John changed into navy sweats and tennis shoes in the front seat of his car, he walked to the baseball fields and headed towards the stout man clutching a clipboard just beyond home plate. The short grass was starting to lose its green luster as the end of October approached, and the field looked sloppy without any bases or chalk lines.

"Hey, John. Come on out." Coach Walker waved John him over. If he recognized John from the fight earlier in the week, he didn't show it. The coach led him into the dugout and motioned toward a bulging bag. "Pick a bat out of there."

As John rummaged through the bag, the coach said, "Your dad told me you regretted quitting baseball last year and wanted to get back in it."

"Actually, I quit several years ago." John pulled out a silver, twenty-six ounce Easton bat with green lettering. "This will do."

"Hmm. Is that right?" Doubt crept into Coach Walker's voice, but he pointed back to home plate. "Why don't you get into the batter's box. I'll get Coach Pope out here to pitch to you."

Coach Pope. The name jarred something loose.

"Ray, come on out here, and bring the net."

Ray Pope. Another name from when the police questioned about Kim's disappearance.

Coach Pope came from left field, carrying a bucket in one hand and a protective net in the other. He set the net up in front of the pitcher's mound and put the bucket of balls next to the rubber. "Whenever you guys are ready."

John stepped up to the plate and dug his feet into the dirt. Once settled, he eyed the tall, lanky pitcher. He wore a red trucker's cap along with blue jeans and a long-sleeved T-shirt. Was it the same Ray Pope the police had questioned him about on the day Kim disappeared? Possibly not, but John assumed it was. The same way he assumed a reason existed for him reliving his high school years.

Who was Ray Pope? What kind of man would this lanky assistant coach become in 1992 when Kim disappeared? How would he know Kim?

John swung over the top on the first two pitches, pulling his head each time.

After missing a third pitch, John stepped away from the plate and refastened the batting gloves he'd borrowed from Sam. He dug his right foot into the dirt, positioned the bat high over his shoulders, and nodded at Pope.

He had a smooth, fluid delivery, and John found it easy to pick up the ball as it left his hand. A fastball right down the middle.

John waited and then swung the bat. He hit a solid line drive into left field. For the next five minutes, he smashed line drives all around the park.

Coach Walker watched silently.

"Four more balls in the bucket," Pope yelled.

John gave a tired nod. He could do four more. The next pitch came in over the plate. He crushed it high into the air, and it sailed over the left field wall.

After a ground ball and a line drive, he hit another one over the fence to finish. He watched the ball bounce and roll on the other side and then took off his batting gloves.

Coach Walker approached him. He spit out a sunflower seed shell and peppered John with questions about his ability to play various positions. Apparently satisfied with the answers, he said, "Okay, John. Come by my office after school tomorrow and we'll talk."

"Who's going to pick up all the balls?" Ray called from the mound.

"You are," Coach Walker answered. "And if you want to finish before dark, you'd better get started."

Ray cursed before snatching up the bucket and heading for the outfield.

John hurried after him. "I'll help you."

Ray stopped at the outfield grass, set the bucket on the ground and eyed John. Beneath the cap, he had wavy blond hair and blue eyes. His skin bore a fading summer tan. "Thanks, kid. That was some good hitting."

"My name's John." He jogged over second base.

"I know, kid."

John shrugged. "Are you an assistant coach?"

"I wouldn't call it that. I help out at practices. They have two other assistants. Coach Walker is really nice though. You'll like him. Thanks for helping. Why don't you go get the balls and throw them in to me. You can work out your arm."

Balls were scattered everywhere in the outfield. John liked how Pope had gotten him to do all the work. He trotted to the nearest ball while Ray moved the bucket over to second base.

"I'm ready." Ray pounded his fist into the glove. "Let 'er rip."

As John threw in the first ball, Ray began his play-by-play. "The runner's rounding first. He's going to try and stretch it into a double. Here comes the throw . . ." He caught the ball and made a swipe tag. "And he's out!"

His enthusiasm was contagious. John hustled after the balls as Ray announced the imaginary game. He uncorked throw after throw, and Ray made a tag on each one.

They finished in no time. Ray was a fun guy in spite of his initial response to the extra work, but a shadow of doubt pricked at John. What did Ray Pope have to do with Kim Addison? Why had the police mentioned him during their questioning?

* * *

Dad and Sam converged on John as soon as he entered the front door.

"How'd it go?" Sam asked.

"Really well. I clobbered the ball. I don't know why, but I can really hit now." John set his bag down by the door. "I'm supposed to meet with the coach after school tomorrow."

"I'm proud of you, son."

A warm feeling rushed through John's veins. "Thanks, Dad."

John spent an hour doing homework and another hour writing a letter to Mark. Then he turned the page back to the list he started the other day.

Ray Pope: Baseball. Enthusiastic.

He put the notebook down and stared at it. He hated it. Why did he have to be here? Yet the list gave him hope. If he just kept forging ahead, he'd find out what happened to Kim.

* * *

John had almost forgotten it was Halloween until Sam and Becky came out of their rooms dressed up in Dracula and Cinderella costumes. They ate a quick supper of turkey sandwiches and chips before they headed out to hit up the neighborhood for candy.

Sam grabbed his bucket and headed for the door. "I'm meeting Jason and Kevin. I'll be back by nine." The screen door slammed closed behind him.

Mom found a flashlight and put on a sweater, and Becky pulled her by the hand out the door. "C'mon, Mom. I want to go to every house in the neighborhood this year."

Still hungry, John heated up a leftover burrito casserole, thrilled to be able to eat with the metabolism of a teenager again. The memory that Thursday nights were *Magnum PI* and *Simon and Simon* night came to him naturally—as though it hadn't been more than twenty years since that ritual—so he set up a TV tray in front of the incredibly small twenty-seven inch Magnavox. Now if only he could watch Tom Selleck on a forty-two-inch screen.

He reached for the remote control to pull up a summary of the evening's episodes, but one glance at the simple device reminded him that the TV didn't have a menu, much less an episode guide. Would he remember them from the first time he watched them? The phone rang. "John, it's for you," Dad called from the kitchen.

"Who is it?"

"I don't know." As he got closer, he whispered, "It's a girl."

"Right. I'll take it in my room." John hurried down the hallway. Evidently, he'd made a big impression on Lanie, and that wasn't necessarily a good thing. "Hello."

"Hi, John. It's Kim."

His heart took off in an entirely different direction.

"Hey, Kim. What's up?"

"I'm eating dinner."

"You're not trick-or-treating?" John propped his pillows against the headboard and sat down on his bed.

"I'm too old for that."

"Where are your mom and dad?"

"They're at a meeting at church."

And she had called him the first chance she got. "Thanks for calling."

"Sure. My parents are nice, but sort of strict. I know why they don't want me to talk on the phone." She giggled. "I know they care, and I respect that."

The doorbell rang, and Dad's hearty greeting to the miniature goblins, princesses, and superheroes echoed down the hallway.

"So, the first chance you get, you disobey them."

"Umm, no."

"Seems like it."

"Let's just say, I trust you."

"Okay." His heart melted. His Kim trusted him. When they dated, she had always said how much she trusted him. "Why do you trust me?"

"Easy. We both know I can't date you. I'm too young. Besides, I don't want to date when I'm sixteen. I don't know if I'll date until I'm in college."

A haunting chill of despair swept through his room like a swirling wind whipping up new-fallen snow. She hadn't had a serious boyfriend until college. He'd been it. He'd been the one she waited for.

The true purpose of the conversation lingered in John's mind. What if he couldn't save her? When he lost her the first time, his world ended. Could he stand to get close to her and risk losing her again?

"Would you like to date me?" He managed to keep his voice calm even though his insides churned with regret and the reality of what would become of her.

"Mmm, I don't know. Let me think."

"You have two years to decide."

"You're funny, John. Do you flirt like this with all the girls?"

"I'm not flirting with you. I was at church, but not now."

"Like with that thumbs-up thing? My dad does that to me all the time."

"Really? That's a coincidence."

"Maybe," Kim said. "Or maybe it's something more."

He squeezed the phone.

She whispered, "Maybe it is destiny."

"Now *you're* joking."

"I know. Let's talk about something else."

"I like talking about you." John closed the notebook on the desk so he wouldn't see the letter he'd begun to Renee.

"Oh no! My mom and dad are home."

He wanted to talk forever. "Can I call you back?"

"I'll call you."

That would have to do. "Okay. Maybe I'll see you at church on Sunday."

"Maybe. Bye, John."

Click. She was gone.

John placed the phone on the receiver. They'd hardly talked at all. And he still hadn't told her she was in danger.

Chapter 11

John woke early enough Friday morning to sit down for breakfast with Dad. "Have you started looking for a job yet?"

Dad sipped at a steaming cup of coffee. "No. I'm in vacation mode right now."

John turned to the sports section in the paper and smiled at the headline over the article about the Game Six call at first base in the World Series. "Ueberroth Agrees Umpire Blew the Call." *Get over it, Cardinal fans. Nothing is going to change.*

On the comics page, he saw an ad for an IBM computer with 256k memory for $2,588. It was nice to see that some things would get cheaper over time. He stared at the computer as an idea formed. It would take research, but it could be done. Maybe he could help his family with his knowledge of the future.

* * *

School flew by, and seventh-hour chemistry approached with the chance to see Lanie again. He might have initially latched onto her to soothe his lonely heart, but his sixteen-year-old hormones didn't exactly agree. He meandered through the crowded hallways, realizing how few people he knew the first time through high school.

As he rounded a corner, someone slammed into him from behind. His face smacked into a locker. *Dennis!*

John swung around, his hands curled into fists. Then he breathed a heavy sigh. Just Willy. "Jerk. You surprised me."

"Oh shut up, you big baby. You thought I was Dennis, didn't you?"

"Yes." John smiled, thankful it *hadn't* been Dennis.

"You picking me up for the game tonight?"

"Umm, yeah." From somewhere deep in his memory, he recalled that Putnam City played Ponca City in football tonight. He pushed aside the urge to take Lanie out to the game. He needed her friendship, not a romance, no matter what his body was trying to tell him. "I'll swing by at six, and we can go to Bueno."

"Perfect," Willy said and disappeared into the throng.

The bell rang just as John crossed the threshold into chemistry class. His heart sank at the sight of Lanie's empty desk. He was surrounded by people he didn't really care about, and the next hour dragged on.

As soon as the bell rang, he hustled to Coach Walker's office.

* * *

John felt pumped and excited as he left the coach. He'd have a chance to make the team when practice started. While he prayed each night he'd wake up at home with Renee, what if he was here for a long time? As each day crept by without any new discovery or any interaction with Kim, it became easier for him to justify diving into this new life.

And yes, the idea of excelling at baseball excited him.

He went straight from school to the batting cages, bought six tokens, and spent twenty minutes crushing 85-mph fastballs. Next stop, Walmart. He found a tub of EAS protein powder supplement. Then he went to the All-American Fitness Center, where his family had bought a lifetime membership when he was twelve. Sam made extensive use of it. This time, he would too. Through the benefit of hindsight he could see what hardcore weight training could do to his body. He lived in an era where every ninth-grade athlete had the chiseled form of a body builder. But in 1985, no one did.

* * *

Cars spilled out of the football stadium's parking lot. They lined the side of the road and even filled ditches, wherever people could find enough space. People walked in droves through the cool crisp air to the cathedral of high school athletics. John loved the atmosphere of high school football. The cacophony of fight songs, thundering drums, and cheerleader chants pounded his ears as they entered the stadium.

As the game began, John and Willy slid into one of the last empty spots along the fence in the end zone, the place to be for people more interested in the game than socializing.

"I can't believe you're trying out for baseball. You hated playing."

"I didn't hate it."

"Sure you did. You complained all the time. Don't lie, now." Willy nudged him with his forearm.

"I hated it because I wasn't any good. I can't explain it, Willy. Last Sunday, when we went to the cages, I hit everything. Maybe I'm just older or something."

"John."

John stiffened at the sound of his name.

Dennis Vance approached with a tall blonde at his side. Carolyn something, a cheerleader in eighth grade. Dennis leaned his elbows on the top of the fence railing. "Sorry about Monday."

"No problem. It's over." As John knew from his long history with Dennis, he had a temper, held grudges, and lacked a moral compass. But he was also the most loyal friend a man could have. Besides that, if John brushed off the fight, perhaps he could learn more about Dennis's ties to Kim. And since his wife worked with Dennis in his real life, maybe he could learn something to help him there too . . . if he ever returned.

"I shouldn't have ambushed you. I should have fought you like a man, given you a fair shot."

"That would have been better."

"No hard feelings then?"

"I'm cool."

"So what are you up to now?"

Dennis shrugged. "A lot of things. I'm working at Curtis Mathis selling electronics. I'll probably be back in school next semester."

He hadn't heard that brand name in awhile. He'd read their laughable slogan in the paper the other day: *It may cost more, but it's worth it.*

"They let you work there? Aren't you too young?"

Dennis produced an ID with the name of Dennis Shaw, a twenty-one-year-old Dennis Shaw. "I'm too young, but he isn't."

"Nice."

"Uh-oh. Touchdown." Dennis pointed to the Ponca City end zone as the crowd erupted.

"There's a party later. You guys should come." Dennis handed Willy and John a hand-drawn map. "You gonna come, Willy?"

"I don't know. We might."

"You can bring your girlfriend. You have a girlfriend, don't you?"

"Shut up," Willy said.

Dennis winked at John. "Are you going to come?"

"I don't know . . ." His insides cringed. Yes, he'd had a few beers in high school, but drinking as a sport appalled him, especially the father inside him.

"Hey, that's okay. I don't mind. You'll regret it, though, if you don't. There'll be lots of girls and lots of beer. Good times."

"I know, Dennis. You always come through."

Ponca City kicked off, and the ball sailed out of bounds.

"You know, Dennis, maybe some good came out of your assault."

"Oh yeah, what's that?"

"I've been talking to Lanie Simpson. She saw the whole thing."

"You impressed her by getting your tail kicked?"

"I think she felt sorry for me."

"I would tell you she's out of your league, but things happened for a reason."

John turned. "What do you mean?"

"Destiny. Maybe she's your destiny."

Kim just said that to him on the phone. *Destiny*. What could being sixteen again have to do with his destiny? And where would it take him?

* * *

As soon as Dennis departed, a loud commotion erupted to the right of the concession stand. Yelling, cursing, drunken loudness.

Ray Pope staggered a few steps away from his friends and cursed at them. Then he doubled over with laughter.

His hat fell off and landed in front of several big guys as they passed by. The one in overalls trampled over it.

Ray spewed a string of foul names after him.

The man stopped and slowly turned back. "You talkin' to me?"

Instead of answering, Ray threw a punch.

Screams of "fight!" beckoned everyone within earshot.

A short guy in Wranglers tackled Ray. They hit the ground and rolled on the gravel, trading punches.

Police officers elbowed through the crowd, broke up the fight, and hauled both of the men away. Ray continued to swear. Blood trickled out of his nose, yet he smiled deliriously.

Drugs? Alcohol? Both? Plus a violent temper. John mentally drew a target on Ray Pope's back. But did Ray even know Kim in real life? And if so, what could she have done to make him want to kill her?

* * *

After halftime, with the game way out of reach for the home team, the announcer called out yardage and names, downs and distance in a bored monotone. John and Willy mingled among the students beyond the east end zone, where students who didn't care about the game came to socialize.

The girls all had thick, wavy hair, the guys had feathered bangs, and John suddenly hated being there. He'd lived this once already. He didn't need to be part of the crowd.

Willy nudged him with an elbow. "You said Lanie wasn't at school today. Well, she's by the bleachers with Tammy Brooks and all those other guys."

John spotted the statuesque Tammy Brooks easily. She would model for Vogue and Cosmo in the early nineties before disappearing from the public eye. At his ten-year reunion, he heard it had been drug problems. Lanie stood next to her, along with another couple of girls and a few guys, including Devon Washington and Phil Prince.

"Go talk to her." Willy shoved him in the back.

The sea of people shifted, and though they were twenty feet apart, John's eyes locked with Lanie's for a brief moment. Then she looked away, and Tammy Brooks stepped in front of her.

John continued to stare. *Come on, Lanie. You're better than this.* Or had he been right about her and her friends in his real high school years, and she really was a snob?

As if she heard his silent plea, Tammy moved several inches to the right. Lanie peered around her tall friend. Her head cocked to the side, and her brown hair lay gently over her shoulders.

Her smile reached through the crowd and grabbed John, even though she tried to hide it by biting her bottom lip. That made it all the more alluring, and the sparkle in her eyes gave her away. Then she darted back behind Tammy and continued talking to the baseball guys and the prom-queen girls.

Willy punched him on the arm. "Dude! Did you see that?"

"Of course, I saw it." John rubbed his arm. Willy always hit him. Someday he should hit him back.

"She smiled at you. She likes you."

Did she like him? In high school, she'd been the dream girl. Now, after reliving high school for a week, he'd connected with her on some level.

She disappeared behind another crowd, and John turned back to the game. She had her friends, her group. He didn't need to try and interfere. Yet.

* * *

Reliving his high school years had never been a fantasy of his, yet here he was doing exactly that. Except, not really. This time, he could hit a major league fastball. And the cutest girl in school liked him. He also had a report he wanted to write for Dad. Hopefully, it would lead to Dad's getting a job with an up-and-coming tech company.

For the first time since he'd been sixteen again, John didn't go to sleep hoping he'd wake up in his own bed. Of course he wanted to go home—and surely he would, eventually. But he was actually having fun. That smile from Lanie had made all the difference.

Then there was Kim.

He didn't doubt the last week had been real. A day actually took twenty-four hours. He had to sleep and shave. He got hungry. He had to go the bathroom. No matter what happened, Kim would disappear in seven years. Could he change that?

He drifted off to sleep wondering if he could really change the past.

* * *

Someone pounced on John's bed. He threw off the blankets and bounded to his feet. Bright light blasted in from the window, and his son rolled around in the covers.

"Mark!" John lunged forward and hugged him tightly. Mark wrestled free, and John gave chase.

Mark rounded the corner and ran through the living room, but John almost caught him before he turned into the kitchen.

His wife stood at the counter in her bathrobe, stirring something in a mixing bowl with a wooden spoon.

"Good morning, Daddy," Sara called from the living room, where she watched cartoons.

John walked around the couch to give her a hug, but she looked bigger. He ran his hands through her hair and bent to give her a kiss. He screamed and jumped back. It was a fourteen-year-old Kim.

"What's wrong, Dad?" asked an eleven-year-old Brad Mullins.

John rushed into the kitchen and turned his wife to face to him. His stare wasn't into Renee's captivating, dark eyes, but into the ocean-blue gaze of Lanie Simpson.

John awoke into pitch blackness. Sweat trickled down his back. He missed his family. Oh, God, he missed his family.

He was losing it. He needed help, and he needed it fast.

Chapter 12

After the nightmare, John lay motionless and wide awake for hours before falling back asleep. He slept until ten and woke miserable and cranky. Each day some small moment, a thought or a memory, threatened his sanity. He couldn't go on like this. He needed help, but who could he turn to?

He also woke to an empty house. Thank goodness. Sam was at a birthday party. Mom and Becky had an event at church. He had no idea where Dad went.

So, how could he spend the day? He roamed the kitchen and found nothing appetizing.

While he fixed a protein shake in the blender, he considered who he might be able to confide in. He poured the shake into a cup and took a sip. Maybe the church's youth minister could help. Buzz Baker exuded gentleness and kindness, but could he handle John's problem?

He wiped off the shake mustache, grabbed some workout clothes, and went to the All-American Fitness Center. He pondered his dilemma for two hours while he ran, swam, lifted weights, and left thoroughly exhausted, both physically and mentally. But he'd come up with a solution that might work.

Next stop, the library. Without thinking, he walked to area where they kept the computers in his real life. Instead, the room was filled with newspapers and magazines. With a sigh, he returned to the front desk and found the large, wooden card catalog with its rows and rows of small drawers. If only he had his iPhone and the instant information gratification it offered. But no one had one, so he opened the drawer containing cards for the topic he needed.

Without the aid of computers, John spent hours doing what could have taken minutes. But he had nothing else to do. He enjoyed the slower pace of 1985, although the lack of instant sports news did drive him crazy.

Only when he approached home did he consider that his family might have worried about where he was. After all, he didn't have a cell phone they could just call.

If they were upset, they didn't show it. Instead, Sam grabbed a couple of gloves and threw one at him. "Let's play catch."

The air was cool and crisp and perfect for practicing in the backyard. He and Sam tossed the ball for an hour.

* * *

John left for church early on Sunday. After wandering the halls for a few minutes, he tracked down Buzz Baker outside the classroom where he taught a junior high Sunday School class.

The balding man stroked his bushy beard as he listened intently to the skinny seventh-grader in front of him.

John waited until the conversation finished before approaching. "Could I speak to you for a second?"

"Sure, John."

John glanced at the back of the seventh-grader walking down the hallway. "It's sort of private."

"Okay. Let's go to my office."

John followed him through the maze of hallways to the office complex on the south side of the building and then took a seat as Buzz settled into the chair behind his desk.

John got right to the point. "I need someone to talk to."

"I understand." Buzz leaned forward.

"It can't be you."

Buzz's brow furrowed. "John, everything you say to me will be completely confidential. I don't know what you want to talk about, but—"

"Stop right there." John held up his hand. "What I want to talk about isn't criminal. There's no sexual abuse or drugs. My parents are great. My brother and sister are fine. I'm fine." Almost. "I'd feel more comfortable talking to someone I didn't know, but someone with a spiritual background. I'll give the person permission to tell you, if he thinks it is necessary or in my best interest. Can you help me out?"

Buzz nodded slowly. "Sure, John. I can do that. Are you in a hurry?"

"Not really. But it would be great if I could do it today."

"So you are in a hurry."

"I guess I am."

"Okay. I think I know a guy. We went to seminary together. Let me dig out his information." Buzz thumbed through a leather-bound address book the size of a paperback. He jotted down a name on a scrap of paper and handed it to John. "He's a good guy. His name is Chad Bailey."

Chills ripped through John's soul. Another name from the police questioning. Another person from his past . . . and Kim's future. How did this new piece of the puzzle fit in?

John left Buzz's office clutching the paper with Bailey's information.

Kim had gone to the Baileys' for a job and disappeared. The police assumed murder, but a body had never been found. No suspects either. But the owner of the property where she last went would be a good place to start.

* * *

Chad welcomed John into his office at St. Paul School of Theology at Oklahoma City University with a hearty handshake and asked him to take a seat. The same Chad Bailey the police asked about during the interview about Kim's disappearance, and the same Chad Bailey who was looking to hire a nanny.

John hid his surprise at the man's youth. Late twenties, probably, with dark black hair, thick eyebrows, and a warm smile.

Bailey sat behind his clutter-free desk. In fact, the entire office looked like a model home: clean furnishings, a lack of personal items, everything in its place.

"Thanks for talking with me." John tried to ignore the butterflies in his stomach. Could Chad be the killer?

"No problem. Buzz is a great friend. I hope everything is okay."

"I'm fine, Mr. Bailey."

He opened a drawer in the desk and took out a legal pad, and then jotted a few words. "What did you want to talk about, John?"

John took a deep breath and exhaled slowly. "Okay. Here's the deal. You're going to think I'm crazy, and that's fine. I'd like you to keep what I tell you a secret, but like I told Buzz, if you think someone is in danger, or a crime has been committed, you can tell anyone you want—Buzz, the police, my parents—I don't care."

"Buzz said as much. I can understand why you wouldn't want to talk to him. It's hard to open up to your friends." Chad leaned forward.

A rush of adrenaline sizzled through John. He wiped his damp forehead with a shaky hand and took a deep breath. He could finally reveal his secret, but to actually put it into words and tell another person was harder than he expected. "Can you listen to all I have to say before asking any questions?"

Chad nodded.

"What if I tell you I know someone who is forty-five years old who woke up one morning in an apartment he lived in when he went to college? He was twenty-three again and a senior in college. This was no practical joke or dream. It was real." In very general terms, John explained the events of the last week as though they happened to someone else.

Chad twirled his pen around in his fingers. His expression didn't change.

John ended by explaining how much his "friend" wanted to go back home. He realized he'd been clenching his fists. He clenched them harder until his fingernails bit into his skin. Finally, he blurted out, "That person is me. Being sixteen again is fun, but it's driving me crazy."

Chad leaned back in his chair and put his hands behind his head.

"What do you think?" John asked.

"I think that's the craziest story I've ever heard." He leaned forward "But I think you'd expect me to say that, or you'd think I'm crazy."

John grinned. "I didn't come here expecting you to believe me; I came for your advice."

"Okay."

"If what I say is true, then I'm trapped here. I haven't seen my wife and kids in over a week. I miss them, Chad." John's eyes burned with unshed tears. "I'm afraid I'm never going to see them again."

Chad looked John in the eyes. "There's no point in debating whether you're telling me the truth. I don't even want to go there. Here's what you should do. Pray."

"Pray?"

"Yes. Every day. Every hour. Every time you think of your wife and kids, pray."

"Do you think God can help me get back to my family?"

"I know nothing about that, but I know God can come to where you are and help you. What that form that help takes, I don't know."

"Could God have anything to do with me reliving the day my girlfriend disappeared or being in high school again?"

"I think we are safe to assume God has His hand in everything."

"God's doing this to me?"

Chad shook his head and pressed his lips together. "No, I'm not saying that. It sounds to me like you need peace of mind. God can give it to you."

"So you don't believe me?"

"Come on, John, of course I don't. You admitted what you're saying is crazy." He closed his notebook and put his pen down.

"Do you want to hear something even crazier?"

"I'm ready. Let me hear it."

"Everything I told you today, I can prove." John spent the next fifteen minutes giving Chad selected information from the future.

Chapter 13

John woke up the following morning in the same bedroom. He buried his head in his pillow and screamed to blow off steam. He wrote in his journal for fifteen minutes, this time to Sara. He found it difficult to write to a four-year-old girl who loved Disney princesses and liked to dance and sing, but he missed his princess.

Feeling better about the day, he got dressed. His talk with Chad Bailey had comforted him. Bailey's advice had been to pray, so John paused to take his advice. *God, I miss my family. Please help me cope with not being with them. If they are aware of my absence, please let them know I will come back. God, please guide me while I'm here. I really believe I will find out what happened to Kim. Please protect me and be with all those I encounter.*

* * *

He breezed through school and especially enjoyed watching *Gone with the Wind* in lit class. In chemistry, Lanie flashed John a quick wave on her way to her seat.

John smiled. In the span of a week, he'd positioned himself inside her circle of friends, and more importantly, she didn't mind acknowledging him in front of others. How different than the first time through high school, when Lanie and her friends intimidated him.

When class ended, she walked out with him. They jostled through the mass of students moving towards the doors. Lanie said, "I saw you at the game Friday night."

"I saw you too."

"I looked for you after the game but didn't find you."

She looked for him? "I came with Willy, and we left early. Did you have a good time?"

"I did. But it could have been better."

Was she throwing him a softball? In spite of himself, he pushed it and tested her to see if he guessed right. "Look, could I get your phone number?"

"Sure." Her response came almost too quickly. And confirmed his suspicion.

He stopped and rifled through his backpack for a pen and piece of paper and jotted her number down. Her smile told him he could have asked her out right then, and she would have said yes. But did he want that? Should he want that?

* * *

When John got home from school, Sam sat on the couch watching TV.

"Do you want to play catch?" John asked.

"No, not today, I don't feel so good."

"Man, its cold in here," John said. The temperature in the house wasn't much different than outside. "Isn't the heater on?"

"It's broken."

John peeked into his parents' room. "When did the heater break?"

Dad looked up from his desk. The checkbook lay open, and his glasses slid down to the end of his nose. "Last night. Cliff Pennington is coming over later to take a look at it. It's supposed to get close to freezing tonight, so hopefully he can take care of it."

His parents' heater never broke in his real life. What did this mean?

Cliff Pennington arrived at six thirty, just after supper. Mom made everyone hot chocolate, and then Cliff went with Dad into the garage to look at the furnace. John did homework in the living room until they came back inside.

Cliff explained the problem. It wasn't good news. They'd need a new furnace.

After Cliff left, Dad swung at the air and muttered under his breath

"We have savings," Mom said. "We can afford to fix it,"

"We don't have savings to fix this," Dad responded. "A new furnace is going to cost us two thousand dollars."

"Are we going to go to a hotel tonight?" She wrapped her arms around herself and shivered.

He shook his head and went to the fireplace, where he unwrapped a starter log. He ignited the gas with a match, and the log went up in flames with a whoosh. "We'll stay here for the night, see how it goes."

"Harold, we'll freeze."

"Becky can sleep in our room. We'll turn on the space heater. John and Sam can set up pallets and sleep in front of the fire."

"We can do that, Dad. It's almost like camping out." Sam's face glowed.

"No problem," John said. He hated to see his parents with money issues. Growing up, they'd never hinted at any type of financial problems. Surely they had some, but they'd kept their troubles away from their kids.

Of course, in real life, Dad never lost his job at Kerr-McGee. If he had, John wouldn't have been able to do anything to help. But in this life, he could. He returned to his room and reviewed the paper he'd prepared for Dad.

*　*　*

With a roaring blaze in the fireplace, the family sat in the living room enjoying the warmth. *That's Incredible* had just gone to a commercial. Monday Night Football would be on soon.

Sam jumped up. "John, do you want to build a big fort like we used to? I'll go get the blankets."

John's first instinct was to say no. They'd probably need the blankets for warmth. Then he smiled. He had a second chance to enjoy a simple pleasure. "Sure. That'll be fun." He waited until Sam left before reaching down beside the chair and fingered the manila folder he'd brought with him. Now was the time. "Hey Dad, I've been working on a report for my economics class."

"Really? Do you need me to look it over?"

"That would be great. It's about Microsoft. Have you heard of them?"

"I think so. Computers, right?"

"Yes, computers." He pulled out the three-page report. "I think they're going to dominate the computer industry for years."

"I don't know about computers. No one ever uses ours." He glanced at the ancient Tandy sitting on a desk in the corner of the living room.

That was true. The Tandy performed no useful functions. "They've just introduced software called Windows, and have plans to put it on every computer made."

"Do they? I've heard rumors."

"You should buy their stock when it comes out."

Dad looked at him beneath his glasses. "You think it's a sure thing?"

"I do, Dad. It's going to be the next Walmart. If you can get in on the IPO, you'll be set."

"You know about IPO's?"

"Sure, Dad. We covered that in class."

"When are they going public?"

"Early next year. March 13, 1986, to be exact."

"Let me see your report. I can look it over for you tonight."

John passed him the folder. "Do you think you'll invest in it?"

Dad frowned. "Oh, I don't know. Probably not, especially if I can't find a job quickly. Most of our retirement is tied to Kerr-McGee. He set the folder on the coffee table as Fran Tarkenton returned to introduce their next "incredible" story.

John bit back the arguments that rose to mind. He held in his response until he reached his room, where he pounded his pillow as hard as he could. Dad was only patronizing him, and he had no way to convince him to listen. What good was it to have knowledge that could change his family's future for the better if he didn't have the power to use it?

Chapter 14

Wednesday afternoon, John faced a new kind of apprehension. After school, fall mini-camp began for the baseball team. Weather permitting, they'd hold several practices over the next few weeks.

Hitting the balls in the cages had been easy. Hitting them to show the coach what he could do was harder. Translating those skills into an actual game situation required an even higher level of concentration and effort. Would he be able to tag up on a fly ball? Could he back up the right base?

When the bell rang, John and Lanie met at their usual spot outside the classroom.

"You haven't called me yet," Lanie said.

"I know. I've been busy."

"Right. Sure you have."

"No, seriously. My family stayed in a hotel last night. Our heater quit on us Monday," John said as they stepped outside.

"Brrr. You must have been miserable."

Low, dark clouds covered the gray sky, but with little wind, it was quite pleasant, especially after such a cold weekend. John said, "We tried to brave out with space heaters and a fire in the fireplace. My brother and I camped out in the living room in front of the fire."

"That sounds fun."

"We had a blast. But in the end, Mom won. She refused to spend one more night in icy conditions. My dad relented, because we're getting it fixed today."

"So that's how it is in your house? What mom wants, mom gets."

"Isn't it like that in everyone's house?" Sometimes, John believed Renee only let him think he had control. His chest shuddered as if a knife jabbed at his heart. Renee. Their marriage had seemed to be cruising along just fine until a few weeks ago. Now they sailed through uncharted waters. She insisted it wasn't something he did, so what happened? Was it another man? Maybe Dennis? She and Dennis worked together.

"It is in mine, by default I guess. My parents are divorced."

"I'm sorry." They waited for a car to pass before crossing into the parking lot.

"It's okay. I still see Dad a lot. I usually see him every other Sunday."

"That's not the same."

She paused and looked at him, her blue eyes the color of the dark sky. "No, it's not."

The deep thought silenced them until they reached John's car. He unlocked the trunk and pulled out his gym bag.

"What's that for?"

"Baseball practice." He looped the bag around his shoulder.

"I didn't know you were on the team."

"I'm not, but I'm going to try out. Come on, I'll walk you to your car."

"Okay." Her lips twisted into a tight grin.

"What?" John kicked at a rock as they walked between cars.

"Nothing."

"You want to say something."

"No, I don't," Lanie said.

"You know a lot of people on the baseball team, don't you?"

"I know a few."

"And you dated a few."

Lanie laughed. "Oh, my goodness. My past finally caught up with me."

"No, it didn't. I don't care who your friends are or who you've dated."

They approached Devon Washington, who stood behind a Ford Bronco with Phil Prince. Devon slung his bag over his back.

"Hi, Lanie," Devon said.

"Hi."

Awkward silence ensued, and John felt bad for Lanie.

"Guys, this is John." She gestured.

"We know John." Devon said it nicely, but tension still floated between them.

"I'll see you guys tomorrow." Lanie offered a short wave and turned away.

He hadn't envisioned leaving her like this. He should have held her hand. No. Yes.

"You're playing baseball now?" Phil said.

"I am."

They moved toward the locker rooms built into the base of the ancient football stadium.

"Didn't you play for the Astros in Little League?" Phil asked.

"I did and haven't played since. I hope you guys will take it easy on me. I'm going to be a bit rusty."

"Sure." Devon said. "I didn't know you and Lanie were friends."

"We have chemistry class together. We actually started talking the day Dennis Vance kicked my tail."

"Oh yeah," Phil said. "If we hadn't stepped in, he would have pulverized you."

"I don't know about that," John said. "I can hold my own."

Devon and Phil shared a glance, and Devon shrugged. "I guess we'll see."

* * *

The locker room smelled exactly as a fifty-year-old locker room should: like wet concrete, wadded-up moldy socks, and body odor. Exposed rusty pipes crisscrossed the ceiling. The worn concrete floor showed several cracks, and the dented lockers squeaked when opened.

John recognized most of the guys. A few acknowledged him with a nod, but most ignored him. He found a corner to dress in and put on a turtleneck underneath a gray Putnam City T-shirt to keep him warm, then gray sweats and cleats.

Ray Pope stuck his head in the door and shouted, "Everybody out on the field in five minutes!"

Guys laughed and cursed. Some snuck a pinch of Skoal between a lip and their gums. This was crazy. John had thought the closest he'd ever get to baseball again would be coaching Little League. Yet, here he was.

"God, be with me," he said quietly before heading out to the field.

The cool weather had turned the grass brown, but the bases were set in their places, the rubber was on the mound, and crisp white chalk marked the foul territory and the batter's box.

John joined several guys stretching in the infield and found it surprisingly easy to bend and touch his toes. He'd never been able to do that. In real life, he was as limber as a two-by-four. Unsure of the proper routine, he copied Devon.

Ray Pope was the last man on the field. He wore baseball pants with actual stirrups and cleats along with a P.C. Pirates jacket. "Are you guys ready? Hope you stretched good, because it's pretty chilly today."

Pope led them in five laps around the field and warm-up exercises, then infield and fly ball practice. It was time to hit. So far, everything had been easy.

Pope and Assistant Coach Ricks lugged two buckets of balls out to the pitcher's mound. "We'll bat three at a time and then rotate from right field," Pope announced.

John spent two rotations in the outfield before his turn. His muscles tightened a little more throughout each. Hopefully his newly acquired skill hadn't left him.

Finally at the plate he picked a bat off the ground and stepped into the batter's box. His performance today wouldn't affect whether he made the team, but he still wanted to impress the guys in the field.

Ricks had taken over for Pope on the mound and threw the first pitch.

John grounded it to third. Okay, the first pitch was out of the way. He took a deep breath and focused. He clearly saw the next pitch as it left Ricks' hand. He started his swing. At the last minute, the bottom dropped out of the ball.

A few guys behind him snickered.

John forced himself not to look. He kept his eyes on the pitcher. The possibility of another curve ball caused him to swing late, and he fouled off the next pitch. He grounded the next one to second and popped another curve up to third. Hitting like that wouldn't impress anyone. He stepped out of the box and refastened his batting gloves. Only a few more chances before he rotated to the field. He stepped back into the batter's box and tightened his grip on the bat. *Come on, John, you can do this.*

When Ricks delivered the pitch, John tracked the seams on the ball as it spun towards him. His hands moved, the ball broke left, and his bat followed. The ball hit the sweet spot of the bat, and John hammered it to straight center field.

The guy playing center field hurried backwards. The ball cleared his outstretched arm and bounced against the fence.

"Good hit," Devon said behind him.

John felt like whooping and hollering, but he still had one more to go.

Coach Pope wrote on a clipboard.

Ricks began his slow wind-up. His arm snapped forward. He put a little extra on this one, and the ball came in extra fast. John blasted it. The ball sailed over the left field fence as the outfielders stood and watched.

This time, he couldn't help but smile as he walked to the dugout to retrieve his glove. He'd been the first one to hit a ball out of the park today.

"Good hitting," Pope said. "You adjusted to the curve ball."

"Thanks."

"You're a long shot to make the team."

"I understand."

"But you'll have your chance. Lanie will be so proud."

John stopped in his tracks. He thought of the cursing-crazy Ray at the football game. He must be a piece to the puzzle. If he could only figure out how it fit together with all the other people the police questioned him about. Then maybe he could go back to his real life.

Chapter 15

Later that night, John's mom stuck her head in his room. "Phone call for you, John," she said with an odd expression on her face. "It's a girl." He dropped the book he'd been reading, jumped up from his bed, and snatched his phone from the corner of his desk. The moment Mom backed out of the room, he closed the door behind her. Finally, he lifted the phone to his ear. "Hello?"

"Hi, John." Kim's voice, even over the phone, electrified him.

"It's great to hear from you. Are your parents gone again?"

She laughed. "How'd you guess?"

Her light response pierced his heart. How had he, the middle-aged parent, come to the point of encouraging a young girl to sneak behind her parents? He shook his head. Well, it was the only way he could influence her in this second chance—or was it his third?—he had somehow been given. Maybe save her life. *If only he knew how.*

Or did he really want to save her life? What would happen to Renee, Mark, and Sara if he saved Kim?

He moved the stack of textbooks from the chair to his desk and took a seat. "I haven't tried to call you since we last talked. Should I have?"

"No. I still think my parents would be mad. No sense in getting on their watch list."

"Good idea. Let's keep our relationship a secret." His conscience jabbed at him again, but he ignored it. He had to try and save Kim. How could he do that if he couldn't even talk to her?

She giggled. "What have you been up to?"

They chatted for a few minutes about John going out for the baseball team. He loved hearing her voice, but he ached to see her again. If only her family would start coming to his church and he could see her every week.

The thought reminded him of the Fall Festival. "All the churches in the city are coming together to hold a Fall Festival at Mission Acres Church in Moore. You should come."

"It sounds really fun, but I think we're going to visit my grandma."

"That's too bad. I could see you without your parents knowing."

"Maybe I want my parents to know. Maybe I want them to know who I see, so if anyone breaks my heart, my dad will beat him up."

"I promise I'd never break your heart. But I could see you breaking mine." The conversation had turned serious. Kim just didn't know it.

She said, "Why do you say that?"

He took a deep breath and dived in. "You're pretty stingy with your feelings. You're nice to everyone but don't really open up to anyone but your closest friends. You guard your heart with a passion instilled by your parents. You won't give it to just anyone, but when you do, it will be completely and without regret."

Kim didn't answer. Maybe she, too, had seen a glimpse of the future they would someday share.

Chapter 16

Fall Festival at Mission Acres Church kicked off at 8:30am, which meant everyone in the Michaels household woke up early. John, Sam, and Becky ate a breakfast of Cookie Crisp Cereal.

"I hear you have a big day planned, Becky," John said between bites.

"Mom's taking me to get my nails done. Then we're going to Penn Square Mall to get a new dress."

"I can't wait to see it. I bet it'll be beautiful."

"You'll miss the big Sooner-Nebraska game," Dad said.

John shrugged. He already knew the Sooners would prevail. "There will probably be a television at the Fall Festival, like last year," Sam said.

John took a last bite of his cereal and put his bowl in the sink. "Ready, Sam?"

"Just a second. Mom, do you have any medicine? I have a headache."

Sam gulped down the Tylenol she gave him, and they headed out the door. In John's Mustang, Sam put in a *Weird Al Yankovic in 3-D* cassette, and they both jammed to "Eat It" and "I Lost on Jeopardy" on the way to Lanie's house.

"You know, Sam, I think Weird Al will be around a lot longer than the artists he parodies."

"Do you think so?"

"Just a hunch." Unfolding a scrap of paper from his pocket, John checked it for directions and then turned onto 63rd. He turned left on Grove and looked for her house number. "There it is."

John pulled in the driveway. "Dude, you're going to have to sit in the back."

"Oh, man," Sam said.

The house was tiny but well maintained with white siding and trim. John rang the doorbell and tapped his foot on the concrete porch.

The door opened, and Lanie smiled at him. A woman followed her out, the spitting image of Lanie only twenty years older, and introduced herself as Lanie's mom.

"Now, where are you taking Lanie today?"

After he explained the Fall Festival in detail, Mrs. Simpson finally let them go. He couldn't explain it to her, but surely he would be the safest date Lanie went out with. He might have the hormones of a teenager, yet he knew what it meant to be a parent. Never mind that those hormones sometimes sought the driver's seat. The forty-five-year-old was in control. For now.

Back in the car, Lanie's fresh scent filled the car as John introduced Sam. She looked so sweet in her red sweater and blue jeans. The desire to pull her closer overwhelmed him. He pushed it aside, but wondered if his adult self had as much control as he thought.

"Sorry about my mom. She warned me she was going to grill you."

"It was nothing. I would have been disappointed if she didn't. She obviously cares about you."

Lanie lifted an eyebrow, but John focused on the road. After an uncomfortable silence, she asked him more about what to expect at the Fall Festival.

* * *

The Mission Park Church was a mega-church before there were mega-churches. Church buses of all shapes and sizes dotted the parking lot, some from as far east as Stroud and as far south as Ardmore.

Everything seemed so familiar because he'd done it all before. The first time, he and Sam played basketball all day, and when not on the court, John and Willy had flirted with as many girls as possible. It has been so fun and innocent. Now he got to do it with the best-looking girl in school.

Inside, rowdy kids bounced off the walls. John repressed the adult side of him and held back the urge to yell at them to settle down. They entered the plush atrium near the sanctuary and got in line to register. Sam registered and then disappeared down a hall with his friends.

John signed in and took the form the woman behind the counter handed him. With a few gray strands in her dark hair and the beginnings of wrinkles around her eyes, she seemed so old compared to the sea of teenagers swarming the church, but she must have been about his real age of forty-five.

Being in a sixteen-year-old body had changed his thinking more than he realized. As each day passed, he became more like the age of his body and less like the age of his mind. He shuddered. What was happening to him?

This Jekyll and Hyde game was really getting to him. The Fall Festival was supposed to be fun. He should enjoy reliving this event that had created such good memories in his real life. He looked at all the kids having fun and resolved to spend the rest of the day just being sixteen again.

They left the main building and entered the gym. The first court already had a basketball game going on each half court. The far court was set up for volleyball. On the middle court, boys and girls from eight to eighteen shot baskets.

"Let's go shoot."

"I didn't bring my gym clothes. I'll just watch."

"Don't be silly. Come on." John took her hand, the first time he'd touched her, and dragged her out to the court. He took off his sweatshirt and tossed it to the side, stepping onto the court wearing Jams, a pair of Nikes, and a t-shirt with the sleeves cut off. He grabbed a shot off the rim and dribbled out to the top of the key. It looked odd with no three-point lines. But that shot wouldn't be legal in NCAA basketball for a few years.

He passed the ball to Lanie.

"What am I supposed to do with this?" She held it as if it were a pumpkin.

"Pass it back."

They passed the ball for a few minutes, and he took a step in and launched a shot. Had his basketball skills improved the way his baseball skills did?

Clank.

No. John chased the ball down and then drove back to made a lay-up before returning it to Lanie. "Your shot. Come on. I know you can shoot." He held the ball out to her.

Lanie dribbled in and shot a free throw.

Swish.

They shot for fifteen minutes until a game started. John joined a team, and Lanie sat on the bleachers. John kept glancing at her as he ran down the court. *How foolish!* He'd done the exact same thing the first time around. He'd spent hours playing ball thinking the girls on the sidelines were impressed. They weren't. His team won, but he quickly found someone to take his place and returned to Lanie.

"Don't you want to play again?" she asked.

"No. I brought you here. It's unfair to leave you on the sideline. Let's go over to the other building. I'll show you around."

* * *

John took Lanie's hand and led her deeper into the church. He didn't think about it, he just did it. When she didn't pull her hand away, his heart puffed with joy, but his mind clouded with confusion.

They rounded a corner and entered an empty, dark hallway. He hesitated as his body and mind waged a war.

"What?" Lanie stopped next to him.

He pushed aside his misgivings. Being sixteen had become his life. Real or not, whether he wanted it or not, he had to live it every day. John Michaels was a teenage boy.

He looked into Lanie's pure blue eyes and pulled her toward him. Gently, he kissed the soft brown skin of her cheek. Then he kissed her on the lips.

It had been a long time since he'd had a first kiss. A long time since he'd first kissed Renee while they stood in the moonlight at the Myriad Gardens. A distant, fading memory. He quickly buried it. That didn't have anything to do with this fantasy life.

He pulled back, smiled, and then laughed. A rush of elation made his soul soar.

Lanie smiled back, radiating pure joy and love for life.

John pulled her into a medium-sized Sunday School room to listen to the soothing tones of a piano. They took their seats as a junior high girl finished her display of musical talent. She returned to her seat, where a woman gave her a big hug.

"Next will be Larkin Connor," announced a woman who stepped in front of the piano and then retreated quickly.

John leaned over as Lanie whispered in his ear, her breath tickling his skin, but sat up straight as the name of the next performer registered.

Larkin Connor.

His adult world crashed in on him. When the police had asked about her, the name meant nothing to him. Still didn't. Yet here she was at the Fall Festival. Had she been there the first time? Should he have met her then? How did she know Kim?

"John, are you okay?"

"I'm fine. Sorry. What did you say?" He wiped his sweaty palms on his shirt.

"I just said 'I'm having fun.'"

He stared intently at the ten- or eleven-year-old girl who began to play the piano. She wore a simple, white dress and had pulled her dark red hair into pigtails.

The reminder that all of this was happening for a reason hit him in the gut. First Ray Pope, then Chad Bailey, and now Larkin Connor. Three people he never knew. Three people somehow connected to Kim's disappearance. Hearing and seeing Larkin convinced him of one thing: he was here to find out what happened to Kim.

So far, he'd enjoyed the ride this fantasy life had provided. But none of it was real, right? It was just some type of dream.

Renee? Real.

Mark and Sara? Real.

Early mornings and late nights at The Coffee Beast? Real.

The hole in his heart from losing Kim? Real.

His heart ached, and his head pounded at the thought of the paradox. How long would he be locked into this fantasy life?

John snapped back to the present after Larkin's performance. "I think the pizza will be here for lunch soon."

"Let's go eat."

They walked back quickly. Lanie's hand latched onto his as they navigated the loud, noisy crowd fighting to get the pizza the sponsors had ordered by the stack.

"Just a second." He held up his hand as they passed a television showing the Oklahoma/Nebraska game. Sooner quarterback Jamelle Holieway scored on a forty-three-yard option run to put the Sooners up 14-0. The crowd erupted in raucous celebration. If only he could see the look on Chad Bailey's face. Did he believe his story now?

He spotted Larkin Connor playing tag by the volleyball net on the third court. She'd shed her frilly dress for jeans and a long-sleeved shirt. He guided Lanie to a table. "I'll get us something to drink."

He walked through the maze of laughing, screaming kids playing tag, stopped by the drink table, and picked up two cans of Coke, which was actually New Coke that tasted a lot like Pepsi. He leaned against the volleyball net pole. Did his kids ever play tag at school? It was a lost art.

John called Larkin's name. Not sure if she heard him, he called again. When she paused, he waved for her to come over. Her forehead glistened with sweat, and the freckles on her nose had brightened from the running around.

"Larkin, I'm John. Can you tell me if Kim Addison is here? You know her, don't you?"

"No."

"Are you sure?"

"Yes."

"She'd be a few years older than you. About fourteen."

"No."

"Okay." Why couldn't there be easy answers? She darted away and quickly rejoined the game.

So much for getting information about Kim that would help him figure out what happened to her.

Kids raced by in a blur. One of them dove on the floor to avoid a tag. Brad Mullins, his pastor in the future, but for now, Kim Addison's best friend.

If Brad was here, could Kim be here too? He hoped not. He turned quickly, and dizziness gripped him. He grabbed the pole to steady himself. The talking and yelling of three hundred kids united into one deafening noise.

"Hi, John." He turned to encounter a face that came to him in the darkest of nights. Kim Addison. She wore shorts and a t-shirt, with her blonde hair pulled into a pony tail. Her face bore a beam of joy he should have welcomed, but instead feared. "Hi, Kim. I thought you were going to your grandma's house."

"I didn't get a chance to call you last night and tell you our plans changed. My parents were on me like hawks."

They stood by the volleyball pole, two individuals in a swirling mass of noisy humanity. John studied his future girlfriend. Her honey-blonde hair was longer than it would be in college. She wore no makeup, and her skin glowed because of the heat in the gym. He could see the woman she would become in the tilt of her lips.

"I rode with Brad's parents, but I'm here alone." Her lips formed a vulnerable smile, and her eyes a hopeful plea.

John shuddered inside. He glanced to Lanie, waiting for him to bring back the drinks he still held.

She rose and started walking towards them.

"There are a lot of people here from our church and from school." John spoke rapidly. "You could hang out with them. I could introduce you to some of the girls."

"Okay." She frowned, and her eyes narrowed.

Lanie joined them and plucked a can of Coke from one of John's hands. She leaned slightly into him, her shoulder nuzzling his. He looked away from Kim, but her eyes drew him like a magnet. He'd chased after his high school dream and played games with the girl he'd known, loved, and lost. Now he'd blown all of his efforts to build a relationship with her in this world . . . and with it, all hope of trying to warn her about her future. Two chances to make a difference, to change what happened to her, and he'd failed both times.

But if he couldn't save her, why was he reliving age sixteen again? His thoughts whirled. What if he couldn't change history? If he assumed only his life with Renee and the kids was real, he'd never be able to save Kim. He could only hope to find out what happened . . . and maybe bring justice.

* * *

Lanie and John finished eating and watched the game on TV. The crowd cleared out, and a basketball game began on Court 2. The junior high kids pushed and shoved each other as they made way for a volleyball game.

"Do you want to play a game?" Lanie asked. "I'll watch. I don't mind."

"Maybe."

They took a seat in the pull-out bleachers against the wall. A parade of junior high kids walked by. Brad Mullins passed them without saying a word. Larkin Connor trailed behind, further back in the line. Bringing up the rear, John saw a face that mortified him.

The face brought his fantasy life to a screeching halt. It brought him face to face with the reality of his wandering heart.

Walking in front of him was an eleven-year-old with dark hair and brown eyes, a girl in the beginning stages of adolescence, who would someday become his wife. A girl he didn't meet in his real life for ten years.

Renee Templin.

Chapter 17

John went through the motions on the basketball court for a few games. He moved his feet on defense, rebounded, kept an eye on the OU game, and kept tabs on Lanie. She watched a bit, talked with Willy, and chatted with some girls he didn't recognize.

Running up and down the court gave him time to think. If he couldn't talk to Kim, why was he reliving age sixteen again? His thoughts whirled. What if he couldn't change history? If this life was fantasy, and only his life with Renee and the kids was real, then he'd never be able to save Kim. He could only hope to find out what happened . . . and maybe bring justice.

His thoughts turned to Renee. They had been married ten years, long enough for the passion to dissipate. Sure he still loved her, he would die for her, but he also took her for granted.

He blocked a player from the other team, yanked down a rebound, and threw a pass to a fellow teammate.

When fate, God, his imagination, or aliens, or whatever, thrust him back into 1992 and the day Kim disappeared, he came face to face with the biggest unfulfilled passion and promise of his life. If relationships could be mapped by peaks and valleys, he and Renee had been up and down several times. He and Kim had reached the top of Mt. Everest before she vanished into the snowy mist. He'd been left to climb down on his own.

John clanked a jump shot.

Then he considered Lanie. Somewhere deep down, his soul told him his relationship with Lanie wasn't real. Sure, it seemed real. Her delicate hands. Her soft lips. Her flowery perfume. She seemed real, and he the shadow. But one thing was certain. Renee had always been real and always would be. His wife, the mother of Mark and Sara.

* * *

At the end of the day, chaos reigned in the parking lot as youth pastors tried to corral their teens into the proper buses. John and Lanie stood outside beneath the cloudless sky waiting for Sam to say goodbye to his friends. Renee and Larkin had already gotten into a Caprice station wagon and driven away. To John's right, a crowd clustered at the curb around an idling brown Camaro.

It had to be Dennis Vance.

John stepped a few feet over so he could see the driver. Sure enough, Dennis talked with Michelle Morton and her friends.

When a guy in a blue windbreaker leaned forward and ran his hand across the top of the car, John froze.

Kim bent down next to the window. She said something to Dennis.

Dennis's laughter thawed John's frozen thoughts until they boiled and steamed. His conversation with Kim's roommate Leslee shortly after Kim's death came back to him as if it were yesterday:

They sat below the mantle of the brick fireplace in Kim's parents' living room. In spite of the abundant misery present in the household, it was nice to be at the Addisons' house. Wallowing in his own despair could only take him so far. It comforted him to be with people who'd shared the same hopelessness for the last week.

"The police talked to me," John said.

"Me too. I couldn't stop crying."

He ran his hand through his hair. His nights consisted of lying in bed and thinking about Kim, getting a few restless hours of sleep, and waking up at dawn. He was beyond fatigued. "I hate that I didn't know anything. I know Kim's heart and her soul, but they asked me so many questions I couldn't answer."

"Did they ask you about Dennis's relationship with Kim?"

"Yeah."

She seemed to expect more. When he remained silent, she nodded and looked away.

"What aren't you telling me, Leslee? Tell me the truth," John said. "Please, tell me."

She stared through the crowd of people milling about in the Addisons' living room and shook her head. "John, it's nothing."

"Tell me anyway. I deserve to know."

"She wasn't hiding anything from you."

"Tell me."

"Dennis called a lot."

The simple words pierced his soul. Kim wasn't cheating on him, but the revelation still stabbed at his heart. He squeezed his eyes shut. "Why did he call?"

"I don't know. Sometimes afterwards, she would be in a great mood. Sometimes, she'd be miserable. I asked her about it, but she always told me she was fine."

John shook his head.

Leslee took his hands in hers. "She loved you, John. But she and Dennis were friends. You know that. She also knew you didn't really trust him. The bottom line is that he's been in and out of her life for many years. But they've always been friends. That's how she is. She's a great friend. The best a person can have."

"They met at college?"

"No, John. They've known each other since she was in the ninth grade."

John stood on the parking lot and swallowed as he continued to watch Kim and Dennis. A lump slowly formed in his throat. They *did* know each other before college. Why didn't she tell him?

Chapter 18

As John walked down the long hallway to Chad Bailey's office, he could still hear the echo of Bailey's words when he called yesterday: *"We need to talk."*

A very different Chad met him. His suit coat hung on a rack in the corner, he had unbuttoned his collar and loosened his tie, and he stared at John from the chair behind his desk as if John were from outer space.

He couldn't help but smile. Someone finally understood that his world wasn't quite right.

"How did you know?"

John shrugged.

"Tell me."

"There are two options. Either it was a wild guess, and I got lucky by telling you OU would beat Nebraska 27-7, Keith Jackson would score on a long touchdown run, and Nebraska wouldn't score until the final minute. Or I knew it would happen."

"Impossible. Both are impossible." Chad threw up his hands.

"Which would you find easier to believe?"

"Neither."

"I agree, but does this make my story any more plausible?"

Chad rubbed his chin. "I guess if I say I believe you knew OU would win, then I would have to believe you have a wife and kids . . . even though you are sixteen."

John nodded and tried to swallow a grin.

"What else do you know?"

"That's about it. I'm a Sooner fan. I always have been. That's how I remembered this season. I don't remember many current events. I don't remember what happened last week, much less almost thirty years ago, which is what this life is to me."

"So you know what will happen next week when OU plays Oklahoma State?"

"I do."

Chad leaned forward, eyes wide in anticipation.

"OU will win 13-0."

Chad scribbled on a notepad sitting on the desktop. "That's all?"

"The game will be played on a field of solid ice during a blizzard. It will go down in history as 'The Ice Bowl.'"

"You're kidding."

"You doubt me?" John lifted an eyebrow.

Chad chuckled and then asked quickly, "What about the next game?"

"They have another one?"

"Southern Methodist."

"Oh yes." John thought for a moment. "I don't remember the details, but OU will win. The score will be 31-14 or something like that."

"And a bowl game?"

John definitely remembered that seminal moment of his childhood. "They'll play Penn State in the Orange Bowl."

"The number one team," Chad said.

"Not for long. OU will beat them."

"Yes!" Chad pumped his fist in the air. "Any chance at a national title?"

John smiled. In spite of himself, Chad believed him. "Maybe you should watch and see."

Chad stood and ran his hands through his hair. "Come on, man, you've got to tell me. You can't leave me hanging."

"Okay. But you can't tell anyone. Confidentiality, remember?" John's mind rushed through all of his sports knowledge. What else did he know about 1985 and 1986? If he hung around much longer, he could use his foreknowledge to help his family financially. No. That would be gambling. But in a world that wasn't real, did it matter? Besides, what if history was different this time around? Maybe what he knew about sports from the last time around wouldn't always hold true.

But so far it had.

"I won't tell a soul."

John nodded. "Miami, the second-ranked team, will lose their bowl game, paving the way for OU to be ranked number one after they beat Penn State."

Chad's jaw dropped. He slowly shook his head. "That's amazing."

"You seem pretty convinced that I know what I'm talking about."

The euphoria of OU winning a national title disappeared from Chad's face. "My mind says what you're telling me is both crazy and impossible. Yet my heart reminds me that everything you predicted about yesterday's game happened, so your story must be true. I'll know for sure after the game next Saturday."

"Yes, you will, Chad."

Chapter 19

The following Saturday John closed the oven on a pan of refrigerated biscuits. Bored, he thumbed through the newspaper while he waited but stopped at an article on page ten, right above a cluster of movie ads that included *Spies Like Us* and *Out of Africa*.

He set his spoon down next to the almost empty bowl of Cheerios and rubbed his eyes. Maybe they were playing tricks on him after the late night watching OU claim its sixth national title with a win at the Orange Bowl.

He re-read the article under the headline "Area Man Killed in Las Vegas." His eyes locked on the name of the victim.

Chad Bailey.

John's stomach did a somersault. He grabbed the table to steady himself. When he could breathe again, he picked up the phone mounted on the kitchen wall. When a woman answered, he asked to speak to Buzz.

"I'm sorry, he's not here," Buzz's wife Jan answered.

"I saw the article in the paper."

She paused briefly before speaking. "You knew Chad?"

"I did."

"Buzz is at their house right now."

"Do you mind if I ask why he was in Vegas?"

Silence greeted him.

"Hello?"

"I'm here," Jan said in a whisper. "I don't know why he went to Vegas. No one knows. And then to die like that, in such a random way. I just . . ."

"Jan, I'm sorry."

"I'll tell Buzz you called," Jan said through sniffles.

John replaced the phone. He'd killed Chad Bailey.

He'd gone to Las Vegas to try and make a quick buck with the info John had given him. Except something happened. Something that never happened in his real life. Much bigger consequences than John making the baseball team or Renee talking to Dennis the day Kim disappeared or even Dad losing his job. This was death. He sank into a chair at the kitchen table. He hung his head until it brushed the table.

But it wasn't real.

What if it was?

A twinge of light crept into John's mind. Kim went to the Bailey's house the day she disappeared. Since Chad was dead now, would Kim ever meet them? Would she go to their house? Would she ever disappear?

Had he just saved Kim's life?

* * *

The next day, John spotted Kim and her parents walking across the parking lot into his church. John waited until Sunday School ended before looking for her. He'd blown it but prayed all was not lost. Rebuilding a relationship with Kim might not help him save her, but it would be the right thing to do.

He waited outside of the high school girls' classroom and then pulled her aside. "Kim, I need to apologize to you. I'm sorry about yesterday."

"What do you mean? I had a great time."

"I feel as if I led you on."

"I don't understand." Kim lifted an eyebrow, showing she understood fully.

"I invited you to the Fall Festival, and when you said you weren't going to come, I invited a girl from school."

He blew out a long breath and dove in. "Look. Here's the deal. I'm going to be honest with you. I like you. We were getting to know each other when things kind of clicked with Lanie. I'm a guy, and you need to get used to guys being clueless in relationships. You may not have been bothered, but it bothered me a lot, and I feel horrible. I hope you can forgive me, and we can continue to be friends."

"Sure." She shrugged and walked away, but stopped before leaving the room, "Are you coming or not?" She flashed him a smile, and he knew all had been forgiven.

On the way into the sanctuary, John spotted Buzz amid a group of people. Next to him stood a woman he recognized from a picture in Chad's office. She must be Debbie Bailey. Another of the people the police had questioned him about.

One of the men looked eerily familiar, as well, and definitely out of place. Murphy Hazelton. He had seen him not long ago, but in 1992, as if that made any sense. He was younger now and had a goatee. John had grown used to seeing people he didn't expect to see.

He had to be here for a reason, so John took the opportunity to find out what it was and introduced himself. "Hi, I'm John Michaels. Are you all friends of Buzz?"

Buzz Baker cut in. and waved a hand to indicate everyone in the group. "We all went to school together." He named each as he pointed around the circle.

"With Chad, too?"

Hazelton said, "I shared an apartment with him. He was a great guy."

John nodded. Another two connections. Two people tied to Kim's last day. "So you went to Saint Paul, too?" He directed his question to Murphy.

"I did."

"Are you a preacher?"

Murphy stole a glance at Buzz, and then chuckled quietly. "No. I lasted a semester and a half. Got kicked out for conduct unbecoming a minister."

"I'll see you after the service, Murph, church is about to start, and Janet is waiting for me and Debbie." Buzz excused himself.

"Why did you get kicked out?"

"It was nothing."

"Seriously, I want to know." John's gaze didn't waver.

Murphy looked away momentarily, as though doing some quick calculations. "Oh, just some fighting and other stuff college kids do."

He was probably the black sheep of the friends. What it meant, John didn't know. "What do you do now?"

"I teach over at Central State. I'm also getting my doctorate in English literature."

"That's a far cry from seminary."

"But it's much more fun." Murphy gave him a wink. "I'd better get into the service. I promised Chad's wife I'd sit with her."

"Sure." John decided he disliked Murphy Hazelton. There was something too smarmy about him.

Chapter 20

When Kim disappeared, John became skilled at burying pain. As the days and months as a sixteen-year-old passed, he used that same skill to bury deep in the soil of his heart the pain of missing Renee, Mark, and Sara. He even followed Bailey's advice and prayed daily. In his darkest moments, he lashed out at God. Then begged Him to send him back to his real life.

But day after day, he woke up in his parent's house, in his sixteen-year-old world.

January dragged into February. He made the best of his situation with Kim by talking with her every Sunday, and he continued to date Lanie. Why not, since this life wasn't real anyway?

He continued to excel at high school. He dropped second semester calculus for journalism. He practiced regularly with the baseball team, and the guys easily accepted him after he hit two home runs in a scrimmage against Bethany.

But beneath it all lay the questions with no answers: Why was he stuck in high school again, and how was it possibly doing anyone any good?

* * *

John hadn't written a note to his family in a week but decided to wait until tomorrow, after their first official game. He crawled under the covers, eager for morning, but this time not because he expected to wake up in his own bed. After a soft knock, the door opened. Light from the hall crept across the ceiling.

"John, can we talk? It's about Sam." Dad sat at the side of his bed.

John's heart deflated. "Sure, Dad." This had never happened in his real life, so it must be important.

"We don't think it's anything, but we're going to have a CAT scan done tomorrow."

"Why?" John's throat was dry.

"You know he's been having a lot of headaches. It's gotten to where nothing can ease the pain. You've probably noticed he doesn't feel like doing anything anymore."

That was true. Sam had stopped going to the cages about a month ago and been much more reserved. He'd noticed Sam's change in behavior but had been too selfish to delve deeper. "What is the CAT scan for?"

"Dr. Rowland wants to check for anything that might be causing the headaches. He wants us to err on the side of caution." Dad spoke softly, and John was glad the lights were off. The darkness hid the fear.

"What's the worst that could happen?"

Dad put a hand on John's shoulder. "We don't want to think about that right now. Let's pray for the best. I'm sure he'll be fine, but he's kind of scared. Maybe you could talk to him a bit in the morning. He's excited about coming to your game."

Guilt rushed through John like a cold wind. For some reason, John knew the test results would be tragic. In real life, Sam ran marathons and excelled in every sport. Why was he facing a thing like this at the age of twelve? John didn't fall asleep for hours. When his alarm clock buzzed, he rolled out of bed, surprised he'd slept at all. He yawned deeply, recalling he'd last seen his alarm clock at 2:30 a.m. Not much sleep.

John dressed, shaved, and then went to Sam's room, where his brother sat on a Dallas-Cowboys-themed bed putting textbooks into his backpack. John sat beside him. "Sam, I had no idea it was this serious."

"It's nothing." Sam kept his head down.

"I think you're right, but I'm glad they're checking you to make sure."

"Me too."

John put his arm around Sam's shoulder. "You're a good brother. The best. I love you." John gave him a squeeze, and then got up. "I'll see you at the game."

"Sure." Sam finally looked up. His expression countered his words. He was worried.

John smiled to reassure him and left, praying it all could end. He didn't need the baseball skills, the new high school sweetheart, or the knowledge of who would win the World Series. He needed his brother healthy . . . and his life back.

Chapter 21

John ran out onto the newly mown field, freshly marked with chalk, and took his place in right field. His first high school baseball game, and he made the starting line-up. The thought put an extra bounce in his step.

Parents and a few students filled half of the bleachers, the ones brave enough to face the gusty wind that made the forty-five degree day feel like thirty. When the umpire called the first pitch a strike, John exhaled slowly. Between pitches, he glanced at the stands, where his parents, Sam, and Lanie sat towards the top. Willy and Nancy watched in the row below them. Becky had opted to go a friend's house, and he didn't blame her for not wanting to sit in the frigid weather.

After the first batter grounded out, Coach Walker motioned for the outfield to shift left. John shuffled several steps to the left and kicked at the brown grass in front of him. It should be Sam out here. Sam was the star, the excellent baseball player. They wouldn't find out his test results for a week or two. It killed John inside to know something could happen to his little brother.

The next two batters struck out, and John sprinted into the dugout. He sat on the bench and put on his batting gloves.

The sun broke through for a brief moment, and the uniforms all looked extra white and the foul lines crisp.

John slipped on a helmet and joined his teammates at the fence. They shouted encouragement as Phil Prince came up to bat.

"Are you pumped?" Coach Pope stood next to John.

"I'm a little nervous, actually."

"Don't be. You'll do fine." He clapped a hand on John's shoulder.

Phil Prince flied out to center field. The next batter struck out. Devon stepped to the plate, and John moved into the on-deck circle, next to bat. As he took some practice swings, it all struck him as familiar, yet surreal. He hadn't played in years, yet this seemed like his destiny from day one in this fantasy world.

Devon worked the count full—two strikes and three balls. The next pitch came in low.

"Ball four," shouted the umpire. "Take your base."

As Devon trotted to first base, the announcer said over the tinny speakers, "Now batting for the Panthers, right fielder John Michaels." John received a smattering of applause and a loud "Go, John!" from Mom. He dug his feet into the smooth dirt in the batter's box and focused on the pitcher.

A skinny kid with huge glasses secured by a rubber strap stood on the mound. He glanced at the runner on first and threw.

The ball sailed in smooth, flat, and a foot outside. Ball one. On the next pitch, the kid buried a curve ball.

John quickly surmised this pitcher wasn't any good. *Come on; give me a pitch to hit.*

Ask and you shall receive. The ball floated right down the middle.

John waited, waited some more, and then swung. The ball exploded off his bat. He took off for first. It all played out in front of him: Devon rounded second, the ball one-hopped to the wall in left center, the fielders gave chase.

John neared second base and ran harder. His foot clipped the bag as his cleats dug into the dirt. It was going to be close. He slid just beneath the tag.

"Safe!" the umpire called.

John pumped his fist, stood, and brushed the dirt off his uniform. In the stands, Sam jumped up, pumping both arms in the air and shouting, "Woo-hoo! Woo-hoo!"

John's joy dissipated. Why couldn't Sam be okay?

In the next innings, John struck out, caught two fly balls, walked, and threw a runner out. At the start of the seventh, Deer Creek clung to a lead by one run. Two innings to go.

John turned his hat backwards like his teammates, accepted a handful of sunflower seeds from one of the guys, and joined the rest of the team at the dugout fence. "Let's go, Murray. Get a hit," John urged as the player next to him smacked on some gum.

Murray hit a sharp grounder right to the short stop, who fielded it cleanly, stepped on second base, and threw to first for a double play. Two outs.

An audible moan arose from the dugout.

Devon launched a home run into the darkening winter sky. He crossed home plate. His teammates mobbed him when he reached the dugout.

John stepped to the plate. By this time, the dirt and chalk outlines of the batter's box had merged into a chalky mess. With one foot in the box, he tightened his grip on the bat.

All eyes rested on him. Sam stood between Mom and Dad. Lanie had bundled up in a blanket, but her soft blue eyes watched him. Her smile warmed John's heart.

His gaze locked with Sam's. This one was for his brother.

After the first two bad pitches, the pitcher began the wind up. The ball started outside, but not as much as the ones before.

John stepped forward and unleashed the bat. He made solid contact with the ball, and a torrid line drive sailed inches over the first baseman's flying leap.

John burst out of the box. If he could get to second base, he could score the winning run on a single. The right fielder ran to the ball, snatched it, and came up throwing.

John ran full speed toward second.

The shortstop covered second base and positioned his glove to receive the throw.

John went into his feet-first slide.

The throw went high, and the shortstop lunged toward John.

John's foot hit the base an instant before his body collided with the shortstop.

The collision brought a blinding flash of pain and then total darkness.

Chapter 22

This was weird. He'd just been at a baseball game where he'd tried to stretch a single into a double and been tagged out. He remembered everything and knew absolutely, without a doubt, he was no longer there.

A ringing, coupled with incredible warmth, told him he was somewhere else. Memories and thoughts not quite his own swirled in his mind, filling his heart and soul with a new existence.

The persistent ringing grew louder. And louder.

John's eyes opened. Darkness surrounded him. Enough moonlight shone through the window to tell him a dark comforter covered him, pictures of children didn't cover the walls, and a TV did not sit on the dresser. He was home, but not his home.

He fumbled in the darkness for the phone and yanked it to his ear. The cord didn't reach across the bed, and the phone console crashed to the floor. "Hello."

"Pastor? Is this Pastor Michaels?"

John instantly knew it was true. He was a pastor. "Yes, it is."

"My name is Derek Simpson. My sister asked me to call you. Dennis Vance was murdered tonight."

* * *

Though John could recite every detail of yesterday—when he played his first, and last, high school baseball game—he knew what he had to do.

He sat up in bed and shook his head to clear out the cobwebs. He hurried to the closet and pulled on jeans and a striped polo. He slipped his shoes, brushed his teeth, and combed his hair. He grabbed his electric razor to shave on the way.

Should he wake his wife and tell her the news? No, they both needed to be fully awake before they talked. He peeked in on Campbell and kissed the baby on her forehead. As he passed through the kitchen, the clock on the microwave flashed 3:15. At least he'd gotten a few hours of sleep. He put on a light jacket, but as the garage door opened, a rush of cold wind almost took his breath away. He unlocked the door to his preacherly car, a silver Buick LeSabre.

Something strange had happened after the baseball play at second base. Not only did he lose consciousness, but a whole new set of memories infused his brain. John still had Mark and Sara in his real life, but now he also had a ten-month-old baby girl. And a different wife. He exhaled deeply. What did it mean? Would it prove to be just as meaningless as reliving the high school years?

He lived in Warrick North housing addition. He pastored Nichols Park Community Church, where they were in the middle of a final push for a fund drive to build a new sanctuary/family life center.

As he drove south on McArthur, John realized he also knew where Dennis Vance lived.

John felt a sudden shudder of fear. The date was October 9, 1999. Seven years after Kim disappeared. Somehow he knew it, but only the date not the day. Yet something else was different. Something didn't seem right. Something he couldn't place.

John pulled into the Lansbrook neighborhood and navigated the circular streets. This would be hard. It always was. He recalled the time the Miniacs lost their baby to a heart defect, and when Carey Norfolk lost his father in the Murrah Building bombing. Tough times, and he'd been there for those families. Well, *he* hadn't been there. But in this fantasy of being a pastor, he had. The memories weren't vivid, as if he'd been there, but thorough, as if he'd read about them in a newspaper.

Weird.

John rounded the corner and turned onto Marlow Lane. The red and blue flashing lights gave the night a creepy, carnival atmosphere. John pulled as close as he could and got out of his car. Frightened neighbors whispered quietly among themselves.

Four police cars, an ambulance, and a few unmarked cars. What had happened to Dennis?

John skirted the perimeter of the corner lot, looking for a police officer. When he reached the front of the house, he stepped between two sets of regal columns that supported a protective overhang along the length of the house and rang the doorbell.

A man with thinning, wispy, blond hair answered the door. His weary eyes intensified the droopy complexion. He looked familiar. "Pastor Michaels?"

John nodded.

"Come on in, I'm Derek, Lanie's brother." Chills shot through John's body. After introducing John to a police officer named Martz, Derek led him to the family room.

John stopped at the threshold. Derek Simpson, Lanie Simpson, Lanie Vance. Why he hadn't put it together? In this life, Lanie had married Dennis. She'd deserved better. But judging by the house and its nice furnishings, maybe she had gotten it.

Why didn't he know about Dennis and Lanie, if he knew his own history of being a pastor and having a different daughter? Maybe some facts were meant to be known, and some to be discovered. Each timeline seemed to have its own surprises.

Lanie huddled on the couch as if she wanted to collapse into herself.

"Pastor John is here," Derek said.

Lanie looked up. Despite the savage beating her spirit had taken in the last few hours, she still looked great. She'd done something to straighten her brown hair, and she'd grown into a thirty-year-old woman with a few wrinkles and a little extra weight. Just like everyone.

She didn't stand. Instead, she reached out her right arm.

When John sat down next to her, she crumpled into him and bawled. He held her for several minutes, and Derek excused himself.

Eventually, the sobbing turned to whimpers. Lanie's raw, fresh pain was a mere illusion to John. He hadn't had time to grasp the complexities of the situation. The Lanie he knew was happy, sweet, and pure. But life had destroyed this Lanie. "Can you tell me what happened?"

She wiped her eyes on the sleeve of her brown turtleneck. She kept her head down and talked quietly between heavy breaths. "When I came home, no lights were on. Dennis should have been home, but his car wasn't here."

She wiped her nose with a rumpled ball of tissue before continuing. "I turned on a hall light and saw the tip of a dining room chair lying in the hallway. Everything was a disaster. Chairs tipped over, the mail and morning newspaper scattered on the floor. A couple of broken dishes. I called for Dennis, but no one answered.

"I turned on my cell phone and entered 911 but didn't dial yet since I didn't know what had happened. I turned on all the lights downstairs but didn't see any other damage. I wasn't thinking straight, really. I hurried up the stairs. I checked our room first and didn't see anything out of place. The doors to the other rooms were shut. We kept it that way. But the guest room door at the end of the hall was open."

Her body spasmed. He grasped her arms, but they continued to shake. She took in several wobbly breaths before continuing. "I turned on the light, and there I found Dennis." She let the last part out in a spurt. Her entire body gave an involuntary shudder. "He lay face down in a pool of blood. I hit dial on the phone and then collapsed onto the floor in the hall. I don't remember much after that. The police came and told me Dennis had been shot twice in the back. Then I called Derek."

So Dennis had a fight in the dining room, and then the tussle continued upstairs, where Dennis was shot in the back. "Why would anyone want to kill Dennis?"

"I don't know."

"Lanie, you have to know something, anything. He was your husband."

She walked to the window, peeked between beige curtains, and then ran a hand down the edge of the bookshelf. She'd only looked at him once. Why?

She returned to the couch, her bare feet brushing the top of the thick carpet.

She sat close to him, too close. Her warm breath tickled his skin as she whispered, "Do you think this has anything to do with us?"

"I don't— What …?"

"I told Dennis about us tonight. I told him I wanted a divorce."

What did she mean? He didn't have an affair—

More facts about this thirty-year-old pastor life poured into his mind. He held back a growl. Why did some facts come to him immediately while other important information obviously didn't?

So, in this life he was an adulterer? Did his fondness for Lanie in his relived high school life have anything to do with it? Then why had Lanie ended up with Dennis? She barely knew him in high school.

Lanie rubbed her blue eyes and squeezed them shut briefly. "What are *we* going to do, John?"

This game, this fantasy, had him cornered. He'd have to play. He blew out a long breath. "Have the police questioned you yet?"

"Just about finding Dennis. They don't know about us."

"Does anyone else know?"

She shook her head.

"Your brother doesn't know?"

"No. What about your wife?"

Fear sliced at his core. "No." Had he planned to tell his wife? Was his marriage in pastor fantasyland on the rocks?

"Good."

Not wanting to continue this line of conversation, he asked, "Is there anyone else I can call? Your mom, other family?"

For the first time, she looked him in the eye. She set her jaw and frowned. "My mom died three years ago. You know that." She pulled away from him, but only took two steps before her body slowly crumpled to the floor, and the sobs came again.

He put his hand on her shoulder, but she violently flung his hand away. "Just go away," she muttered.

John left her there and found Derek in the kitchen. He sipped a cup of coffee and offered John one. He accepted.

"How is she?"

"In shock. Devastated. Broken-hearted. About what you can expect." John cringed at the partial lies. At this point, he hated his other self for putting him in this situation.

"Is there anything I can do?"

"Just be there for her. Will you be able to stay a while?" John sipped the coffee.

"I can take time off work, sure."

Then John asked, "Is the body still here?"

"No. Just left before you got here, but the CSI guys are here, doing their thing."

"Any idea what happened?"

"No idea." Derek took a seat at the cluttered kitchen table.

"Could this be random?"

"I don't see how. Lanie said she had nothing of value, and none of the electronics or jewelry were taken."

John examined a collection of pictures taped to the refrigerator. "Was Dennis involved with something?"

"That's what we'll have to find out."

Chapter 23

As John pulled his Buick onto the highway, the sun peeked over the horizon before disappearing behind a cloud.

Dropping into the day Kim disappeared had traumatized, yet focused him. That failure landed him in the surreal world high school again . . . with a few changes. Although much remained the same, all that mattered had changed. And this life was completely new.

But the changes weren't all good. His brother got sick, his dad lost his job, and he hurt Kim. He momentarily lost his sanity and confided in a man who then got himself killed.

Why? Whether real or only in his mind, there had to be a purpose. He prayed every night for God to reveal it to him. That had yet to happen.

But maybe there were clues. For starters, he had to discern whether new discoveries in this fantasy life actually happened in his real life. It all tied back to the police interview.

"Did she ever mention Professor Hazleton?"

"What about Larkin Connor?"

"Did you ever hear about Chad or Debbie Bailey?"

"Ray Pope?"

Names he never heard in his real life had become familiar in his teenage life. And Renee crossed his path much sooner than in his real life.

Renee Templin sat on the couch talking to Dennis Vance.

So many connections. So much confusion. What did it all mean?

* * *

Driving through his neighborhood, John stopped behind a school bus picking up a group of sleepy students. Anxiety scampered through his body like a spider on a web. Would his wife be awake?

He parked in the garage, retrieved the newspaper from the driveway, and entered through the laundry room. The house was eerily quiet, with all the lights off downstairs. It didn't matter. He'd do what he had to do.

Since his wife hadn't come downstairs yet, he decided to answer some questions before telling her about Dennis.

He popped the rubber band off the newspaper and opened the front section. Chills of regret slid down his spine. Today was Friday, and another OU/Texas game loomed tomorrow. OU would lose 37-27. As much as he enjoyed the Sooners and football, he hated the day they played their biggest rival. It always brought him back to the day he lost Kim.

He folded the newspaper and turned his focus to more urgent matters. Sunday would be here soon. He'd have to get in front of people and preach. He couldn't do that. Besides his own secret fear of all types of bugs, he feared public speaking more than anything. A sheen of sweat formed on his forehead. John wiped it away and forced the fear aside. He didn't have time to worry about that right now.

He picked up a cream-colored photo album from a bookshelf in the living room. His new memories didn't tell him what was inside. The opening page proclaimed "Christmas, 1998." John flipped through the pages. The photos progressed from decorating their house to Christmas morning, to Christmas with their families. His parents looked happy, and Sam and Becky were both there with their spouses.

John smiled at a picture of him and Sam standing side by side, bodies straight, each trying to be taller than the other. More importantly, Sam looked to be in perfect health. No hint of the headaches that had caused such concern in his 1985 life. Relieved, John returned the album to the shelf and headed up the stairs.

A shrieking cry came from Campbell's room. It must be morning diaper change time.

John paused at the edge of his daughter's door, wondering if he was ready for this. The potent fear that had first appeared as he drove to Dennis's house gripped him. He didn't understand it, and he couldn't explain it. He took a deep breath to fortify himself and stepped into the nursery. "Hi, Kim."

The second the phone call startled him awake, he'd known Kim was his wife, just as he knew he was a pastor, where Dennis Vance lived, and that Campbell was born on February 12th with a full head of dark hair.

But he knew nothing about his relationship with his own wife, so he studied her as she finished dressing the baby.

She shot him a quick glance. Her eyes narrowed before she snapped Campbell's pants into place. A furrowed brow and pursed lips. Not a loving look. Uh-oh.

When she faced him, a lump formed in his throat. He'd never seen Kim after age twenty-one, and now here she was in front of him at twenty-eight. Other than the trendy short haircut with dark highlights that made her look extremely stylish, she hadn't changed a bit. She stepped forward and handed him the baby.

He cradled Campbell on his shoulder and patted her back.

"What was it this time?"

"Dennis Vance."

Kim stopped. A wave of fear cascaded across her face. "What?"

"He was murdered last night."

The whole world seemed to come to a stop. Kim's eyes narrowed and then shut before she opened them. Watery, red eyes below a brow furrowed with unimagined pain. She sprinted from the room and down the stairs, followed by sounds of her scurrying about.

A minute later, the front door slammed shut.

John stepped to the window and watched Kim speed away in her red Accord coupe.

He didn't really know this Kim. Surreal.

He had the knowledge of a full life as a pastor, a husband to Kim, and a father to the baby he held, yet he felt no emotional bond to them. Although he loved the Kim of his college years, this Kim had lived a different life, one he hadn't truly shared.

His memories of Renee, Mark, and Sara tore at him. They were real. Kim wasn't really his wife and Campbell wasn't his daughter. He wasn't a pastor. He wasn't having an affair with Lanie Vance, and Dennis Vance wasn't dead.

Except he did have a different daughter. He held her in his arms. A real baby. His baby. Campbell Dawn Michaels. The warmth of her skin penetrated his shirt. Her soft breath tickled his neck, and she smelled of baby shampoo. Her muscles momentarily gave way, and her head flopped to the side. She brought her head back up with a jerk and resumed looking around the room with her dark brown eyes.

John took her downstairs. In the corner next to the bookshelf, he found everything needed to occupy her. He spread a yellow blanket on the carpet and put Campbell down in the middle of several Fisher-Price toys.

A black, Samsonite satchel rested on the counter. He flipped through the papers inside. He found a Bible, a daily planner, and a cell phone. John pocketed the phone and sat down at the kitchen table to thumb through the planner.

He spent forty-five minutes going back through his life as a pastor, a life he hadn't quite lived yet understood completely: staff meetings, hospital visits, committee meetings, board meetings, and meetings about meetings.

He found the notes he'd prepared for his next sermon. His heart thudded to a stop. He couldn't preach. He became fidgety and clammy when asked to read a scripture in his Sunday school class. He couldn't talk to a large crowd for twenty minutes, let alone about a subject he knew nothing about.

Wait, what was this. John found another set of notes, and relief erased the fear. On Sunday, a missionary from Haiti was scheduled to share his adventures with the congregation.

He reviewed his notes for a few minutes before tossing them aside. He got down on the floor next to Campbell. On his back, he gripped her sides and lifted her up and down, up and down. She giggled and laughed as he made faces and jabbered like a silly daddy. He put her back on the floor and watched her explore her world. She touched, grabbed, slobbered and grunted. Adorable!

Soon her eyelids began to droop. He changed her diaper, fed her Similac, and put her down for a nap. She fell asleep without fussing, a feat he never thought possible after Mark and Sara.

John tiptoed about the silent house, studying the rooms and the furnishings. His study creeped him out. The bookshelf contained hundreds of books on religion, spirituality, and several editions of scripture commentaries. He never would have read any of those books in his real life.

But that wasn't the creepy part. The wall had a vintage movie poster of Hitchcock's *Rear Window*, starring Jimmy Stewart and the beautiful Grace Kelly. Right next to it, he'd framed a poster of *Dial M for Murder*, also staring Grace Kelly. The same two posters were in his real home office, where he took care of The Coffee Beast's business. He took a seat in the same Aeron chair he owned in his real life.

He kept his pens, pencils, and scissors in an old Dallas Cowboys coffee mug. The computer was centered perfectly on the desk, the mouse on an OU Sooners mouse pad. To the right of the computer sat a haunting family picture. Not a studio shot, but a portrait someone must have taken for them. John stood hand in hand with Kim on a beach somewhere, with the sun setting behind them in a splash of red and yellow. His heart twitched in pain, as if a hidden hand had squeezed it. The familiar pain surprised him. It had appeared at random throughout his life. At the most innocuous times, he'd be reminded of Kim and what could have been. Now he was living it, but it wasn't what he'd imagined.

Chapter 24

John microwaved a pot pie and carried it upstairs to his desk. He checked on a sleeping Campbell while his food cooled. Then he fired up the computer and spent several minutes trying to figure out how to get connected to the Internet via their Net Zero dial-up, frustrated again that this life didn't come with every memory intact.

He had finished his pot pie and started munching on a Little Debbie honey bun when a continuous squawk told him he had achieved Internet success.

The front door slammed, and footsteps pounded up the stairs.

His mind flashed to the damaged furniture and the lifeless body of Dennis Vance. Could someone be coming for him? John swiveled in his chair in time to see Kim flash by in a whirl.

Moments later, she began banging around in the closet, which shared a wall with the room he was in. He should go talk to her. He stood and then stopped. He had no idea what to say. He'd let it play out.

After several minutes of noise, Kim stopped outside his office door.

Her eyes were bleary red and her hair was frazzled. A large duffle hung from her shoulder. The vibrant life he knew had been sucked out of her pale skin. Could she be this distraught over Dennis? What did she know?

"I'm taking Campbell. I'll call you later." She marched off in a huff down the stairs and then stomped back up again and down the hall to Campbell's room.

The baby woke with a slow cry that Kim comforted away with soft words as she passed by John's office.

"Bye, John," Kim called from the bottom of the stairs.

He jumped up. With a sudden urgency, he hurried to catch her. She was really leaving! This wasn't really Kim, but yet it was. It could be her. Either way, he couldn't stand to see her in so much pain. What if this was a test? What if his actions now somehow determined his future fate? He couldn't let her leave. "Kim, wait!" he hurtled dangerously fast down the stairs. He skidded to a stop in the living room.

Halfway out the door, she carried Campbell in the baby carrier with one arm and a second duffle in the other arm. She glared at him. "I won't be at church tomorrow."

"Kim, please."

"I'll be at my mom's. Don't call me," she said as if she hadn't heard him. Then her eyes became more narrow and piercing. Through gritted teeth, she said, "I want a divorce."

* * *

The apathy with which John had greeted this new situation quickly dissipated. Kim's anger and hatred for him—yes, hatred—tore at his heart. This wasn't the same Kim he'd loved, but maybe there was still something left to save.

The phone on the wall in the kitchen rang, and John answered.

"Hi, Mom." He let out a sigh, relieved to hear a friendly voice.

"They have a lawyer who's agreed to help them through the foreclosure process. So that's good, I guess. They have two weeks—no, I think it's three. They were looking at apartments, but that won't work, so they're probably going to stay with a couple from their church, the Robinson's. You don't know them—"

"Who are you talking about?" John managed to intercede.

"Your sister. They expected it. Henry's working two jobs right now and looking for a third. I think they're going to be okay. She didn't want me to tell you anything, at least that's what she said. But I think she knew I'd tell you, and wanted me to. I know there's not really anything you can do. Money is tight all around. Your dad and I are helping where we can. I think we might tap some of our retirement money. Of course your brother would be of no help at all. He's in worse shape than they are . . ."

John tried to wrap his mind around Mom's litany. If he was thirty, that made Becky twenty-two. And already in foreclosure? How long had she been married? And how could Sam be worse off? Was it the same medical problem he had when John relived high school? Becky and Sam both looked happy in the pictures he'd looked at earlier.

But . . . wait. Maybe he could help. "When is the foreclosure, Mom?"

"In a couple of weeks."

"Okay. Maybe I can help. Don't tell them, though, okay?"

"Sure, John. I won't say anything."

John talked with Mom for a few more minutes. He didn't ask about Sam. One thing at a time . . . if he remained in this pastor life much longer. Maybe he'd wake up in the morning with his own wife and his own kids, and the insanity of the last several months would become a distant memory.

Chapter 25

John followed the same route he'd driven earlier, his soul reeling as if it had been a target dummy for a dodgeball team. He could shrug off Kim's hatred, Dennis's murder, Lanie's insinuations, and his family's difficulties. After all, none of it was real. But he needed an anchor, and those close to him had changed.

As if on cue, something tugged at his conscience. Of course. God could be his anchor. John shook his head and chuckled. He'd been such an idiot. He'd started off following Chad's advice to pray, but it had fallen by the wayside.

He'd thought this nightmare couldn't be God's plan for him. It must have been random or something. God couldn't have chosen for him to leave his family and to relive life in so many different variations. But that was foolish too. The God of miracles could do anything.

John gripped the steering wheel. Why was he here? Somewhere deep in his mind, he always believed he'd endured this for a reason. That was why he agreed to take Lanie to the church for a funeral planning session. All of the people the police had questioned him about—people he hadn't known until living through these fantasies—they had to be the key.

A crowd of neighbors lingered across the street from the Vances' house. Yellow police tape cordoned off the front door. The garage door stood open, just as Lanie said it would be. He took out his cell phone and called her.

"Give me a minute," she said.

John stepped into the garage, where he found signs of Dennis's life everywhere in the organized mess of yard tools, canned food, and stacked boxes of who-knows-what. It all conflicted with the Dennis he knew. That Dennis had never been married, though he always had a woman or two around. He went from job to job, moving from one scheme to another. A few stuck, like the vitamins he sold. He'd spent time in jail and would disappear from John's life for years at a time.

This fake Dennis had structure. A large upright freezer stood next to the door that led to the house. John opened it, and a blast of cold air momentarily took his breath away. It looked as if an entire cow had been butchered and stored in the freezer. The shelves were stocked with steaks, hamburgers, ribs, and hot dogs. The lawnmower sat in the corner next to a red, five-gallon plastic gas can. A weed eater, blower, and hedge trimmer hung from the wall.

John picked up one of several boxes labeled "Nutridyne." He shook the light box, and its contents rattled. He counted twenty-five boxes. Wasn't Nutridyne a network marketing scheme that had been popular back in the 1990s? A lot of people were promised financial freedom, but most hopefuls faded away after a few months of disillusionment.

Dennis had sold something similar in real life.

There were two mountain bikes. John pictured Dennis and Lanie riding on the trails at Lake Hefner, the wind blowing their hair as they flew past joggers and rollerbladers. He fingered a nice set of Calloway golf clubs, stepped over a paper sack full of tennis balls, and admired an Easton baseball bag. He nudged it with his toe to see if it held a bat. It did.

Did he still have the baseball skills from his last fantasyland, or had they been replaced by the skills needed to conduct a funeral service?

Lanie moved briskly through the door. He had to hurry to keep up with her as she walked over the lawn to his car. He couldn't help but admire her figure in the blue jeans and tan fleece shirt she wore. But the dark shades covering her eyes reminded him of the tragedy at hand. Before pulling from the curb, John asked if she should shut the garage door.

"No. The police will shut it."

"When will they be done?"

"Today, probably."

John stopped at the stop sign and pulled out onto McArthur. "Have the police told you anything?"

"They've told me a lot. What do you want to know?"

"Any ideas who did it?"

"No. A random intruder, most likely. They're in the process of interviewing all friends and family. They're going to schedule the interviews around the funeral." She reached under her sunglasses to wipe her eyes with a crumpled Kleenex. With no inflection in her voice, she said, "They'll want to talk to you too. I told them about us."

"You did?" John didn't know what to say to that.

"Of course. What we did may have been wrong, but it wasn't criminal."

"No." John said. At least, not legally. Neither said anything for a few more minutes.

"Have they found his car yet?" John finally asked.

"No."

"A weapon?"

"No, but I found something."

The church steeple rose through a grove of trees ahead. "What."

"This." Lanie reached into her purse and pulled out an earring. It was a double hoop of gold, with tiny diamonds cut into the surface. It looked familiar. Did Renee have a pair like it?

"Is it yours?"

"No. Dennis was seeing someone." Lanie's tone was drenched in scorn.

John didn't point out that Lanie was too. "Just an earring? That doesn't prove anything."

"We've slept in separate rooms for months. He stays out late, he never calls. I don't need more proof. This is confirmation."

He automatically pulled into the parking spot for the senior pastor at Nichols Park Community Church, the church he went to while growing up. He attended there in his real life with Renee and the kids.

* * *

Lanie's family had gathered in a conference room adjacent to John's office on the south side of the church. He held the door open and ushered Lanie in. "You go on in. I'll be back in a minute."

He shut the door all but a crack and remained at the doorway and listened. Maybe he'd learn something.

"What are we going to do about his clients?" a hushed voice asked.

"I don't know. We should definitely wait a little while."

"Dennis did great at the meeting in Norman. There'll be a lot of money out of that one."

"Have the police told you anything?" John recognized the voice from his teenage fantasy.

The entire room became quiet. John pictured every head turning.

"It's still early," Lanie said as John got a glimpse of her through the crack in the door. She exhaled slowly. "They think Dennis knew his killer." John sensed distance in Lanie's voice, as if her heart wasn't in it.

Silent shock permeated the room and confounded John. Why would Lanie tell him one thing and Dennis's family something else?

John took a deep breath and lightly knocked on the door before stepping into the room. "Hi, everyone, I'm John Michaels, the pastor of this church. I'll be performing the memorial service. I knew Dennis well, but not like most of you did. My hope for today is that we can all talk and share about Dennis and how much he meant to each of us."

He saw Derek, Lanie's brother, amidst several people he didn't recognize. His gaze stopped at a man in the corner, the man whose voice he'd recognized. His thick dark hair had begun to thin on top, and his goatee had more gray hair than black. Unlike in John's life as a high schooler, this Chad Bailey was still alive.

"Let's all take a seat, and we'll get started." After a quick prayer, John opened up the table to comments.

"I guess I should go first." Lanie shot him a narrowed glance. Whatever intimacy they'd shared this morning had vanished. This Lanie seemed vicious and vindictive. Had he had a hand in making her that way?

"Dennis was a great man and a great husband." She refused the tissue Derek offered. "A perfect example of his character would be the Angel Tree project. Every year, Dennis organized this. He loved delivering the gifts to the families. He always made sure the children had something they could use like a new coat or a new pair of jeans and a fun toy."

That didn't mesh with the Dennis John knew.

"As you know, Pastor, Dennis loved working at the New Hope Shelter." A middle aged woman spoke. Her pleasant features sagged from grief. "He and a small group from his Sunday School class went every month to serve lunch. He talked with them, knew most of them, and treated them with respect."

John nodded even though he didn't know. For an hour, he took notes as everyone at the table gave their own take on Saint Dennis, and he formed a rough outline for the funeral.

After the meeting, people formed clusters again and continued talking. John caught Chad Bailey before anyone else could get to him. "Could I talk to you in private?"

"Sure."

He took Bailey to his office and offered him a seat. "I noticed you didn't say anything during the meeting."

Bailey shrugged. "I think they covered it all."

"How did you know Dennis?"

"Work." Bailey paused and stared at a spot on the floor-to-ceiling bookshelf to his left.

John looked too. Did he have all the knowledge contained in those scholarly works?

"Well, not actually work." Bailey said. "I know Dennis through Nutridyne."

"Tell me about that."

"I invited Dennis to a Nutridyne meeting. He came, tried the product, and took some samples home. I didn't hear from him for a few months, but then the commissions poured in. Dennis was on fire. In a few months, Dennis set meetings up all over the city, and then at the universities and junior colleges. He didn't care what people thought about him, which is good if you're going to be calling up your friends and asking them to buy a box of vitamins for thirty bucks."

The college campus angle seemed the way to go. Dennis and Kim must have been connected in real life, since Dennis kept showing up in these relived lives. Chad too. He was a direct link to Murphy Hazelton, and perhaps the last person to see Kim alive.

"More professors than college kids," Bailey said as though reading the direction of John's thoughts. "Most students didn't have any money, but Dennis signed up some real go-getters who were suited to selling Nutridyne."

John wanted to drop names to see if they were involved with Dennis in this life, but he couldn't tell Chad how he knew the names. "Did any professors come from OU?"

"A couple, but they are on my team not Dennis's."

"Was Murphy Hazelton one of them?"

Chad's gaze finally left the bookcase and turned back to John. "I'm sorry?"

"Murphy Hazelton? Was he one of them?"

"Yes, he was. How did you know?"

"Lanie and I talked a lot this afternoon. She told me about Dennis's friends. She was rambling really. Did Dennis get into any trouble?"

Bailey's eyes narrowed. "What do you mean?"

"I need to know what kind of person Dennis Vance really was. For the sake of his friends and family here, and for my congregation."

Chad glanced toward the ceiling and then spoke slowly. "Everything said in that conference room was true."

John could almost see the wheels turning.

"But there's a lot more that wasn't said," Chad stated. "A lot that perhaps shouldn't be said of the dead."

John reached for a notepad and pen. "How was their marriage?"

Chad stifled a chuckle. "I'm not the expert here. I only have opinions."

"Everything you tell me is confidential. But I need to know."

"Their marriage was terrible. I think it began when they learned they couldn't have kids. That caused all kinds of issues. Dennis cheated on her, mostly with college girls he met at the meetings. I tried to get him to stop, but he wouldn't."

This stunned John, yet at the same time it made sense. Dennis was the kind of guy who would cheat on his wife. "When did you last talk to him?"

"The day before he was murdered."

"What about?"

"It was personal. About something that happened a long time ago. I told the police everything, but I'd like to keep some of this to myself."

"Okay, sure." John tried not to show his disappointment and moved on. "How was Dennis with these women, or girls? Was he violent?"

"Dennis had a temper, but not with the women. Unless he was fooling us all, I don't think he ever hurt Lanie. When their marriage fell apart, Dennis became distant. I think the rift in their marriage was mutual."

What role had John and his "affair" with Lanie played in that? He couldn't wrap his mind around this alternate self as a pastor and a womanizer. This version was definitely not "him."

"So you don't think Lanie harbored any anger toward Dennis? You don't think she could have been involved?" John asked.

Chad's gaze bored into John. A slight smile crossed his lips. "I think Lanie had the capability to do a lot of harm to Dennis. But not physical. She had other ways."

"Like what?" John leaned forward.

"She, too, was having an affair."

John's mouth became dry.

"Dennis knew about it," Chad said. "And he knew who it was with."

Silence hung in the air.

"But he didn't tell me who it was."

John hesitated. Did Chad notice? "Lanie found something in her house. She thought it belonged to one of the girls Dennis was sleeping with. Do you know any of them?"

"No, I don't. Sorry."

They talked for a few more minutes. John had gotten all he could out of Chad, and it amounted to nothing.

Chapter 26

After spending the evening preparing for the funeral and a restless night sleeping in a new house, John returned to the church at seven-thirty. Somehow he wasn't nervous at all. In his mind, he knew the Sunday schedule and what he should do. He couldn't explain it, and he didn't want to think about it.

His pastor-self always went to each classroom and prayed for the people who would meet there in a few hours. Then he retired to his office to go over the service one last time. Finally, he met with the staff to talk about the line-up for the service to make sure it flowed correctly.

Today, he didn't do any of that.

Instead, he read the newspaper and surfed the Internet to find information he could use to help his sister. The incredibly slow dial-up made him want to kick the computer. He closed out the last window just as someone knocked on the door.

"Come in."

Brad Mullins walked in and closed the door behind him.

"Hey. You're just the person I needed to see."

"Really?" Despite his upbeat reply, Brad's face remained serious.

John quickly calculated that Brad would be twenty-five. He had never let as much as a whisker show on his face in real life, but now he bore a nice bushy mustache.

"Have a seat." John motioned Brad to take one of the chairs in front of his desk and turned the other to face Brad.

"Is something bothering you?"

Brad scooted back in his seat and crossed his ankles. "I needed to talk to you about something important."

"Sure. You and I are good friends, right?" John desperately needed a friend.

"We are, John, and that's why the board asked me to talk to you."

"The board?"

Brad nodded. Weariness and pain lined his friend's eyes.

John met Brad's gaze. He had a feeling he knew what Brad's bad news would be. "I understand. You go first."

Brad clasped his hands together and exhaled slowly.

The tables had turned. Brad had been John's pastor and spiritual mentor for years.

"This is the hardest thing I've ever had to do in my life, so I might as well get right to it."

"The church board is meeting after the service this morning. They're going to discuss your future at the church."

"Okay." Of course. They couldn't have a man like him as their leader.

"I believe they are going to ask you to resign."

John nodded.

"They know about your affair, John."

Brad stared out the window. When his gaze returned to John, it held a mixture of contempt and compassion. "Why did you do it, John? You've let a lot of people down. You've let *me* down."

"I . . . I don't know." Even though he'd done nothing, the weight of disappointment threatened to crush his spirit.

"I'm coming to you on my own. The board doesn't know. I hope there's a way out of this. Maybe you can come up with a reason why you're resigning. The truth will tear the church apart."

What could he say? He hadn't created this situation, and he didn't think he'd be around long enough to see it through. But he couldn't just throw aside the feelings of those he encountered. In real life, they were best friends. They probably were in this life too.

John glanced at Brad's left hand. Married.

"Who told you?" John said, his voice resigned.

"Why does it matter?"

"Was it Kim?"

"That's the worst part." Brad paced across the room. "You have a daughter. Kim loves you. She *still* loves you. Can you believe that?"

Silence descended on the room like a heavy cloud. John searched his heart and finally said, "I'm going to do the right thing."

Brad turned back to him, meeting his eyes for the first time.

"But I need your help. I still need to talk to you."

Brad slowly nodded. "Sure."

* * *

John sat on his living room floor alone. The service had gone well. The missionary speaker spoke until twelve-fifteen, which made the congregation anxious to get out of the sanctuary and off to lunch. He didn't mind. The church board had to meet to decide his future, and he had to explain Kim's absence to several people.

In front of him was a photo album. He had never been a picture-taker. Renee wasn't either. They'd bought a digital camera and now had plenty of unexamined pictures stored on their computer's hard drive. Kim, on the other hand, had always taken pictures.

After Kim disappeared, John had taken all the negatives her roommate Leslee could find. He took them to MotoFoto and had the pictures developed. Then he put them in a shoe box and taped it shut.

The box was still in his attic at home. He'd never looked at them, but he cherished the idea that he still had a piece of Kim with him.

John started at the beginning of the album. The pictures were just as he remembered from his real life. Nothing had changed. The pictures brought back the memories of the happiest time of his life, a time he'd buried in the deepest recesses of his heart.

He smiled at a picture of them all at Brothers on Campus Corner in Norman. They sat at a long table and hoisted their drinks in a toast. Willy had his arm around a girl and a goofy smile on his face. Everyone looked happy. He flipped through pictures of football games and parties, dorm life and night life.

The pictures changed in the fall of 1992, when he and Kim began dating. He counted five pictures where a waiter took their picture as they posed over their finished dinners. John studied Kim's eyes. They radiated a joy and innocence he'd forgotten existed.

Oh, Kim. Why did this happen?

Next were pictures of the OU home games. He'd never missed one. Then, at the bottom of the page, John found the last picture ever taken of them in his real life. He had his arm around Kim, and they stood in front of his Grand Am outside his apartment. He stared straight into the camera, with a cheesy smile plastered on his face. The picture caught Kim mid-sentence, her mouth contorted as she spoke. Would he have looked at Kim instead of the camera if he knew he would soon lose her forever?

When he turned the page, he viewed scenes from a future he had never had never lived. A future that might have been his if she had lived.

Kim, Leslee, and a bunch of girls in outrageous Halloween costumes at a girls-only party. John smiled at a picture of himself and Willy dressed as Bill and Ted from *Bill and Ted's Excellent Adventure.*

He opened a new album and relived their wedding. Kim looked beautiful in her strapless wedding gown. Her face radiated joy. It looked as if they had an awesome honeymoon at a Sandals resort.

Another album covered their first apartment and their first dog. John enjoyed seeing Kim able to live life as an adult. It could have been his life, but this pastor fantasy he now lived proved it wasn't. The Kim in this life wasn't real. Just as he'd moved on from the day she disappeared to his high school baseball life, he'd move on from his pastor life and lose Kim again.

At the rumbling of the garage door opening, John sat up. A door creaked and slammed shut. Kim walked through the kitchen but stopped when she saw him on the floor. She held Campbell in her left arm. Her gaze took in the photo albums scattered on the floor. "So, you're reviewing our life together to see what you screwed up?"

"Not exactly, but . . ."

"Here, hold Campbell. I'm packing some things." She handed him the baby and ran up the stairs.

Campbell was bright eyed and wide awake. She flashed him a smile. He held his baby close to his chest and kissed her on the forehead. He could love this little girl.

A sudden flash of anger jolted him.

This wasn't fair. Why, God? Yes, he blamed God. Why did you put me here? He should be with Renee and Mark and Sara. His heart ached to return to them, yet he now held a soft, precious little girl who had already captured his heart. His girl. Would he lose her, too?

John cradled Campbell like a football and hurried upstairs. He found Kim in their room, her suitcase on the bed.

She moved around in a flurry, grabbing clothes out of the closet, from her drawers, and from the laundry hamper in the corner.

"Slow down," John said.

She glared at him and then disappeared into the bathroom.

He turned Campbell around so she could face the room. When Kim appeared again with her hair dryer and shampoo bottles, Campbell cooed and kicked her arms and legs in a whir of excitement.

"Where are you going?" he asked.

"My mom's."

"Are you coming back?"

"No."

She entered the bathroom again and returned with a small bag strapped over her shoulder.

He couldn't stand to see her leave his life again. "I don't want you to leave."

"You should have thought of that sooner," she snapped.

"I'm sorry."

Kim dropped her bag onto the bed, where it bounced once before falling over. Her face withdrew into withering hatred. "Sorry? You're telling me you're sorry?" Her words came out tight and slow, as if it was the only way to keep a torrent of pent-up rage from erupting. "It's a little too late for that, John. You've ruined our life. You've destroyed everything we've worked for, everything we've dreamed of."

Her words grew louder, stronger. "You betrayed me. I know you, John. I like to think you have no idea what you've done to me or you wouldn't have slept with Lanie. But the damage is done. I can never look at you the same way."

"I've changed."

"Oh, really?" Her cheeks turned darker shade of red, and she marched up to him. "Was the speaker good at church today? Were the songs extra holy?

"No, I . . ."

Kim spun away and stalked out.

John cradled Campbell close and kissed her on the forehead. His heart ached for Kim, for the pain his pastor-self inflicted on her, and for his loss of the real Kim.

A heavy depression and a lifetime of pain filled the room. It became incredibly clear what he had to do. While this life wasn't real, Kim's pain was very real. He might soon leave this life and go to his own, but this version of Kim might in pain forever. He had to do something.

Chapter 27

John met Brad at Mona's Café on McArthur, a restaurant where the kind and hospitable staff went a long way to make a man forget how ordinary the food tasted. In his real life, Mona's existed, but the strip mall behind it had become home to abandoned store fronts, pawn shops, and vapor stores. In this pastor life, the strip mall thrived with two clothing stores, a discount shoe shop, and a pizza place.

Needing a constant in his life, John ordered a cheeseburger and fries. So did Brad. They sat in a corner booth in the near-empty restaurant. "Thanks for coming."

Brad nodded. He hadn't said much.

"I'm going to resign."

Brad looked up, his gaze curious. "I'm glad you're not going to fight this."

"I'm not going to fight it, but I didn't do it."

Brad's eyes creased into doubt. "Come on, John. Kim came to me. Why would she lie?"

"I hesitate telling you this because you'll think I'm crazy." John leaned forward in his chair and whispered in a conspiratorial tone. "I'm not who you think I am." Brad wouldn't believe him, so why not tell him?

A flicker of curiosity replaced the doubt in Brad's eye. "What do you mean?"

"I'm married and have two children, but I'm not a pastor. I'm a small business owner. And I'm not married to Kim. I'm married to Renee Templin."

Brad smiled, then snickered, then laughed. "You've always been able to make me laugh. But I expected you to have a deep theological reason to explain why it wasn't you who cheated on Kim. I thought maybe God had convicted you and you already repented. Maybe . . . I don't know. What's your point?"

"I don't know what my point is. Something strange has happened to me, and there has to be an explanation. God has to be involved somehow."

Brad shook his head and blew out a deep breath. "Tell me about it."

John looked around the room. A few old-timers wearing trucker hats. Regulars. Brad was waiting.

"When I was in college, my girlfriend disappeared. She was never found, and everyone believed she was murdered."

"I didn't know that." Brad sounded genuinely surprised.

"You wouldn't, because that didn't happen in this life."

Brad's face crumpled.

John stared directly into his friend's eyes. "I don't want to lose your friendship. I need you to hear me out. I need someone to trust, or I might go crazy." Or was he nuts? He'd killed Chad Bailey in his high school life. But he needed a friend. Maybe if he was more careful about what he said.

"Okay. I promise to listen." He munched on the last few fries on his plate.

"About four months ago, I went to bed, and I woke up back in college on the day my girlfriend disappeared. I tried to save her, but I couldn't. I think all of this is happening so I can find out who killed her." He kept his voice low so the couple at the nearest table couldn't overhear.

John told Brad everything. He sipped from his glass of water and asked, "What do you think?"

"Even if this were true," Brad said after thinking for a moment, "there's is no way I could believe you."

"I understand," John braced himself. "But I can prove it." He jumped from and grabbed the newspaper off the corner of the counter. He thumbed through the sports section until he found it what he was searching for. "Okay, the Sooners just lost to Texas. Who do they play next?"

Brad shrugged. "I don't pay attention."

"Here it is. Texas A&M. OU will kill them; 52-7 or something like that. OU will lose to Ole Miss in the Independence Bowl, and Florida State will beat Virginia Tech in the national championship."

John looked up at Brad, expecting to see amazed shock. Instead, Brad's wide eyes revealed sympathy. "Of course, you won't believe me until these things start to happen. Let's see, what else can I find? Oh, here, the NFL. The Rams are doing great. Who played in the Super Bowl last year?"

"Umm, let me think. Denver, and they won. I don't remember who they played."

"Doesn't matter. The Rams will go to the Super Bowl this year and beat the Titans. Next year, or maybe the next, they'll lose to the Patriots."

"Okay, anything else?" Brad raised an eyebrow.

John looked up. Brad's demeanor remained calm. Did he need more proof, or had he lost him?

"George Bush will be the next President," John said.

"I can believe that." He grinned.

"Yeah, but you'll never believe how it'll happen."

"Try me."

"It'll all come down to Florida. Bush will win, then Gore, then Bush. Lawsuits will fly. It'll go all the way to the Supreme Court. A 5-4 decision will give Bush the presidency."

Brad cracked a smile. "You have a great imagination, John. I can't wait to see if any of this comes true."

"You only have to wait until OU plays A&M." John flipped to the entertainment section. He found the movie listings and searched for familiar titles.

"*American Beauty* will win the Oscar. I know that. Not sure about the other awards." He thumbed through more pages. When nothing else triggered a memory, he moved the paper aside.

John looked Brad in the eyes. "Here's what I'm trying to tell you. The John Michaels everyone knows may have cheated on Kim. I'm sure he did. But *I* didn't. I also don't think I'm going to be here forever. Someday, I'll go to bed and wake up in a different house, in a different world."

That sounded preposterous and seemed unfair to give this life such little credence. "I'm struggling here, Brad." He looked down at his hands. "I miss my family. I miss my kids, and I can't tell anyone about it. Can you help me?"

Brad shrugged and laughed, a strained sound, chopped off short. "I guess I can help you, John, but I'll never be able to believe you. Here's what I'll do though. I'll listen and pray for you. I'll try and help you figure out what's going on. If it turns out you're crazy—and you might be—I'll try to find out what to do then as well. Deal?"

"I can accept that."

CHAPTER 28

John performed Dennis's funeral with emotional and pastoral precision. He even managed to ignore the undercover policemen in the building. After the funeral, he tried to track down Lanie. They needed closure on their affair, especially if he was going to make things right with Kim, but every time she saw him she went the other direction.

A man from the funeral home gave John the guest registry and the remaining programs and asked him to give them to the family. He thumbed through the registry. Perhaps someone who came to the funeral could help him in his quest for the truth. He looked for Buzz Baker or Murphy Hazelton, but didn't see either. How could he find out more about Dennis, Nutridyne, and the OU Norman campus?

Another name made him stop. *Larkin Connor.* Why had she been at the funeral? How did she know Dennis?

John caught Lanie as she left the church with her brother and the rest of her family. He ran to catch up to them. "Mrs. Vance, I wanted to give this to you." He handed her the items from the funeral home. "Could I talk to you for a second before you leave?"

The look in her eyes implied no. Instead, she nodded. "Go on ahead," she told the others. "I'll be out in a minute."

Now wasn't the time to talk about their personal situation, so he got right to his immediate concern. "Could you do me a favor and look through the names in the register? There might be someone you recognize, or don't recognize, who might be of interest in Dennis's death."

"The police already asked for a copy."

"Okay. I saw the name Larkin Connor. Do you know her?"

Her eyes flashed suspicion. "No. Why?"

"What about Buzz Baker or Murphy Hazelton?"

"No. Were they here too?"

"No."

Lanie sighed. "Do you think I should ask the police to look into those people?"

"Maybe. I don't know."

They talked for a few more minutes about how the service went. They gave each other a civil hug, and John whispered into her ear, "I'm sorry, Lanie, sorry for everything."

* * *

John stayed late that night during the scripture-based grief recovery program hosted at the church. He ate a Subway meatball sub and read through every file he could find. Fascinating stuff. He learned a great deal about the church, and most of it wasn't good. Maybe that was the wrong way to put it. The church was like everyone else. Not perfect.

Around eight-thirty, he peered through the room's small window. The meeting should be about done. The chairs were arranged in a circle, and Brad Mullins led the discussion. But John couldn't take his eyes off the young woman sitting to Brad's right.

Larkin Connor.

John stepped back and leaned against the wall. What did he know about her? The police considered her relevant enough to ask about her during the investigation of Kim's disappearance. If he was thirty now, she'd be about twenty-five. During his high school life, she was a junior high girl who lived in his church district. He saw her at the church festival, the same day he saw Renee, and they left together. Maybe Larkin had some answers.

He sat on a nearby couch and waited for the meeting to end. It dragged on, but he didn't dare move. John rubbed his eyes and yawned.

Finally, the door swung open, and people straggled out in groups of two or three. Larkin didn't come out for five more minutes, but then she appeared at the threshold with Brad. Larkin's shoulders slumped as she spoke to him. She looked down and wrung her hands. This was a defeated woman.

He retreated into the darkness of the hallway.

Brad listened and nodded. Then he embraced her in the type of hug John saw him use every Sunday at church. He was a compassionate man. He put his hand on her back and guided her down the hall to the exit. He was probably going to walk her to her car. John had to act. "Hey, Brad."

They both stopped at the door, and John ran to catch up with them. "Are you the last two here?"

"I think so. I usually lock up after our meetings."

Larkin took a step backwards, like she'd turn and run if she could.

"Hi, I'm Pastor Michaels."

She looked up at him, her dark eyes hiding so much. "I'm Larkin Connor," she said softly.

"I was walking her to her car," Brad said.

John addressed Larkin. "Could I talk to you for a minute, Larkin?"

Her gaze darted to Brad, her eyes pleading.

Brad studied John.

"It's about Dennis Vance."

Larkin's entire body froze, and stared at him with wide eyes.

Brad started to speak, probably to decline on Larkin's behalf, but John beat him to it. "It'll only take a second. Brad, you can wait for us outside my office if you like."

Brad didn't answer.

"It's important." John stared down Brad.

"Fine."

John walked down the dark hall towards his office. Brad and Larkin followed in silence. He stepped into the foyer and motioned for Brad to sit at a chair against the wall.

"It'll just be a minute," he said to assure both of them.

John opened the door for Larkin and closed the door as she took a seat in one of the chairs.

John circled around the desk and slid into his chair. The wheeled chair rolled backwards, and he grabbed the front of his desk. Larkin gazed about the room, perhaps taking in his vast collection of books and colorful array of photographs of the ideal family.

Either she'd be comforted by the setting or scared to death.

"Larkin, thanks for seeing me. I'll try to be brief." Hopefully his calm demeanor would put her at ease. In her early twenties, she still retained a girl-next-door freshness. Her short brown hair was either some type of current trend or an untamed mess. Her pretty face was devoid of makeup, but her darting eyes told the story.

"Was this your first night at one of our meetings?"

"No, I've been to a few." She spoke softly.

John instinctively leaned closer to hear her. "I hope you'll continue to come. I'd like to invite you to our church this Sunday."

She offered a meager smile.

"Could you tell me how you knew Dennis Vance?"

The color drained from her face. "Umm . . ."

"I saw your name in the funeral register. I didn't know you knew Dennis."

"You don't know me. I've never seen you before in my life." She twisted the ring on her pinky.

John's fists clenched. He'd made a mistake. "I'm sorry; I didn't mean it that way. I just wanted to know how you and Dennis were acquainted."

She shook her head and pinched her lips. "Why does it matter now?"

"He was murdered, Larkin. Have you talked to the police?"

She snapped. "I'm not talking to the police. You can't make me." Her eyes blazed.

"I'm not going to make you do anything." John held up his hands. "Please understand, I'm on your side. I just want to find out about Dennis."

"I knew him. A long time ago."

There had to be a reason Larkin came to the funeral. Something personal. He hated pressing her, but he hated even more not having answers.

"Do you know someone who would've wanted to hurt him?"

"I don't know anything."

"Would Dennis have any reason to have a pair of your earrings?"

"I don't wear earrings. My ears aren't pierced." She pulled the hair back to show her ears. "What kind of question is that? I haven't seen Dennis in years."

It was a long shot. The earring in Lanie's possession must not have been Larkin's.

"Did you meet Dennis at the Nutridyne meetings?" John's foot tapped up and down beneath the desk.

"What's Nutridyne?"

"Something Dennis was selling. You never went to any meetings?"

"No."

So Larkin was in and out of Dennis's life a few years ago.

Do you live around here?

"No. I live in Norman."

"So, you're in school?"

"I was. I'm working now at Hastings." She frowned.

Probably not in management, either.

"Was Dennis nice to you?"

Her face morphed into defensive anger. "I don't understand what you want. Dennis is dead. Leave me alone."

A flash of heat rushed through John's veins. He took a deep breath and spoke evenly. "This isn't about you, Larkin. I'm trying to find out about Dennis. Did he ever hurt you?"

"No." She wiped a few strands of hair away from her eyes.

"Hit you?"

"NO!" Larkin stood. Her bottom lip quivered.

John stood too. He needed to reassure her. "You'll never be safer than you are at our church. I don't care what you've done in your past, what you've seen or how you've been hurt. God can help you. I care about you. Brad cares. God loves you. Do you understand that?" The words flowed from his pastoral mind, but John realized he believed them too, regardless of what life he was in.

She nodded once.

"I need your help. A few more questions. Do you know Buzz Baker?"

She shook her head.

"Kim Addison?"

Again, no.

"Okay. What about Murphy Hazelton?"

"Yes."

Interesting. She knew Hazelton, but not Bailey, yet Hazelton, Bailey, and Buzz Baker were all related.

Then a thought hit him.

"Renee Templin?"

Larkin's eyes froze.

"You know her?"

Larkin reached for the door. It opened, and she stumbled into the lobby and into Brad.

"What do you know about Renee?"

"Leave me alone. Don't ever talk to me again." She begged, her eyes masking a deep, hidden pain.

"What's going on?" Brad demanded.

"Everything's fine." John said.

"It doesn't look fine. Come on, Larkin." Brad took her hand and pulled her into the hall.

John's face tightened. "She knows something."

Brad stepped closer.

John clenched his fists. Over Brad's shoulder, Larkin retreated to the exit. Confusion marred her face.

"Forget it, Brad." John returned to his office and slammed the door.

Chapter 29

The clues Larkin had dropped teased him. He couldn't erase the image of her face when he mentioned Renee. He turned off the lights in his office and peered between the blinds. The overhead lights illuminated Brad and Larkin walking across the parking lot in a fog of evening mist. They talked for a few minutes, and John half expected Brad to kiss her. Instead, Larkin got in a navy Honda that had seen better years and drove away.

John waited until Brad left as well before grabbing the master keys from his desk. In the lobby, he unlocked the file cabinet and pulled the recovery program file. He opened the file, and found what he wanted right on top: a record of last week's attendees and their home addresses.

John copied Larkin's address on a sticky note, opened the phone book, and consulted the yellow pages map. Five minutes later, he drove off in his Buick and got on I-35, heading south. John kept the radio off during the entire thirty-five minute trip.

After turning north onto McGee, John slowed to five miles per hour. Larkin must live in the large apartment complex on the left. Before he reached the complex, he came on a turn-in for another, smaller complex. These apartments consisted of two long rows of single-story off-white brick units.

John glanced at the sticky note affixed to the console. Apartment 1132. Larkin lived in the second building, the apartment at the end. Her unit backed up to a privacy fence missing several planks.

He killed his lights and shifted into park. A shadow of movement crossed the front window of Larkin's apartment. Other than having nothing better to do, why did he come here? On the drive over, he expected Larkin to have the answers to all of his questions, or at least know what questions he should ask. Now he shook his head. What foolishness. But he continued to stare at the window. She was his best hope. His head dropped to his chest and jerked up again. It had been a long day. He ought to go home.

Still, he didn't want to leave. She was hiding something, information that might help him put the pieces together. He drove across the parking lot and reversed into a space so he could easily watch Larkin's place. He would leave when she turned off her lights. Over the next thirty minutes, a few cars entered the complex, and Larkin's lights remained on.

Larkin's door opened. She stepped out into the night wearing jeans, a heavy coat, and a backpack looped around one shoulder. She hopped into her Honda and drove right past him.

He waited until she exited the complex before starting his own car.

He remained close enough to keep her taillights in view. When she turned onto Highway 9, he punched the accelerator to get to the intersection. He couldn't lose her now. When he turned, he breathed a sigh of relief. She was easy to spot on the empty road.

He settled into a comfortable distance behind her. Except for a few cars they passed, they were alone. He suddenly knew where Larkin was going.

Chad and Debbie Bailey's house.

After a few miles, Larkin put on her signal and turned right at the gas station near the Baileys'.

John pulled into the gas station and turned off his car. He needed to think. He also needed food. The sandwich he had earlier hadn't been enough to hold him this long. He hurried inside and bought bottled water and some peanuts.

He finished the peanuts and tossed the package and the empty water bottle onto the floor. He pulled out onto 108th street and drove until he spotted the drive to the Baileys' house. Pulling past the drive, he angled his car into the roadside ditch.

The crisp air and brisk wind chilled his ears and nose. A knot of eager anticipation welled in his stomach. He'd never do this in real life; he had too much to lose. He couldn't die in a fantasy world, could he?

Buoyed by his own invincibility, he crept up the Baileys' driveway. A heavy mist hung in the air. Darkness surrounded him. The wind picked up, and John wiped the moisture from his face.

Why did Larkin lie about knowing Chad Bailey?

Larkin had parked her Honda behind two SUVs. The Baileys obviously hadn't become environmentally aware yet. Living in Oklahoma, they probably never would.

A light by the door illuminated the porch, and light glowed through curtained windows. Keeping the SUVs between himself and the house, John edged closer to the house, sprinted to a window on the side of the house, and found an angle where he could see through a crack between the curtains.

Chad Bailey sat on a leather couch and Larkin in a matching recliner. Her hands flew as she spoke.

When Chad responded, John tried to read his lips. It looked as if one of the words he said was "police."

Larkin commented and then stood and disappeared from John's view.

He caught a shadowy movement out of the corner of his eye. He crouched and tried to disappear behind a foot-high bush. No luck. But the person darted straight to the porch.

John scooted along the wall, stepping carefully over a tangled mess of plants. At the corner, he crouched low and peered around the edge.

The tall, lanky man standing at the door wore dark clothes, and his baseball cap kept his face in shadows. But what drew John's attention was the gun in his hand.

He started to speak, but the words stuck in his throat.

The man opened the door and disappeared into the house.

John charged to the porch. His foot caught on a bush and he stumbled forward. He hit the concrete porch hard but broke his fall with his hands.

Two gunshots shattered the cool innocence of the night.

Larkin!

John stumbled to his feet but didn't rush into the house.

Glass crashed inside the house.

"I'm calling 911!" yelled a woman, probably Debbie Bailey.

He peeked inside the open front door and looked down a long entry hall that led to a room where Chad Bailey stood, his back to John and his hands in the air.

"Put the gun down," Chad said slowly, but a tremor in his voice betrayed his fear. "You're never going to get away with this."

Another gunshot hurled Chad's body against the wall. He staggered forward two steps and crumpled to the floor.

A wailing agony echoed through the house, a misery only known by watching a loved one die.

I could die tonight, too. Would a fatal gunshot permanently separate him from Renee and his kids? Maybe. Maybe he already was. But he couldn't leave Larkin and Debbie to be slaughtered. He hoped both were still alive.

He rushed through the living room and down a hall. Family pictures blew by in a blur as he glanced in each room. Debbie must still be in the room with the killer. He had to focus on Larkin. "Larkin, "he whispered. "It's John Michaels. I'm here to help."

Screaming, shouting, and crashing furniture in the front room interrupted him.

"Larkin, we need to get out of here."

"It's not too late; we have to call the hospital!" More desperate pleas from Debbie Bailey. She didn't have much longer to live.

John rushed into a bedroom. He tore open the closet. Empty. He darted into the master bedroom across the hall.

The phone on the nightstand had been overturned.

In three giant strides, John entered the walk-in closet.

Larkin huddled in shivering bundle with her head buried in her hands.

John brushed aside several dresses and knelt next to her. "Larkin, it's John. We need to go." He pulled on her arm, but she pulled away from him. He put his hand under her chin and forced her to look at him.

Her dark eyes were wide with fear.

"Do you understand? We have to leave. Now!"

No response.

He moved closer, their faces inches apart. "Larkin. Let's go. Answer me!"

She gave an almost imperceptible nod.

John pulled her to her feet. They had two options for escape. The single window in the bedroom, or back into the hallway.

Did the window lead to the front or the back yard? Had another killer remained outside? What if the killer had disabled his car? If he didn't know they were here, maybe they could stay in the house.

Another gunshot exploded in the night.

John jumped, and Larkin yelped. John's heart thudded in his chest. Larkin's hand shook in his.

The noisy boom receded, and an eerie silence spread through the house.

"All right, who else is here?" called an angry voice. "I'm coming to get you."

John snapped out of his indecision and dragged Larkin to the window. "Come on, we've got to get out of here."

He yanked the string on the wood blinds. They rattled to the top of the window frame. He pulled up on the window, but it didn't budge. Locked. John prayed for steady hands and snapped the two locks open.

The window slid easily. Cool air rushed past them, and a dog barked in the distance.

John punched out the screen, which landed silently on the ground. "Larkin, go," he whispered. When she didn't move, he grabbed her wrist and pulled her toward the window and up onto the blanket chest next to it. Larkin stepped onto the window ledge before dropping two feet to the grass. He followed.

Maybe the killer wouldn't know they'd escaped.

A gunshot shattered the window and showered them with bits of glass.

Larkin screamed, while John stifled a curse. They both ran. It would be a race. He reached for her hand, and pulled her along with him.

The killer leaped through the window, cursing the whole time. The wind whipped the words away.

John looked back to see him stumble as they reached the corner of the house.

"My car," John sputtered.

They picked up speed as they ran across the front yard. When they reached the drive, they hurried past the two SUVs and Larkin's old Honda.

Two more bullets pinged off the larger SUV, only a few feet away.

Fear hammered his heart as he ran by. They had a straight shot to 108th Street. The killer would have to run at an angle before he'd have a good shot.

John still held Larkin's hand. The wind whipped against his face. The cold night air burned his lungs.

Larkin stumbled, and he lost his grip on her hand. He slowed to let her catch up, and he resumed running.

As he ran, the last few minutes tore through John's mind. Had he done something to bring that killer to the Baileys' front door? Why would anyone want kill the Baileys? Could it be the same killer that killed Dennis Vance?

Low-hanging limbs brushed against John's head as he sprinted down the sloping hill. He dug in his pocket for the keys as they reached the end of the drive. He skidded to a stop and aimed the key fob at the car.

The locks clicked open.

John took a moment to glance up the hill. The killer was halfway down the slope. He stopped beneath a large tree and raised his arms.

John didn't wait to see what would happen. Larkin was already in the car. "Hurry!" The first words she'd spoken.

As John threw himself into the front seat a bullet banged against the rear of the car. Then another.

He shifted into drive and pushed the accelerator to the floor. The car leaped forward. It bounced, bumped, and went airborne briefly before John slammed on the brakes at Highway 9.

John turned left and merged into traffic. A safe distance away from the house, he allowed his tensed muscles to relax. He breathed heavily, and his heart pounded.

Next to him, Larkin stared straight ahead in an almost catatonic state. He didn't blame her. His own nerves were frayed, and his heart pounded.

"Where should we go? What should we do?" John mumbled, more to himself. After driving for miles in silence, he pulled into a 7-Eleven and parked in front of a pay phone.

"I think I should call the police."

Larkin stared at him, her dark eyes glossy.

"I'm not going to tell them our names." He fumbled for change on the center console, hopped out of the car and made the call. When a harried-sounding woman answered, John told her what had happened.

The operator asked for more information and begged him to remain on the line, but he hung up.

* * *

John pulled into his driveway after midnight and led Larkin to the upstairs guestroom. "The bathroom is across the hall. Can I get you anything?"

Her eyes were still glazed with shock, but she shook her head.

"Are you sure you don't want to talk about what happened?" He desperately needed answers.

She shook her head again.

"Food? Something to drink?"

Larkin took a deep breath and exhaled slowly. "I'm fine. I appreciate everything you did. You saved my life. I just want to go to bed now, but I'll talk to you in the morning. I promise."

Once she settled in, John went back out to the garage. He knelt by the right rear panel and ran a hand over the two holes. Only a few inches lower, and the bullets would have blown out the tire.

Chapter 30

His mind numb from the evening's events, John caught a glimpse of a family portrait with Kim and the baby in his peripheral vision. A picture of a family never his, a life he never had. By the time he reached his room, his anger had morphed into rage. He needed an outlet.

His gaze swung around the room and landed on a lamp sitting on the dresser. He grasped it, picked it up, and got ready to heave it at the wall. Then he stopped. Larkin would hear, and she was already in a fragile state.

Tears filled his eyes as he let go of the lamp. He didn't fight them. He couldn't stop them if he wanted to. He dove onto the bed and buried his head in the collection of pillows. The sobs racked his body. He cried and cried, not worrying about regaining his composure. The fear had always been there, ever since he woke up from a nap and became a college student again. He couldn't shake it or dampen it. What if he never saw Renee again? What if he never saw Mark or Sara again? His kids needed him.

Fatigue finally exhausted him. He fell asleep fully clothed on top of the covers and slept without dreams. He woke up abruptly to bright sunlight that gave the room a splash of color. A conviction that he needed to get something done overwhelmed him.

Larkin! Was she still here?

His alarm clock read 9:30. He hurried to the guest bedroom. The bed looked as if it had never been slept in. Larkin could disappear if she wanted to. She didn't have to talk to him.

He retreated back through the living room and then stopped. Larkin sat at the kitchen table sipping a cup of coffee. An empty bowl sat to her right. She still wore the same clothes, but her hair was wet, so she must have taken a shower.

"I thought you were gone," John said.

"Why would I leave?"

"I didn't think you wanted to talk to me."

"I have no one else."

The simple statement broke John's heart. How could a young, pretty girl like this have no one to turn to?

He poured himself a cup of coffee and sat across the table from her. He cleared his throat. "I don't know where to begin."

But he saw much more than a woman. He saw an answer, a link to his past, a feeling that he couldn't explain.

"Why did you follow me?"

John clasped his hands together. If only he could tell her the truth. She might even help him try to find the answers he needed. But he couldn't. Instead he said, "I know Dennis's murder wasn't a random killing. He was killed for a reason; I just don't know why. And then the way you reacted when I mentioned Renee. I knew you were hiding something. I think the two things are related."

"You still shouldn't have followed me."

John nodded. "I know. I had nothing but unfounded suspicions to go on. But I'm glad I did."

She looked out the window. The sun was out, and an easy breeze caused the leaves on the trees to flutter. "I'm glad you did, too."

"Did you see the man who killed the Baileys?"

Larkin wrapped her hands around the coffee cup. Tears spilled down her cheeks. "No," she whispered. She obviously wasn't going to elaborate.

A car door slammed outside. The garage door rumbled open.

"Oh no."

"What?"

"My wife is home." He hadn't seen her in four days.

Larkin flashed a bemused smile. "Why are you panicking?"

"I'm not pan . . ." John's shoulders slumped. "Okay, here's the quick version. She moved out. She thinks I cheated on her."

Kim came through the garage door. She only glanced at John before her gaze landed on Larkin. She looked like a wounded animal that had been beaten again. "Is this another girlfriend?" she said in a raspy voice.

"No, no, no," John assured her. He took her arm and guided her to the chair he'd just left.

John stood between the two. "Kim, this is Larkin Connor. She goes to the grief recovery meetings at our church."

Kim's eyes narrowed into cynical beads. "Part of the job, right?"

"Last night, a man killed Chad and Debbie Bailey. Chad was at Dennis's funeral."

Kim's features softened a bit. "I heard about the killings on the radio."

"Larkin would have been killed, too, but I got her out of the house. She was in shock and had no one to go to, so we came here. I think the same person who killed Dennis killed the Baileys."

"You were there? Why were you in Norman?"

"I followed Larkin."

Kim sat up straight. "That's weird, John."

"I know, but I had a hunch Larkin knew something."

Kim shook her head and put her arms up in mock surrender. "I don't know what to say. If it's true, I'm glad you're both okay." For the first time, Kim acknowledged Larkin. She eyed her as though she were a rival, even though she was leaving him. "What did you know?"

Though he hardly knew this Kim, it felt good to have her take his side. But he still half believed that if he reached out to touch her, his arm would pass right though.

"Nothing," responded Larkin.

"Why did you go to the Baileys', Larkin?" Kim asked.

She looked down at the table and slowly raised her head. "Brad knows everything. You can ask him."

"I don't need to," John said. "I trust you."

"Chad and Debbie are—were—good friends. Chad was an attorney. He helped me with some legal issues."

"Do you think the person last night was after you or the Baileys?" Kim continued the questioning.

"I have no idea."

"How did you hear about the Baileys?"

"One of my professors at school. His name is Hazelton. You asked me about him at the church."

Another piece to a puzzle with no solution.

"What's your plan now, John?" Kim stood and put her hands on her hips, as if daring him to say something smart.

"No plan. No idea. I don't know what to do."

"Well, I still need to get my stuff. Let me know if you need my help regarding these awful murders. Otherwise, don't call me. Let's meet on Saturday and discuss our future."

"What future?"

After a quick glance at Larkin, Kim said, "I think you know."

"I do know, and I want you to know it's not going to be easy for you."

That got Kim to look at him in the eye. "What do you mean?"

"I don't want a divorce." He didn't care if Larkin heard their conversation. She wasn't real. This wasn't real. He imagined he was speaking to the Kim he last saw in 1992. "I don't want to lose you."

She bit her bottom lip and squeezed her eyes shut.

Had he broken through?

"You don't have that choice." Kim stared at him for a moment and hurried up the stairs.

"Sorry you had to witness that," John said.

Larkin shrugged.

John paced beside the table before raiding the pantry for something to eat. He found a pouch of instant oatmeal, added milk, and put it in the microwave.

"I have to go to work. Can you take me?" Larkin asked.

"Sure." John retrieved a spoon from a drawer. "No, wait. You shouldn't go to work. The police are probably looking for you because we left your car at the Baileys."

"I don't know what to do."

John ran his hands through greasy hair. He needed a shower, but he didn't have time. If the police were going to be involved, he needed to do some things first. "Do you trust Brad?"

"I do," Larkin said.

"I'll take you to his house. I want you to tell him everything that happened, and then do whatever he wants you to do."

* * *

After dropping Larkin off at a curious-and-confused Brad's house, John dialed his sister from his cell phone. He knew nothing about his sister in this life. Another unexpected gap in his memories. But whatever was going on, she needed help.

"Hi, John." Her voice seemed different. Like it was infused with pain. Why?

"I was going to come over. Is it okay to stop by in a few minutes?"

"Sure."

He parked on the street in front of her tiny, wood-sided home. The lawn had recently been mowed, but not trimmed, and weeds and grass had overtaken the flower garden.

John knocked and waited. How would Becky be different, and what would it mean? She was only twenty-two and already married. In real life, she didn't get married until she was twenty-seven. Was her new husband a jerk? Had she made a bad decision in high school? In college?

What was taking her so long? He tried the doorbell. The chime reverberated through the house.

Still no one answered.

He put his ear to the door to listen for footsteps.

"Come in," a faint voice hollered from inside. "It's unlocked."

Maybe she was in the bathroom. John stepped inside to a mess that a flea market merchant would be proud of. The room smelled of cardboard, paper, and dust. In the far corner of the living room, rows of boxes stood four feet high. More boxes covered a thrift-shop sofa. The clutter of loose papers, books, boxes, and paper sacks obscured the border between the living room and the small kitchen.

"Sorry about the mess," Becky called from the hallway. She rolled into the kitchen in a wheelchair and deftly maneuvered around another two boxes next to a microwave cart. She opened the refrigerator door, retrieved two cans, and offered one to John. "Pepsi?"

John stared in heartbroken silence. His sister in a wheelchair. Another new life, another family tragedy.

He took the cold can, unsure of what to say.

Becky didn't seem to notice his uneasiness. She wheeled past him, stopped at the recliner, and moved a plastic storage bin from the chair to the floor. "Have a seat."

"Sure." John slowly sat down, and then opened his Pepsi. Becky positioned her wheelchair across from him, grabbed a huge stack of papers from a box, and put them on her lap. After studying each paper, she either placed it back in the box or threw it in the trash can next to her wheelchair. She didn't seem to notice his stare.

No obvious signs of an injury. Her legs appeared fine. No cast or boot or brace. He glanced around the room for clues. He didn't know what he expected to see, but there had to be an explanation. How could she go from a successful attorney in real life to wheelchair-bound, financially insecure, and married twenty-two-year-old? If she still planned to be an attorney, she wasn't starting out on the right track.

"We have to be out of here by next Friday," Becky said. "Maybe you could help us move."

"I'll be here."

"Mom told me about Dennis Vance." Her gaze never left the papers in front of her. "I know he was one of your friends from high school, but I don't remember him very well."

"They still don't know who killed him."

"I hope they find out. You never know if this could be your last day on earth. I'm just thankful for what I have."

"I know." That was all he could say before a gigantic lump formed in his throat. His life wasn't perfect, but he'd taken for granted how good he had it. Maybe he'd already spent his last day in his real life. Were his last words to Renee, Mark, and Sara really so mundane that he couldn't recall them?

He'd been given the chance to relive parts of his life and make new choices, but so had other people. Dad lost his job, Sam got sick, Becky was in a wheelchair. Second chances didn't always make life better.

Becky dropped the last of the papers on her lap and leaned back. "How's Kim and Campbell?"

"They're both good. Campbell's great." *Oh, and I've been forced to resign from my job as a pastor because I supposedly had an affair with Dennis's wife. Kim found out, and she is going to divorce me.* Tonight would be a great night for him to wake up back in his own forty-five-year-old world.

Nothing he did here would be adequate. He couldn't save Kim again. She hated him. He couldn't protect Larkin. He couldn't heal his sister. He couldn't convince Brad he didn't have an affair. What good was reliving his life if he couldn't do anything? He wanted to scream.

"I'm glad they're doing fine. I need to get by and see that baby. Maybe this weekend?"

"Sure." He should tell her that Kim and the baby moved out, but not yet. He'd tell her before she came over. Or maybe he'd just leave town. He could vanish. Run away. Move to Vegas and win a fortune. He didn't know the results of every game, but enough to make a lot of money. Which was why he was at Becky's house. Putting that knowledge of the future to good use. "I came over because I want to help you out."

Becky extended her arms wide and smiled. "Knock yourself out. Everything you see must go."

"No. I don't want to help you leave. I want to help you stay."

Her smile disappeared. "That's not possible."

"It might be."

"No, John. Absolutely not. I don't know what you're thinking, but it's not. Didn't mom tell you we didn't want any help?"

"She did."

"I know you don't have the money, John. We've made our own decisions, and we'll deal with it."

"Becky, you need to let me do this."

"I can't." A tissue appeared in her hand. She sniffled and wiped her nose.

"My life isn't going so great either, but I don't want to burden you with that right now. Let's get your house situation fixed, then maybe you can help me. Deal?"

She nodded.

"Anyway, I came into some money. It's not my salary; it's not my retirement; it's not Kim's. It's extra money, money I'm going to give you and your husband. You don't have to pay it back. I want you to take it in the spirit it's given. In love."

Becky wiped away tears.

He took an envelope out of his pocket. "There's a cashier's check in here for your house. You can pay it off." He held it out to Becky.

The grateful sadness in her eyes retreated before stunned disbelief.

She opened the envelope and pulled out the check. Her jaw dropped. Her head rose slowly. "Where in the world did you get this kind of money?"

"Maybe I'll tell you someday. But all you need to know right now is that nothing pleases me more than to help you." But he knew he'd never tell her the truth. It involved maxing out credit cards, an online betting service, and the knowledge that the Oklahoma Sooners would lose to the Texas Longhorns 37-27 last Saturday. Something a pastor probably shouldn't do. But this life wasn't real, so it wouldn't really mean anything, right?

CHAPTER 31

After spending two hours at Becky's, John returned to an empty house. Clouds covered the sun, and a sharp wind rattled the trees in his front yard. He walked through silent darkness inside his house. Loneliness descended upon him like a heavy fog. He needed a connection to reality.

He searched the guest bedroom. Larkin left no sign of ever being there. What remained of Kim's things were nice and tidy. The baby's room still smelled of talcum powder and baby wipes. But nothing reached out and enfolded him. It still wasn't *home*.

Back downstairs, he found some lettuce. He reached for a knife to chop it and saw an envelope on the counter with a sticky note attached to it.

John, I meant to give you this sooner. Kim.

Her signature tugged at his heart. She used to write notes to him all the time and signed them with the same extravagantly curlicued signature.

He tore off the end of the envelope and took out a folded piece of notebook paper. A handwritten note to "Pastor." At the bottom, it was signed, "Dennis."

He leaned against the counter and read slowly. The tiny, hand-written print was hard to follow at first.

I'm sorry about all I have done. Lanie would never forgive me. You've always preached that a man can hide for only so long, but eventually the type of person he truly is will be revealed. I'm tired of the cheating. I can't hide anymore.

Please don't tell Lanie. I want to tell her on my own, when I have exorcised my own demons.

A knot formed in John's stomach. He stared at the logo on the refrigerator. Dennis obviously had no inkling about his impending death. Another avenue yet to be explored. Who were his enemies? He refocused and started reading again.

I know where the body is buried.

A cold flash spread through his chest. He finished reading the details in the letter, folded it, and put it in his pocket. His hands shook. He couldn't do this alone, but could he trust anyone?

He pulled out his primitive Nokia 8210. The tiny display informed him that he'd missed three calls. He clicked on the number. "Brad, it's John."

"Where have you been? I've been trying to call you. I tried your house, your cell, and the church. You need to . . ."

"I was at my sister's and turned my cell off. Sorry."

"Larkin's here. You both need to go to the police and tell them what you saw." Brad's voice rose. "I'm glad you're okay, but why didn't you go to the police last night? You witnessed a murder. More people may be in danger."

John let Brad vent.

"That was stupid. John, I'm trying to be supportive, but every decision you've made lately is one you wouldn't have made a month ago."

"I have a bigger problem now, Brad. I'll be at your house in ten minutes." Before he left, he rummaged through the garage for the gear they'd need.

* * *

The door flew open immediately when John knocked. Inside the long front room, Larkin sat on the couch next to Brad's wife, a blonde he didn't recognize. Larkin looked refreshed in a different pair of jeans and a sweater.

Brad crossed his arms. "What's your *big* problem?"

John handed him the letter.

The color washed out of Brad's face. He passed the letter to his wife and turned back to John. "You want to go out there, don't you?"

"I do."

"No way."

"I have my reasons, Brad."

"You need to go to the police."

"We will. We can even call and have them meet us out there. I don't care. I want to see this for myself."

"No, absolutely not." Brad pivoted to face his wife. "What do you think?"

She shrugged as she passed the letter to Larkin. "I don't know, honey." She briefly made eye contact with John before saying, "It probably wouldn't hurt to call the police first. Why didn't Dennis call?"

"Like the letter said, he wanted to talk to me about it first. But I think he would have gone to the police if I suggested it." He took a deep breath. The same sharp feeling that pierced him when he first read the letter still pecked at his insides. "Under normal circumstances, I agree it'd be insane not to go to the police . . ."

John caught Brad's eye and tilted his head toward the door. They retreated to the small entryway. "Brad, this is just like what happened to Kim."

"It's a body buried in the woods. How can it be the same?"

John spoke quietly, "The letter said the body is behind the old York Recreational Center."

"So?"

"That's off Highway 9, less than half a mile from Chad and Debbie Bailey's house."

That jerked Brad to attention "The same place where Larkin and you were almost killed."

"Yes, and, the same place where Kim was last seen in my real life."

"Interesting. But it could be dangerous."

"Come with me. We can see if there's anything that can help me figure out what happened to Kim."

Brad closed his eyes rubbed his chin. "Okay. I'll go."

John smiled in relief. "Thanks."

They stepped back inside. "I'm going to go with John to look around," Brad informed the women as he retrieved a jacket from a tiny closet.

"I'm going with you." Larkin stood.

"You should stay here," Brad said. "When we get back, we'll call the police."

She walked to the door. "I know whose body it is."

John's heart thudded.

"It's Renee Templin."

Chapter 32

No one spoke in the car until they reached the highway. A slight drizzle began to fall, and John turned on the windshield wipers. "Tell me about Renee."

"I didn't know her that well." Larkin looked out the window.

Brad remained quiet, and the silence seemed perfect. They were all here for different reasons. Brad tagged along out of obligation, and Larkin came because she knew something. The darkness, the pit-pat of the rain, and the swish-swish of the windshield wipers gave John a soothing peace. For the first time in ages, his soul felt rested. Something deep inside told him he was nearing the end. He'd soon be back with his family. Why did Kim and Renee share the same fate but different lives? One was real, one was not.

"Renee and I grew up on the same street." Larkin's quiet voice knifed through the silence.

The rain came down harder, and John put the wipers on high.

"We played all the time, and we were best friends. But we didn't know any better. She was my friend because she lived close. We weren't anything alike. In junior high, we went our separate ways, but we remained friends."

Brad slid to the center of the back seat and leaned forward so he could hear over the pelting rain.

"What changed between you?" John asked.

"I changed. A ninth-grader named Casey raped me."

The wipers rhythmically whipped across the windshield, adding a beat to the silence that grew heavy with Larkin's revelation.

John swallowed.

"I didn't do anything about it. That's why I came to the meetings at your church. They've really helped, Pastor."

After a moment, John realized she'd been talking to him. "I'm glad."

The wind whipped against the car, and he had to fight the tug of the steering wheel.

As he drove past the exit for the airport, Larkin spoke again. "After eighth grade, Renee moved. We went to different high schools, and I never saw her. I didn't think I'd ever see her again, and I didn't care to."

"Why?"

"We were different."

Larkin didn't continue, and John asked her to elaborate.

"I hung out with the wrong crowd. I did the wrong things. Renee studied hard, went to church, and never disappointed her parents."

"How did you know this?"

"She told me later. I only managed to get into college because of my dad."

"He had a lot of money?"

Larkin cut off a laugh. "No. He didn't have any money. He tried to straighten me out. He believed in me. He shouldn't have, though, because I didn't change once I went to college.

"Anyway, I *tried* to straighten up. I went to class. I spent a lot of time in the library. I think I was fortunate that my roommate got sick the second week of school and had to go home, because I spent days at a time alone. It's really easy to do when you're surrounded by thousands of freshmen."

John slowed to wait for two cars to pass before merging onto I-35. They'd be in Norman in fifteen minutes and at the York Recreational Center in twenty. Rain continued to pound the car. The wipers worked furiously to clear the heavy drops from the windshield.

"One day I passed a wall in the Student Union with a bunch of fliers. One was for the Christian Youth Association. I decided to go. The meeting, or party, or whatever, was a lot like the ones I went to in high school, only dialed down a notch. Everyone was nice to me. I ate snacks and wandered around the big, old house. In a large room in the back, I saw Renee sitting in the corner with a group of people. I recognized her instantly. She still had the same dark hair, freckled nose, and kind eyes."

"When was this?" John asked.

"September."

"What year?"

"1992."

Probably a few weeks before Kim disappeared.

"When Renee saw me, she jumped up, ran across the room, and gave me a hug. It embarrassed me, but I felt good inside that she still cared about me. She dragged me back to her group of friends and introduced them: Kate, Leslee, and Willy."

"Willy and Leslee," John interrupted. "What were their last names?"

"Mmm, why? Do you know them?"

"Maybe."

"Let me think."

The heater in the car had won the battle with the cooling temperatures outside. John turned it to a lower setting.

"I only remember Leslee's. It was Williams. She and Renee were roommates, I think."

The parallels smacked John between the eyes. It was as though Renee had taken over Kim's life in this pastor fantasy.

"The last person she introduced was Dennis Vance." Larkin paused to look at John. "Renee made me feel welcome. She talked, laughed, and her skin glowed with energy. I hung out with them and enjoyed being with a friendly group of people. I kept expecting a service to start, since it was a Christian meeting, but it never did. We were probably there until about eleven, just talking and meeting people."

"Tell me about Dennis?" John accelerated to pass a slow-moving semi.

"He knew everybody. I remember that was why I watched him. Something was going on between Dennis and Renee. When he handed her a can of root beer, he whispered something in her ear. I couldn't hear what he said because of the music, but it seemed intimate. They lingered close for a few minutes, talking, whispering, and touching in ways that said they were more than friends."

"They were dating?" He gripped the steering wheel tightly. *Dennis!*

"They weren't at the time. I found that out later. But they had dated before. Quite seriously."

Not much shocked John since his life sank into the canyon of despair he was currently in. But this intrigued him. How could all these fantasy-life events be tied to events in his real life?

He flicked on his blinker and took the looping exit onto Highway 9. They'd be there in five minutes, and he needed answers. "How do you know we're going to find Renee?"

Larkin looked at him with narrowed eyes. "I just do. She disappeared shortly after I met her at that party."

"Early October?"

"Something like that? The weekend of the OU–Texas game."

John nodded. Probably many more similarities, only the victim had changed. No sense beating around the bush. "Did Dennis kill her?"

Larkin didn't hesitate. "No."

"How do you know?"

"He loved her. Renee told me they began dating when she was in ninth grade. He went to church with her, which made it easier to ignore the age difference between them. He became the prince that swept the princess off her feet."

"I think we need to turn right up ahead." Brad leaned forward and pointed.

John squinted, trying to identify where to turn through the sheets of rain. "But he still could have killed her."

"I don't think he did," Larkin said.

"How did he know where the body was?" John tapped the brakes.

"I think he just found out."

That jived with what Dennis's letter said, or didn't say.

"That has to be what got him killed. And the Baileys."

He recalled the enraged man chasing them through the darkness. He'd killed Dennis, the Baileys, and Renee? What about Kim? It made no sense.

He slowed and pulled onto the shoulder to look for the entrance to the York Recreational Center. He stopped at a worn gravel path overtaken by weeds. "This must be it."

His headlights illuminated what used to be a park filled with kids playing Little League baseball. John killed the ignition, and the windshield wipers skidded to a stop. The rain on the hood grew louder. With the headlights off, the abandoned fields vanished into a mist. Only the flicker of headlights passing on the street behind them broke the darkness.

"Maybe this isn't a good idea," Brad said.

"We'll be fine. Nothing will happen to us. We'll just get a little wet."

Larkin stared out the window. This mysterious girl had revealed so much, yet somehow he knew she'd left something out.

"Larkin?"

She faced him, her expression hidden in the shadows.

"Is there anything you're not telling me? What happened after Renee disappeared?"

No answer.

"Larkin," John prodded.

"They never found her."

"I understand. Were there any suspects?"

"Dennis."

"But that went nowhere?"

"I guess. He loved Renee. He always had. It tore him apart."

"What happened with you and Dennis?"

Brad had rested his chin on the seat as though drawn by the topic of conversation.

"We became good friends."

John's cell phone vibrated in his pocket. He checked the display but didn't recognize the number.

"We dated," Larkin continued. "I got pregnant and had a baby."

The new revelation stunned John into silence. Before he could put words to his surprise, Larkin continued.

"I gave the baby up for adoption. Chad Bailey helped me. He was a nice man and . . ." Her voice cracked.

That explained Larkin's appearance at the funeral and her trek to the Baileys' house after he asked her about Dennis and Renee. The Baileys were much more than her legal counsel, they were her friends.

John contemplated the depth of Larkin's loss. How had her relationship with Dennis changed over the years? He'd fathered a child with her, and then married another woman. Was she angry? Bitter?

"I'll get the gear out of the trunk." He popped the trunk popped open, took a deep breath as if about to plunge into the ocean, and opened the door.

The deluge drenched him as quickly as a fall into a dunk tank. He grabbed the raincoats and duffel bag in one swoop, picked up the two shovels, and leaned them against the car.

He returned to the front seat and slammed the door. "Should we wait till the rain lets up?"

Larkin shrugged and then looked at Brad.

John tapped the steering wheel. The terrain would be muddy and dark, the odds of finding a decomposed body slim. But he seemed so close to answers. "Let's go. I know we'll find it."

No one complained as John handed out the raincoats. He zipped up and asked, "Ready?"

Larkin answered by opening the door and stepping outside.

John pulled two flashlights out of the Walmart bag he threw into the car earlier and handed one to Brad. John stepped out into the downpour again and grabbed the shovels before joining Larkin in front of the car.

The rain had let up a bit, and the wind had slowed. John and Brad pointed their flashlight beams in a crisscross pattern toward the entrance to the ball fields.

John took the lead and, with his first step, found a puddle. His foot made a sucking sound as he pulled his tennis shoe out of the mud. Already soaked from head to toe, he shivered.

They passed a worn wooden stand where John imagined overweight men taking admission fees from captive parents. The flashlights illuminated glimpses of bleachers, chain-link backstops, and a building. From what he could tell, the York Recreational Center consisted of four baseball fields, with the concession stands and bathrooms in the center.

The last part of Dennis's letter said they should go past the concession stands and through the outfield gate between the two south fields. There they would find a maintenance shed.

John found solid footing on a gravel path and stayed on it. Larkin and Brad followed.

The rain fell harder and then softer. The wind picked up and blew the rain sideways. Then it stopped. Typical Oklahoma weather.

Ahead, he spotted the fence. He flashed the light toward it and was able to pick up a change in its pattern and the outline of a shed behind it. That must be the gate. "Over there."

A rusty, corroded padlock fastened the gate latch closed.

"We'll have to climb over," John said.

Brad shrugged. He scrambled up the eight-foot fence and landed gracefully on the other side.

"Do you need help?" John asked Larkin.

She looked at John, then at the fence. "I don't think so." She drove her foot into the fence and pulled herself up. Her step made the fence leaned forward. As she took another step, the fence sagged further. She swayed and fell back. Her feet hit the ground, and she stumbled.

John dropped his flashlight and the shovels and rushed toward her but tripped on a rock and lost his footing. They tumbled together into a swath of squishy mud.

"Guys, down here," Brad called. "There's no fence here."

John gathered the equipment and followed Brad's voice. Twenty feet to their right, a section of the fence was missing. They walked right through and then back to the path. It disappeared at the threshold of a dense forest.

Brad hung back. "Are you sure about this, John?"

John nodded. "Let's go."

The weeds and brush thinned as they entered the thick knots of trees. The high branches above acted like a roof and held back the rain. Water only pelted their raincoats when a strong gust of wind rustled the limbs.

John recalled the rest of Dennis's note. *There is an abandoned truck just south of the fields.* He led the group, careful not to veer too far from a straight line. As they slowly covered more ground, he turned around to see if he could spot the maintenance shed.

Nothing.

They sloshed through standing water, and mud coated their shoes, but John didn't dare veer from a straight line.

"Do you see anything?" Larkin asked.

The flashlight beams seemed powerless against the mist and overwhelming darkness.

"Not yet."

He forged ahead, keeping his head down to avoid low-hanging tree branches, but looked up frequently to scan ahead. He saw the shadowy form ahead.

"There it is." Larkin hurried around him.

They quickly gathered around an old, rusted-out pickup. How did it even get way out here? Maybe a trail existed at one time. Now for the hard part.

Once you reach the abandoned car, walk south to the creek. Just beyond it, the trunk of a large tree has split. Dig at the base of that tree.

So vague. In the total darkness, could they find the tree? Could they even find the creek?

"We need a compass," Brad said.

"We came in from the east," Larkin said, "so that way is south. Follow me." She grabbed Brad's flashlight and led them forward.

John's phone vibrated. By the time he dug it out, it had gone to voicemail. Another missed call from Kim.

A burst of wind caused a wave of raindrops to fall from the trees. John wiped the water from his eyes and tucked his phone away. With Larkin about ten feet in front of him, he waved the flashlight back and forth, searching for the creek.

Would they have to wade across? He hadn't considered that. Had this been a mistake? How could they find a body buried in the middle of a forest? It had been seven years ago. They should have waited until tomorrow. They should have called the police.

He pushed the doubts away. Every morning he risked jumping away from this version of his fantasy life. It had to be now.

Larkin stopped. John and Brad hurried to her side.

"Is this the creek?" asked Brad.

Their flashlights illuminated nothing but a dip in the terrain, filled with mud, sticks, and fallen leaves. Not even a trickle flowed in either direction.

"It might have been at one time," Larkin said.

"That's the tree." John focused his flashlight on the tree directly across from them. Thick at the base, the trunk split about eight feet up and continued high into the air. Roots furrowed out of the ground like thick ropes and then burrowed back down.

John handed the shovels to Brad. "Toss them over after me." He backed up, took a running leap, and flew over the creek bed. He landed halfway up the other side. His foot squished into mud to his calf.

"Over here, Larkin," Brad said. "We can step across here."

By the time John struggled up the incline, Brad and Larkin waited for him at the base of the tree.

"Where do we dig?" Brad handed John one of the shovels.

"I don't know." John kicked at a root. "I don't see how anything could be buried under these roots. This tree's been here for decades." Wind rushed through the trees and pushed his hood back. The air cooled his hot skin. "Let's look around."

The three studied the section of ground illuminated by the flashlights as if looking for a lost quarter.

John bent to look at a twisted root more closely. Surely there would be something to tell him where to dig. A marker. An indentation. A clearing. But he found nothing.

His phone vibrated again but stopped before he could pull it out. He grimaced. He had wanted to talk to Kim if she called again.

This time she left a message: *"John, where are you? I've been trying to reach you. Call me back. The police are looking for you."*

He crammed the phone back into his pocket. She'd called him. Maybe there was hope. He shook his head. Why did he still care about salvaging the relationship? He loved Renee. He needed *her*, not Kim. This whole surreal fantasy was driving him crazy. If he tried to battle his heart, he'd never win. Regardless of the memories from his real life and Renee, they weren't here. Kim was here, and she was his wife in this life. He couldn't let that relationship crumble without doing something.

"Hey, guys, check this out," Brad said.

John aimed his flashlight at the point lit by Brad's flashlight, about five feet to the right of the tree. He and Larkin joined Brad, and they all looked at the ground.

They stood over a freshly dug hole, about three feet wide and two feet deep.

"Someone's already been here," Brad said.

"Dennis," John said.

"Or the Baileys," Larkin offered.

John tried to think. Did Dennis know where the body was buried because he'd put it there? Or had someone else told him?

A flash of light made him look up. Lightning? No. The trees blocked all view of the sky.

There. He saw it again. "Hold up guys; we're not alone."

Brad almost jumped out of his shoes. Even in the shadows of the flashlights, John could see his face turn white.

Larkin craned her neck silently, as though she expected evil to be lurking overhead.

To John, the wet silence felt ghoulish and mysterious, but not threatening. Little scared him anymore. Except for the possibility of never seeing his kids again.

"I saw it too," Brad said. "Someone is out there. Let's leave and call the police." He and Larkin scurried past the tree and over the muddy creek bed.

John followed, brandishing his shovel in case they needed a weapon. When he caught up with Larkin, a voice boomed through the forest.

"Freeze! Police!" A strong, focused flashlight beam preceded two uniformed policemen.

Everything that followed happened in shadows. The officer who smelled strongly of tobacco called in over a radio, but John couldn't make out the words. Another asked them to drop their shovels. John and Brad did as they were told.

John tried to think of an innocent explanation for being in the woods. No. He needed to tell the truth and show them Dennis Vance's letter.

They all furnished identification when asked. The taller officer examined their IDs carefully in his flashlight beam. It also lit up his face, a face John recognized from his high school fantasy. Ray Pope.

Ray stepped away and spoke into the radio again. When he returned, he asked, "Are you John Michaels?"

"Yes."

"You are under arrest for the murder of Dennis Vance."

Chapter 33

The gray walls and floor sucked the life out of the interview room. The warm air in the confined space made John's shirt stick to his back. The officer's icy glare as John placed his only phone call made him want to crawl into a hole.

After he told Kim where he was and why, she greeted him with silence.

"Kim. Hello. Are you there?"

"I'm here," she said in a shaky whisper. Then stronger, "I can't help you tonight, John. I can come by tomorrow after I drop off Campbell."

"Okay. I really need to talk to you."

"I'll be there." The finality in her voice scared him.

"You don't think I killed Dennis, do you?"

She took too long to answer, and then spoke in measured tones. "The person I married would never have done it."

"I'm still that person."

"You cheated on me."

"I didn't."

"How can you still deny it?" she hissed.

"Kim, it's just that . . ." He stopped. He couldn't tell her over the phone. "I'll tell you everything tomorrow. The one thing I promise is that I'm not going to lie to you."

"I'll see you tomorrow. Bye, John." The line went dead.

*   *   *

John sat alone on a metal bunk. This was a first, something he could tell his kids about when they were older. "Let me tell you about the time your dad was thrown in jail . . ." Or maybe not.

He didn't really know or care where he was. What he really wanted to do was talk to Ray Pope. Not about the charges, but about who he was. In John's baseball fantasy, Ray had been an overly enthusiastic baseball coach who liked to leer at the high school girls. Now he was a Norman police officer.

If only he could say everything was coming together. But it wasn't. Tons of clues and connections, yet nothing made sense. It was all crazy.

John allowed himself a smile and wondered when he'd be a free man again. He reclined on the bunk and folded his hands across his chest. The sooner he fell asleep, the sooner Kim would come to see him . . . and the sooner he could pour his heart out to her.

Chapter 34

No thoughts, no dreams, nothing... until a shrieking alarm snapped John awake. He'd slept well. Surprising, considering the jailhouse suite he occupied.

Beep! Beep! Beep!

Except they didn't have alarm clocks in jail cells.

He wasn't in jail anymore. He was home!

John threw off the covers and jumped to his feet. The sight that greeted him made him slump back down as if he'd been shot. Dirty laundry formed a pile in the corner. A Compaq 386 computer sat on top of the rickety computer desk that had taken him hours to put together. A TV rested on a milk crate. He wasn't home.

He turned off the alarm and picked it up, ready to hurl it across the room. But wait. Since he'd jumped to a different time again, maybe he was getting a lot closer to finding out what happened to Kim.

He glanced at his lean, college-age body and shook his head. This crazy journey back in time had started in this dusty apartment, and here he was back again in 1992. Maybe this journey was a circle, and he was almost home. If there was a reason he woke up here, he had to act on it. But first, *when* was he?

The digital clock read 2:04 p.m. Was it the day Kim disappeared again? He rummaged through the backpack next to his bed and found a copy of the campus newspaper.

October 8, 1992.

The day *before* Kim disappeared. Unless that was yesterday's paper. He picked up the phone resting on the dresser and punched in a number. "Kim?"

"She's not here, John." It was her roommate, Leslee. John let out a deep sigh. Kim was still alive.

"Does she work on Wednesdays?"

"You're a day off, John. It's Thursday." Leslee laughed. "I don't think she worked today, but she did mention something about going in. I'm expecting her to be home for dinner, though."

"Thanks. Tell her I called."

John threw on the same jeans and sweatshirt he'd worn last time, grabbed his keys, and left the apartment. He headed to the campus in his Grand Am.

As usual, traffic moved at a snail's pace on a weekday afternoon. He used the time to try and remember where Kim had gone the day before her life came to an end. Had they gone out to dinner, or maybe a movie? Had they talked on the phone? It must not have been memorable.

He decided to retrace his steps and look for Kim. He parked a few blocks away from Gittinger Hall and resisted the urge to run. He moved swiftly past meandering students and walked the last fifty feet on the grass when a throng of men dressed in suits failed to move fast enough.

Once inside, a burst of cold air gave him chills. The cold followed him down the hall to the quad of offices where Kim worked. A few classes were in session, but many classrooms stood empty. Distant voices roamed the halls, but nothing drew his attention.

Today felt different. Randomness had vanished. Whatever he needed to find, he'd find. He had to. The end felt close.

He opened the door, expecting to find Kim sitting at her desk and talking on the phone or typing a letter. The same faded wood paneling and stale carpet met him, but no Kim. The doors of all four offices were closed.

Frustrated, John clenched his hands into fists and punched at the air. He needed results. He needed something to happen.

He checked out the desk. *The Bodyguard* soundtrack case sat next to the phone. The Six Flags picture was in a frame by the typewriter. Sticky notes adorned with Kim's handwriting covered the top of the stapler. She hadn't quit yet.

The same issue of the *Oklahoma Daily* John had at his apartment rested on the corner of the desk.

John read the headline: "Fourteen Freshmen Charged in Cheating Scandal." Apparently a few individuals thought it would be fun to steal exams and sell them to students. So far, the university had only identified the cheating students, not the thieves.

A door squeaked behind him and brought John away from the paper.

Professor Murphy Hazelton stepped out of an office and fumbled to lock his door. He carried his leather satchel in one hand with his tweed blazer draped over the other arm. He jumped slightly when he turned around and noticed John. He lowered his head as he walked toward the door. Not exactly the attitude John expected. But then, an ingratiating smile wouldn't have meshed with his flushed cheeks and the gleam of sweat on his forehead.

Now that John had become more familiar with the man, something didn't feel right. "Excuse me, Professor Hazelton. Do you have a moment?"

"I'm sorry. I'm late for an appointment." He spoke with a forced calmness.

Then John saw something that raised the hackles on his back. A ripe, red gash on his neck. A fresh cut, like someone scratched him.

Hazelton hit the door to the hallway and kept walking.

John followed. "I'm looking for Kim."

Hazelton ignored him.

John matched his stride. "Kim Addison. She works for you."

"I know who she is."

"Have you seen her today? It's important."

They reached the front door and skirted around a few students before going outside.

"No." Hazelton put on a pair of sunglasses.

"Who scratched you?"

Hazelton stopped. "What?"

"Who scratched your neck? That's fresh. It just happened."

"It was an accident and none of your business." He started walking again, faster now.

"Was it Kim? Was it another student?"

Hazelton didn't answer, but his wide, shifty eyes gave him away. He reached his car, an elongated Caprice tank. He pulled keys out of a pocket. He dropped them and then scooped them up quickly.

John stepped close. "What happened? Where's Kim?" As Hazelton opened the door, John realized nothing had happened to Kim. Not yet. She wouldn't disappear until tomorrow. Kim would die tomorrow.

Hazelton slipped into the car, slammed the door shut, and gunned the ignition to life. The engine roared.

"Wait!" John slammed his fists down on the hood. The large car lurched backward out of the space. An oncoming car had to slam on its brakes to avoid hitting it. Hazelton tore out of the lot as though he were an extra in a Steve McQueen movie.

The car disappeared around a corner. Had all the answers he needed disappeared with it? He exhaled, and air rushed out like a deflated balloon.

Students nearby stood with backpacks slung over their shoulders, stunned expressions on their faces. Then they resumed walking and talking, and the car Hazelton almost hit took his parking place.

John ran to his car and dropped into the passenger seat, not even winded. Nice to be young and in shape again.

He took solace in knowing he could still see Kim this evening. But he couldn't wait.

He turned the corner and approached Dennis's house. Unlike the last time, the driveway and yard weren't littered with cars. Instead, a campus police car parked in front. Two officers walked across the lawn.

John parked across the street but didn't get out. When the officers knocked, someone answered the door. John strained to see who, but couldn't see.

The officers disappeared inside.

A memory stirred to life in the back of his mind. This had happened before. Dennis had been expelled from college shortly after Kim's disappearance. His occupation as party-drug supplier to the frats and sororities had finally caught up with him. From the looks of it, life was repeating itself in front of his eyes.

John waited. Where could he search for Kim? Perhaps he could drive out to the Baileys' house. Something interesting always seemed to happen to him out there. But he remained at his spot underneath the large tree across from Dennis's house.

His thoughts wandered. Where was Renee? There was something about seeing her talking to Dennis the last time he'd been here that he didn't understand, some piece of vital information just outside his reach.

The murder of Dennis Vance. John had been arrested by two Norman police officers. The officers talking to Dennis now were campus police. That was different.

The door opened again. John expected Dennis to be led out in handcuffs, but instead only the two police officers emerged. The tall one said something to a figure at the door and then waved goodbye.

John's mouth drew into a tight line. He studied the tall one, but there was no denying it. He was the same guy who'd arrested him for Dennis's murder. Different times, different jobs, but the same man: Ray Pope.

* * *

John stood on the front porch next to a bulging trash sack filled with crushed beer cans. He shook his head. They had to make room for the new ones.

Dennis answered and stepped aside to let John in. The room smelled of old food and stale beer.

"Why were the police here?"

"Dude, you saw that?"

"I waited outside till they left. I expected you to be in front of them, with your hands behind your back." John sat on the gold sofa and pushed aside a pizza box.

"Yeah," Dennis chuckled halfheartedly. "I need a drink. You?"

"I'm good."

John followed his friend into the kitchen. Dennis grabbed a bottle of Coors, twisted the cap off, and took a long, slow drink.

"You in trouble?"

"Ah, no. Not really. I'm always suspected of something."

"Because you're always doing something."

Dennis raised his glass. "And getting away with it."

"How do you know Renee Templin?"

Dennis lowered his glass, his eyes narrowed. "Why?"

John couldn't explain how he would see them both tomorrow, so he just shrugged. "I was just wondering."

"She's a friend." Dennis tossed his bottle into the trash and walked down a narrow hallway. He had a lot of secrets, and John needed to learn about this one.

"What about Kim? Have you seen her today?"

"Nope." Dennis turned into his room and rummaged in his closet.

John leaned against the door frame. "She's not at work."

"Do you have big plans tonight? I heard she was mad at you for going to the game with Willy."

A bolt of panic shot through John's heart. "No, she isn't."

"Is too."

That couldn't be. John racked his brains. Kim had wanted him to go to the game, hadn't she? She didn't care about football. "I don't think she is."

"Maybe not," Dennis said, his back still turned. "But I think you're crazy. I'd take Kim to Dallas any day over Willy."

"What about Renee?" John countered.

Dennis ripped a shirt off a hanger and threw it on the closet floor. "What about her?"

Why did the visit by police bother Dennis so much? "Do you know her?"

"Yes. But I didn't know she knew you."

"I think I have her in a class," John stared at a wad of twenty-dollar bills on the dresser.

"I don't want to talk about it." Dennis threw the hanger on the floor.

What was going on? What would cause Renee to be here, in this room tomorrow, having a heart-to-heart with Dennis? "Is she involved in something she shouldn't be?"

Dennis whirled around and stalked toward John.

John braced himself, ready for a punch, but Dennis blew by him. He grabbed his backpack off the table. "I gotta go, John. I'll see you tomorrow when you come and get the tickets."

"Do you have them now?"

"I thought I would, but no. Sorry."

Dennis waited by the front door until John stepped onto the porch. After locking the door, Dennis got in his car and drove away. John considered following him, but his heart wasn't in it. He needed to find Kim.

Chapter 35

John cruised around a commercial area looking for a pay phone. He drove so slow at the intersection of Lindsay and Jenkins that a knot of pedestrians crossed in front of him.

In real life, John hated cell phones. He hated being dependent on a small, expensive device that no one had twenty years ago. But he was, and he paid a fortune so he and Renee could have iPhones with all the features. Now he really needed a cell phone and didn't have one. He finally spotted a pay phone outside a strip mall on Lindsay. While he dialed, a group of college kids wandered into O'Connell's. He'd spent many evenings there during college. He could use a burger right now.

Leslee answered.

"This is John. I'm still looking for Kim."

"She came by, but left for the library. She said she'd be home by about eight thirty."

"Thanks." John trotted towards the library. With its location in the middle of campus, it'd be faster to walk. He crossed the street and circled around the south side of the football stadium. He paused just inside the library. Without having an idea where Kim might be, he'd never find her. He took the stairs down to the lower level and got a Snickers and Pepsi out of the vending machine. He returned to the front desk.

"Could you use your intercom, I need to find someone."

The thin girl with stringy hair and thick black glasses hesitated. She turned around but couldn't find anyone to come to her rescue.

"Please. It's an emergency. Her name is Kim Addison."

"Mmm, okay." She picked up a phone and pressed a button.

"Would Kim Addison please come to the front desk. Kim Addison, please come to the front desk."

John thanked her and wandered away to wait by the water fountain in front of the restrooms. The clock ticked, and the minutes passed slowly. Maybe Kim wasn't here.

She hurried down the stairs and burst into the wide-open lobby, her eyes wide and cheeks flushed.

Relief flooded John. Living with a tormented, angry Kim during his pastor life had messed with his memories. All of his love for her rushed back. "Kim, over here."

"John, what's wrong?" She hurried to him, her tense shoulders slacking just a bit.

"Nothing, I . . ."

Redness washed over her normally blue eyes.

"What's wrong with you?" John asked.

"Nothing."

"No, something's wrong. I can tell."

"Okay. You're right. I'm in the middle of helping someone with something right now. I'll tell you about it later. Why did you page me?"

"I needed to see you." Because she was going to die tomorrow.

Kim sighed. "Let's meet at eight. Pick me up." She stepped away.

He couldn't let her go, yet it seemed right. Something was going on with Kim that hadn't happened in real life. He'd never seen panic, maybe fear, etched into her face like this. "Okay. Sure."

Kim hurried up the stairs. She didn't look back.

* * *

The time passed slowly, but John used it to grab a bite to eat at the New York Bagel Shop on Campus Corner. He also returned to the pay phone and made arrangements for a nice dinner later. It cost more for a private table in the back, but he charged it. No point in worrying about the future.

At quarter 'til eight, he retrieved his car and drove to the apartment Kim shared with Leslee. His curiosity nagged at him the entire way. What was going on with Kim?

She greeted him with none of the apprehension from earlier and gave him a fierce hug.

John let her arms swallow him and treasured the warmth of her body and smell of her hair.

She locked the door behind her. "Can we go somewhere to talk?"

It was hard to find a quiet place on a college campus, so John drove west on Lindsay. "You hungry?"

"Sure."

John pulled into Legend's Restaurant.

"This is kind of expensive, isn't it?"

"You wanted to talk, didn't you?"

They sat at a table for four, ordered water, and talked about John's upcoming trip for the game. He had a lot more on his mind, and Kim's tentative and short answers said she did, too.

John ordered a steak, while Kim ordered the same thing she ordered every time they went to a restaurant, a chicken sandwich.

Kim's girlish smile had vanished, replaced by a grimace. A layer of innocence had been stripped away, and he wanted to know why. "You had a rough day?"

"Yeah, I did."

"Want to tell me about it?"

"I do, but I don't." Kim fiddled with her straw. "Do you understand?"

"Can I ask you about it?" He unfolded his napkin and put it in his lap.

She nodded.

"Let me see your hands."

She held them out. His insides shuddered at the intimacy of taking her hands. After several months of being away from Renee, he needed something real. He examined her hands then looked at her.

"What are you looking for?"

"Professor Hazelton had a scratch on his neck today."

She pulled her hands away and cast her gaze downward. Rosiness crept up her neck. "How did you . . ."

"I looked for you at your office, and Hazelton came out. He seemed flustered and didn't want to talk. I saw the cut on his neck. It was fresh, and when I mentioned it, he rushed to his car. He wouldn't answer my questions."

Kim rubbed her eyes as if she could massage away whatever anguish she was going through. "I didn't do it."

"Who did?"

"A student." Her eyes focused on something over his shoulder.

"Who?"

"I don't want to talk about it."

"Why? You can tell me anything."

"I know, but I feel like I'd be violating someone's trust." She took a drink of water. "Why did you have to find me?"

John hesitated.

"You said you had to find me."

"I'm worried about you."

"Why?"

Their waiter passed brought the salads that came with their entrée choices. He nodded his thanks, and Kim put her napkin on her lap. They both arranged their silverware. When he left, John picked up the conversation again. "I had a dream today, during my nap."

Kim nodded.

"We were married and had a baby named Campbell."

A broad smile lit Kim's face, a smile that told him she could envision the same.

"Yeah, that was the good part. In the dream I was cheating on you and you wanted a divorce."

Kim frowned. "That would never happen."

"No, but in the dream, the pain was very real. I so wanted to salvage our marriage, to tell you how much I loved you, how much I cherished you."

Kim held his hand again and squeezed hard. She smiled with happy, watery eyes.

"I wanted to apologize to you and tell you I never meant to hurt you, but I didn't get the chance."

"That's amazing, John. We were meant to be. I needed to hear those words so badly."

"I had another dream," he said.

"Tell me about it."

"It's simple really. I went to the game this weekend, and OU lost."

"No way."

"I came home, and you were gone. You'd been murdered."

Kim froze, fork midway to her mouth. "That's horrible."

"Yeah. It was." Could she hear his voice crack?

The waiter brought their food. They moved their barely touched salads aside so he could place the plates in front of them.

Steam simmered up from juicy steak and the buttery baked potato.

This could be their last meal together. Maybe he was saying farewell.

"What are you doing tomorrow?"

"I don't know yet."

Maybe he could ask Kim what he needed to ask without freaking her out. He prayed he could. "Work?"

"No." Kim shook her head. "I may be looking for another job."

"Like what?" John tried to catch her gaze, but she focused on her French fries.

"I don't know."

Like being a nanny for the Baileys. "I was considering not going to the game."

She looked up. "Don't be silly."

"I'm not. I'm worried about you. The dreams I had, and now you're troubled by something." He kept his tone light.

"That's sweet, but you'd regret the rest of your life not going to that game."

The knife of regret that always remained in his heart twisted again. A day didn't go by that he didn't ask himself if Kim would have lived if he hadn't gone to the game. "I keep going back to that dream."

"Okay." Kim tilted her head and gave an amused but caring smile. Her wavy curls fell gently across her forehead. "We can talk about it."

John took a bite of his steak and decided it was so good, it didn't need any A-1 sauce. "I don't believe dreams can tell the future."

"No, of course not."

"But my dreams got me thinking. We're young, we're in college, and we have our entire lives ahead of us. That's what everyone tells us. But, what if we don't? What if something happens to me, or to you? What if you die tomorrow? What if I don't come home on Sunday?"

Kim sat her fork down. "Wow. This is serious, and I'm glad."

"Really?"

"Yes. I'd love to talk to you about it."

"Okay."

"I'll go first." Kim licked her lips. "I am not afraid to die. I've made peace with God and know that when I die I will go to heaven. It's devastating to think about how you and my family would feel, but honestly, I can't wait to go to heaven."

John stared back, speechless. His tongue caught in his throat. Kim continued.

"We've been friends forever, and we've been dating for a few months. Every night before and after we started dating, I prayed that God would bless me and give me wisdom as I dated and looked for my future husband. I believe He answered my prayers with you. But we never talk about God or our spiritual lives, and that bothers me. I think I don't bring it up because I'm afraid of what you'll think, but that shouldn't matter. Does it?"

"Does it what?" John stammered.

"Does talking about God bother you?"

John shook his head, still finding it difficult to give voice to the words forming in his head. What Kim had said was big, for so many reasons, and he had trouble getting his mind around it, partly because he didn't want to accept it.

"No. It doesn't bother me." Or it didn't bother him now that he'd learned to pray. He was a different man from the one who first woke up back in college on the day she died. He should say something, but if he did, he might start bawling like a baby. He finally, choked out, "Kim, you're amazing. I don't think you know how amazing you are."

"Thank you." Kim smiled at him and then seemed to drift away.

Okay, where now? He still needed answers.

"I guess after talking about life and death, I can tell you a little about my problems," she offered.

Maybe he wouldn't even have to ask again.

"I wasn't supposed to work today, but I left my literature textbook in my desk. After Dr. Bartlett left, I spent a few minutes tidying my desk. I thought I was alone until I heard something break in one of the offices. It sounded as if a vase had crashed to the floor. The door burst open, and a girl almost knocked me over in her rush to the door. She disappeared into the hallway at a sprint. I didn't know whether to check the office or go after the girl. Something was obviously wrong, so I chased after the girl.

"I thought I'd lost her, but just outside the building she'd stopped at a bench and buried her head in her hands. I sat down next to her and laid my hand on her shoulder. She continued to cry for a while. Then I asked her what happened.

"She didn't say anything, but eventually she looked at me. Beneath her red eyes and smeared mascara, I saw a scared girl."

"What happened to her?"

"She didn't tell me at first, but I eventually coaxed it out of her. We spent all afternoon figuring out what to do."

"Who was the girl?"

"I can't tell you."

"The teacher was Hazelton, right?"

Kim looked away, and a tear escaped when she blinked.

John pictured Renee talking with Dennis asking him what she should do. That would happen tomorrow? Did it relate to today? Another parallel? "Kim, was the girl Renee Templin?"

"Who's that?"

That set John back. He thought he had this figured out. "She's friends with Dennis."

She rolled her eyes. "A lot of girls are friends with Dennis."

John threw out another name, because somehow all this had to make sense. "Was it Larkin Connor?"

Kim's eyes grew wide and then narrowed. "Did you follow me in the library?"

"No, of course not."

"Then how do you know?"

"It's something I really can't explain right now."

She studied him and seemed to accept it. Her spirit deflated. "He tried to rape her."

"Right there in his office? Are you sure he tried to rape her?"

"Of course I'm sure. She wouldn't lie about it."

"I'm sorry."

Kim shook her head. "I don't know what I'm going to do."

"You work with Hazelton?"

"I don't. I used to, though."

"Really? What happened?" Since they became friends, Kim's life had been an open book. Had he missed something? "You never told me you had any problems with a professor."

Kim took a drink of water. "It's a secret, John. We all have secrets."

Chapter 36

After paying for dinner, John walked Kim to the car and opened the door for her. Silence filled the short drive back to her apartment.

It was his big opportunity to change history and keep Kim from dying. He could ask Kim to talk to him all night, maybe about Hazelton and Larkin Connor. He could stay home from the Sooners game. He could protect her.

The faces of Mark and Sara floated through his mind. He could smell Sara's raspberry-scented hair and Mark's tinny sweat after a Little League game. Could he give them up for this dream of keeping Kim alive?

He took a deep breath. He couldn't make a choice like this. He loved Kim, he cherished his ideal of her, and he regretted losing her. But tonight, his heart told him to back off. If he woke up in the morning still a college student, then he'd try to save her tomorrow.

"I need to call Larkin," Kim said. "We can talk after that."

"No, that's okay. I'll see you tomorrow."

He parked in front of her apartment, and she leaned over to kiss him. He met her lips, but his eyes squeezed closed, and his muscles tensed as though he were about to receive an electric shock.

She didn't notice.

He opened his eyes and took in the moment: her closed eyes, the freckles on her nose, the mascara on her eyelashes, the smell of her shampoo. He relished the feel of her soft lips on his again. The tenderness, the love, the trust.

She pulled away, smiled, got out, and closed the door. She bounced up her apartment steps and flashed him a quick wave before disappearing inside.

He drove home feeling lower than he ever had before. He'd climbed the highest mountain, fought the longest battle, braved the fiercest storm, and had nothing to show for it. Even if he woke up tomorrow, saved Kim, and stopped the bad guy, there would be no happily ever after. Not until he got home to Renee, Mark, and Sara and repaired the problems in his marriage.

He took a thirty-minute shower, not even seeing the point in getting out, drying off, and going to bed. Eventually, he crawled under the musty sheet and soft maroon comforter. He'd forgotten how infrequently he washed the sheets while in college.

Regardless of his resignation about tonight's events, tomorrow would be a new day. He'd give his life to save Kim if he had to. First, he'd call Dennis and find out where he could acquire a gun. Perhaps Dennis could follow them around all day, watch for any one suspicious.

Or he could kidnap Kim and take her on a romantic getaway. She'd love that.

Whatever it took, he'd figure it out.

Part Two

Chapter 37

There were no clouds of smoke or wispy dreams. After the deepest and darkest sleep, his eyes popped open.

He recognized the wall-mounted television, the picture-adorned walls, the heavy comforter.

Home!

Immeasurable joy welled up inside him. He clenched his jaws to contain the scream of elation fighting to burst out. He lay on his back and soaked in the realness: the ceiling fan whirred above him, another fan buzzed on the dresser, and the alarm clock next to the fan displayed 7:24 a.m. in bright red numbers.

He took slow, deep breaths, and squeezed his eyes shut. Tears ran down his cheeks. When he shifted, his arm brushed against something warm.

Renee rested on her side, her back to him. Her dark hair cascaded across the pillow.

She'd come back to their bed.

He'd made it back to his life. The crazy journey had ended. He was home.

It could have been any day or any month. Had time continued while he'd been gone? Did his family know he'd been gone? Would they be happy to see him?

The sleeping lump next to him exploded out of the covers and disappeared into the bathroom before he could open his mouth. "John, I overslept. Could you get the kids up?"

He looked around the room. The laundry hamper sat in one corner, the desk in another, covered with orderly stacks of papers and bills. The dust-free dresser featured framed photos and a stack of magazines Renee planned to take to work for the break room. In the bathroom, she turned on the shower.

His image stared back at him from the mirror above the dresser. Unruly brown hair and more wrinkles than he'd seen in the months he'd been gone. He was forty-five again.

Renee stuck her head into the room, her reflection in the mirror. "Hurry, John." She disappeared before he could turn. He stared at his goofy grin. Time to wake the kids.

Before going to the kids' rooms, he grabbed his cell phone.

Wednesday, July 18.

No new texts. Only two new emails.

John exhaled slowly and deeply. He hadn't missed a thing. He'd gone to sleep on July 17th and had a six-month-long dream.

He stopped at the doorway of Mark's room. Beneath the jumbled covers, his beautiful boy rested on his tummy, with his gangly limbs spread out in all directions. John beamed with overwhelming pride at the joy of having a son. The weight fell from his shoulders, the vise around his heart loosened, and guilt evaporated. The fear was gone.

John navigated his way through the toys scattered about the floor like a minefield. One misstep and he'd crush a Transformer with his bare feet. He sat down on his son's bed and gave him a hug. "Mark, time to wake up," he whispered in his ear. He tried to say it again, but his voice caught in his throat. He ran his hands through his son's short, thick brown hair. "Wake up, Mark."

Mark stirred a little and stretched his legs.

"Wake up and put on your clothes. Then come into the kitchen for breakfast."

At the door, John took another look at his son, who had rolled onto his side. He rubbed his eyes and stretched his arms over his head. He flashed John a quick grin, and John couldn't hold back a big smile.

In Sara's room, the morning sunlight filtered through the blinds. As usual, Sara had wiggled out of the covers. Her wavy, golden hair covered her face so much that John couldn't tell if she was facing him or the wall. She was getting so big, but she was still his little girl. He wrapped his arms around her, gave her a tight squeeze, brushed the hair away from her face, and kissed her cheek.

He wanted to pick her up, hold her, squeeze her, dance with her, and twirl her in his arms. She always slept like a rock, so he refrained. Instead, he whispered in her ear to wake up, gave her another kiss, and went to the kitchen.

He set out two bowls, filled them with Fruit Loops, and then poured two cups of apple juice. Everything seemed so familiar, as if he'd never left. But he *had* been gone . . . and he learned many things. About Kim, about Renee, about himself.

Since time had not changed with his family, they had no idea how much he missed them. Every minute felt as if it were a special gift from God.

* * *

Mark came in first and first devoured his bowl of cereal, then a Pop Tart.

John helped Sara get dressed and carried her to the kitchen table. While she ate, he squirted her hair with water and detangler spray and brought out a comb.

Still no sign of Renee.

Time for coffee. The tile floor felt cool on his feet as he opened the cabinet for a mug.

An arm grabbed him from behind.

His heart thudded to a stop. The coffee mug fell from his hands as Renee's lips brushed against his cheeks.

The thunk of the mug on the counter brought him back. He caught it before it fell to the floor.

Renee stepped into the living room, picked up the newspaper, and stuffed it into the trash, but the smell of warm skin and hairspray lingered.

"Sorry, I didn't mean to scare you."

"You didn't."

John followed her every move. She moved her large purse to the kitchen table and kissed Sara's forehead. Sara ignored her mom, instead intently watching the television in the living room. SpongeBob.

A confused mixture of memories rushed back. Renee's lips on his cheeks. A kiss. Lanie. Her hair. The kisses they shared. He squeezed his eyes shut. Renee had been a memory then, a dream, an apparition. Lanie had filled the void of loneliness that had descended upon his soul, and . . . He swallowed heavily and opened his eyes.

Renee grabbed a muffin and stuffed it and a water bottle into her purse. She picked through some old mail and threw several pieces away, and then put away a box of Triscuits. She picked up this, rearranged that. Her behavior seemed more obsessive than he'd remembered. But maybe not. Typical for Renee, everything had to be in its place. Everything had to be perfect.

After closing the pantry door, she said, "I really need to go." She paused and cocked her head to the side. "What?"

"What?" John said.

"You look different. I don't know." She studied him as if his face would reveal what she didn't understand.

He shrugged. If he looked anything like he felt, he probably looked like an idiot. "It's nothing. I'll tell you later."

"Okay." Renee went through the kitchen and living room, told each kid "bye," then disappeared through the garage door. Neither kid took their eyes from the television.

But he wasn't ready for her to leave. He caught the door just before it closed. "Renee?"

She'd opened the door of the Tank—a Ford Expedition that drove like a tank and guzzled gas like one too. Renee loved it. "What?" she asked with one foot in the door.

"Umm."

She tossed her purse onto the front seat. "What?" She exhaled, her eyes pleading.

He stood in the door and fished for words to say. "You came back to bed last night."

Her features softened a bit. "Yeah, I did."

"Why?"

"I was being a fool. I'm sorry." She paused and then climbed into the car.

"Why did you leave?"

A frown. "I can't talk about that right now."

"So . . ."

"Tonight?"

"Okay." It would have to do.

Chapter 38

With Renee gone, John did a quick mental inventory of what he was supposed to do today. It had been so long. Could he remember the simple things? The middle of the week in July. He'd need to be at The Coffee Beast by lunch. Before then, he'd drop Mark and Sara off at the day care center. Renee would pick them up later.

After a little bit of teasing and cajoling, he got the kids to wrestle around on the floor with him. Then Mark played the Wii, and Sara colored while John prepared to go to work.

He needed time to ease back into the flow of things, but life didn't slow down. He dressed in his normal work attire of denim shorts and a T-shirt. He spent a few extra minutes getting used to his forty-five-year-old body again. He was no lean, mean, twenty-something, but he'd aged well.

Life couldn't come fast enough. He couldn't wait to re-enter his life, to be with the kids, with Renee, to go to work, to go to church. But life couldn't come slow enough either. He didn't want to waste a minute or take one second for granted.

* * *

After dropping the kids off at the New Hope Learning Center, he drove north to the Kilpatrick Turnpike. The question that had ricocheted around in the back of his mind all morning took center stage.

What now?

Was anything he'd experienced real? Could he really hit a baseball? Did he really date Lanie, marry Kim, and cheat on his wife? Was he really a pastor?

No. And yes.

He'd get a one-way ticket to an insane asylum if he tried to convince anyone of what had really happened to him. But his experiences in those other lives raised valid questions. In his real life, while he had thought of Kim and her demise every single day, he had pushed away the desire to find out why. He'd shut down when the police questioned him, awash with regrets about going to the game with Willy, and he'd stayed that way.

As he turned off at the Penn Avenue exit, he added up the facts. Dennis knew Kim in high school; they'd met at the church youth fest. He also knew Renee in college. Now John also knew a lot about Larkin Connor, Professor Hazelton, Chad Bailey, and Ray Pope. So many people the police had asked him about. Now he had his own questions . . . and he might be able to find out what happened to Kim.

He pulled into a parking space in front of The Coffee Beast, which shared space with picture studio, a golf discount store, and a cell phone outlet in a long strip mall. A prime location with anchor stores like Old Navy and Lowe's, and plenty of chain restaurants sharing the half-mile-long parking lot.

John opened the door to the coffee shop and breathed in the aroma of mocha. Pleased to see the place already half full, he straightened some of the black wooden chairs and tables near the door. On one of the two HD televisions hanging in the corners of the room, a reporter droned about the economy. The other—which John insisted always be tuned to a sports channel—was on mute. On the way to the counter, he picked up a *People* magazine to put back in the rack. He put his laptop bag in a corner in the back.

"Good morning," Gina said. "Try this." His newest employee handed him a cup of coffee. The literature major working her way through the University of Central Oklahoma had several ear piercings, one nose and one tongue piercing, and the customers loved her.

"Thanks." He took a sip. "This is great. Is it new?"

"We just got it in," Mitchell called from the back.

"Hey, Mitch. Good to see you."

"Hey, boss." The barrel-chested workout freak with broad shoulders was another customer favorite. He flirted with the female customers, and they didn't mind.

The lunch crowd filed in, and John quickly stepped back into the routine of taking orders and serving food. He loved it.

Late in the afternoon, he sat at an empty table beneath one of the televisions and prepared a list of items they'd need to purchase at Sam's. Kim wandered into his mind. Hard to believe he'd just been with her yesterday.

"It's a secret, John. We all have secrets."

What were Kim's secrets?

Since she'd disappeared, the regret had been his cross to bear. He'd kept it inside, buried it, and tried to ignore it. Doing so allowed him to live with the pain of losing her . . . and to live without ever knowing what truly happened.

Suddenly a revelation came to him more clearly than ever. He was free!

That burden had been lifted. The pain still existed, but the fear had vanished. He could explore Kim's final days and not be afraid.

Why?

I am not afraid to die. I've made peace with God and believe that when I die I will go to heaven.

Because Kim wasn't afraid.

* * *

John found a seat in the corner of the coffee shop and booted up his laptop. While it was loading, he grabbed a cup of coffee and a snickerdoodle cookie.

He clicked on the Firefox logo, and the browser opened to his Yahoo homepage. Ah, the Internet. He sure didn't have that in 1985 or 1992. John clicked on his Yahoo! Inbox. No new messages.

He opened the search box, typed in "Murphy Hazelton," and hit enter. Maybe he'd find a Facebook link or a LinkedIn account or a faculty website page.

"Professor acquitted in rape charge," read the first link.

Whoa. John took his eyes away from the screen and looked around the dining area while the news sank in. Patrons sipped coffee and nibbled on pastries. Mitch clanged away, cleaning up the dishes, and Gina wiped down tables.

John snapped the laptop shut. He needed to visit the professor.

CHAPTER 39

John bowed out of work early so he could be home when Renee arrived with the kids. Once home, he searched again for Murphy Hazelton. He scanned an article from a 2001 *Daily Oklahoman*. It only named one victim, Abigail Winters, a twenty-four-year-old research assistant in the English department where Hazelton worked. No mention of Larkin Connor.

He clicked on other links, found a few phone numbers, and made a few calls. Could he get Hazelton to call him back?

The time in the corner of the screen said 4:30 p.m., which gave him an hour to whip up a spectacular dinner. He pulled out the *Italian Cooking for Dummies* book Renee gave him for Father's Day—a book he'd requested—and looked for something simple. He settled on chicken marsala. Delicious, and he could probably make it.

With the chicken soaking in marinade and ingredients lined up on the counter like a parade, John's cell phone rang.

"John, could you pick up the kids? Work is crazy right now."

"Sure, no problem. What's going on?"

"I may be late tonight. Really late."

Her tone rubbed him the wrong way. She worked at Country Springs Sports Center, where they sold hot tubs, swimming pools, tanning beds, saunas, and everything else you needed for summer fun. The store closed at seven, and Renee, as the controller, never worked past five thirty.

"Past seven?"

"I don't know. I'm sorry." She hesitated and added, "Financial irregularities. I've got to get on top of this before I explain it to Ron."

John frowned. Her boss was a bitter, spiteful old man with an occasional nice streak. "Sure, I'll get the kids." His mind flashed to her nights in the guest bedroom.

"Thanks. Love you. Bye."

* * *

Mark and Sara squealed with joy when John pulled into Chuck E. Cheese after picking them up. The night got even better when he took them to Family Video and they rented Monsters University.

While John microwaved popcorn, the kids took all the cushions off the couch and created their own seating arrangements. He laughed along with them at Sully and Mike and had a great time.

The phone never rang, and Renee didn't come home from work.

So thankful to be back home, John didn't want to question Renee about the reason behind her absence and break the semblance of his perfect world. His gut told him that the next time he saw her, his life could be turned upside-down. But he held onto hope, held out trust. He needed life to be the way it had been. He'd waited six months to be home. He could wait a little longer.

* * *

Renee came home at 8:30 while the kids were in the bathrooms showering. Her heavy eyes, faded make-up, and slumped shoulders told John the day had defeated her.

They exchanged a tight hug. "What's going on?" he asked.

Looking down at the floor, she shook her head.

"Renee?"

She met his eyes. "Let's talk after the kids are in bed."

"Sure."

Renee flashed him a smile of relief and walked down the hall. "Hey, how's my little sailor doing tonight?" she said to Mark as she entered the master bathroom.

John thoroughly enjoyed the tag-team effort it took to put the kids to bed. So many times before, the tedious routine had drained him. But now he cherished every moment.

Renee read from a Bible storybook and prayed with the kids while John rocked back and forth in his recliner. With the lights off, he waited for Renee in the soothing darkness.

When she entered the room, she stopped. "What are you doing? Shouldn't you be watching SportsCenter?"

He shrugged. "I've been waiting for you."

"The kids want to tell you goodnight."

He hopped up and spent five minutes with each, what had to be the best ten minutes of his life. As he left Sara's room, he chastised himself for all the times putting the kids to bed felt like just another chore. They wouldn't always need him.

When he returned to the living room, Renee sat on the sofa, still in her work clothes, her legs crossed beneath her and her arms folded across her chest.

John opted to leave the lights off. He returned to his recliner across from Renee and leaned forward. The ceiling fan whirled slowly above them. "What happened tonight?"

"Remember Gabe Alverez, the accountant Ron hired to be the finance manager?"

"Sure."

"He was looking over the QuickBooks accounts or something, auditing on his own—I really don't know what he was doing, but he found some money missing."

"What? How much?"

"Around forty-five thousand."

"Is it really missing?"

"It is." Renee looked down. "Gabe, Dennis, and I spent the evening trying to figure out what to do."

Dennis Vance. Ron Stout had hired Dennis at Renee's urging. Though irresponsible and amoral, he could sell anything to anybody. How much time did Renee really spend with Dennis? If their relationship dated back to college, what else didn't he know? "What did you find out?"

Renee looked back into the kitchen, where the icemaker rattled and hissed. "I don't know what we're going to tell Ron."

"He might be behind it," John said. "You said he was slimy, that you never trusted him."

"No, he didn't take it."

"What about Dennis?"

Renee snorted dryly. "He could have. But he didn't."

He rubbed his sleepy eyes. "Does this have anything to do with you sleeping in the guest room, or your talk with Dennis? Just tell me, Renee. What's going on?"

"Oh, John," she whispered. With her eyes squeezed shut and her mouth pulled tight, she appeared to be in intense pain. "I'm so sorry."

John moved to her side and wrapped his arms around her. "What? Tell me. How can I help you?"

"You can pray for me," she said with her face burrowed into his neck and shoulder.

"I will."

"Ron or Dennis didn't take the money," she said. "I did."

Chapter 40

Renee called in sick on Thursday. They stayed up until one hashing out plans to talk to a lawyer and pay the money back. John ran The Coffee Beast, but Renee—the numbers person in the family—handled most of the finances.

"Could you open earlier, or stay open later?" she'd asked.

"That would be a break-even proposition at best."

"What about new menu items? More expensive?"

"That's a possibility." John nodded slowly.

The bottom line was there would be no quick fixes. Sure, the Beast was profitable, but when you had a mortgage, two nice cars, and two kids to raise, sometimes you fell short. At least that's what Renee claimed.

John didn't have time to dwell on it now. The compulsion to find out what happened to Kim still pulsed deep within him. He drove to work with the radio silent and his hands tight on the steering wheel. At the Beast, he took up a corner and booted his laptop.

On Facebook, he searched for "Larkin Connor" in Oklahoma, hoping she was one of the many women who included their maiden name. After studying the pictures, he identified her as Larkin Hooper of Mustang. So, she was local. He could be in Mustang in twenty minutes.

He sent her a friend request. Maybe she checked her account more often than he did. After snacking on a chocolate-chip muffin denser than a brick, he returned to the computer and checked Facebook. Nothing.

He pushed the computer away from him. This was foolish. Why wait when he knew her name and what town she lived in? He looked her up on Whitepages.com, found she was married to a guy named Jerry Hooper, and punched her number into his cell.

"Hello?" Her voice bubbled with a suppressed giggle.

"My name is John Michaels. We've never met, but I was calling to ask you about a person you and I went to college with."

"Okay, sure." The sound of running and children laughing flowed through the receiver.

"I wanted to talk to you about Kim Addison."

John braced himself. Would she hang up on him?

The sounds faded, and then a door closed.

"Sorry, I wanted to get to my room. You knew Kim Addison?"

"I was her boyfriend."

Larkin didn't answer at first. "I don't know anything."

"Can we talk?"

"You're not a reporter?"

"No." John began formulating an argument to try and convince her to talk to him.

"Okay. I'll talk to you."

"Great. When would be a good time?"

"My husband's home. You can come now." She gave him the directions.

He ran his hand across his forehead. It came away damp, but a cool wave of relief swept over him.

* * *

The drive on the sparsely traveled western leg of the Kilpatrick Turnpike reminded John of some of things he took for granted, like his GPS. It was nice to be back in the 21st century.

His stomach churned in with guilt. Renee sat at home with the kids. He should be there for her. He should be by her side, carrying her through this.

No. She was the one who should feel guilty. White, hot anger flared in his heart. He hadn't put words to his feelings yet, but it felt good to admit the truth. She'd messed up, made an immoral choice to do something illegal, and he had every right to be mad. Her foolish actions threatened him, their family, and their life.

His heart ached to be with the kids right now, but not with Renee. As he exited the turnpike and caught Mustang Road, his fists tightened around the steering wheel. Why had she done this? They—he—could lose everything.

As he drove into the heart of the charming, flat city of Mustang, nerves replaced guilt. After dipping his toes in the water by looking up Hazelton, he was about to take the plunge into finding out what happened to Kim. He'd find out if his descent into his own past had any relevance to Kim's disappearance.

Or he'd find out he was crazy.

Larkin Hooper's neighborhood consisted of newly built houses, a scattering of empty lots, and houses under construction. He turned into a cul-de-sac with freshly sodded lawns and fledgling shade trees and parked on the street. Her front yard looked like his own, littered with toys: a Spiderman sprinkler attached to a hose, two Nerf balls and a spongy bat by the front door, and a big-wheel tricycle and squirt guns in the driveway.

He knocked on the screen door, and within seconds a man with wavy black hair, broad shoulders, and strong arms that held a squirmy toddler answered. "Are you John?" he asked with a broad smile that forced John to smile back.

"I am." They shook hands.

"Come on in. Larkin's in the kitchen."

She had her back to John, putting plates and bowls in the dishwasher.

Her straight, shoulder-length hair still held its reddish-black sheen, and her petite figure remained trim. She turned to greet him while drying her hands on a paper towel. "Hi. I'm Larkin. Have a seat." She pointed to the kitchen table.

Her husband kissed her on the cheek. "I'll be outside with the kids." He gave John a sidelong glance before going out the patio door.

"So what do you want to talk about?" Larkin took a seat and leaned forward, her eyes warm circles.

John tried to form a coherent response out of his jumbled thoughts. The Larkin he knew had left the Fall Festival with Renee, so she knew his wife. But in his pastor fantasy and relived college day, her life took a downward spiral.

This smiling, self-assured woman wasn't the same Larkin, any more than he was the pastor who had an affair with Lanie.

"Let me tell you a little about myself first." He filled her in on his life, minus the information about Renee's embezzlement. Finally, he brought it back to the point of this meeting. "In college, Kim and I were friends for a couple of years. Then we started dating in the fall of 1992. She disappeared a few months later."

"I remember those days. They were hard for everyone in the English department."

"So that's how you knew Kim?"

"At first, anyway. She worked in one of the offices, and I saw her a lot."

"Were you friends?"

"I got to know her a little bit, but not until right before she disappeared. We never hung out or anything." She involuntarily wrinkled her nose, but then smiled, showing the dimples in her cheeks.

John shifted in his chair. "Over the years, I've buried my memories of those difficult days, but now I feel the need to know what happened to her. I may never find out, but I want to talk to the people she knew at the time."

"Oh, that breaks my heart." She put her hands over her chest.

"I guess I want to know if you could tell me about what the police asked you, or anything that might indicate what happened to her." He leaned forward and studied every nuance and tic of Larkin, hoping it would tell him something.

She glanced out the patio door. The muted sounds of whiffle bats and balls and laughter brought a smile to her face, but it faded when she looked back at him. "I can only tell you what I told the police. But I imagine you already know that."

"No, I don't. I don't know anything." John's heartbeat quickened.

"Okay, let me think." She drummed her fingers on the table. "I couldn't tell the police anything about her personal life or friends. I only had one thing to talk about."

He gave her a little nod to encourage her to continue.

"One afternoon, I had a meeting scheduled with Dr. Bayless, my English teacher. It was around three in the afternoon. When I knocked on his office door, he wasn't there, so I waited in the lobby. I sat across from Kim's empty desk. I thought I was alone.

"I began reading a magazine I had with me. Soon, I heard muffled voices. At first I thought they came from the hallway. I quickly realized they were coming from one of the offices."

"One of the four offices," John said.

Larkin nodded. "I couldn't make out what they were saying—and didn't really care—so I continued to read. Then I heard a crash, followed by shouting. Then a scream."

John's mouth dropped open at the parallels.

"I heard nothing for probably ten seconds. Then the door burst open. Kim flew by me and disappeared out the door. A man came out. His face was flushed, and he had a bright pink scratch on his neck.

"I sat there, frozen. I didn't know what to do. He stared at me, started to say something, then left. I followed him because I wanted to see if he'd chase after Kim. He didn't. He just got in his car and drove away."

"Who was the man?" But he already knew.

"I didn't know it at the time, but it was Professor Hazelton."

Of course it was. Except, this time he attacked Kim, not Larkin. "And you told all this to the police?"

"I did."

"And the police did what with the information?" He asked it more to himself.

"I don't know. I mean I assume they talked to him. I followed the case as much as I could. It was in the papers for a while."

John's mind drifted back to the days after Kim's disappearance. He didn't go to class. He didn't talk to friends. He hibernated in his apartment, waiting for the phone to ring and his life to be okay again.

Larkin shook her head and sighed. "Yeah, I know nothing much came out of the investigation."

So Hazelton attacked Kim, but she hadn't quit her job yet, at least as far as he knew. Why not? She'd been looking for another job in his fantasy life. Had she been looking into a job with the Baileys in real life, too? He cleared his throat. "When did this happen?"

"I don't know the exact date," Larkin said. "Close to the day she disappeared, though."

"Did you see her after that?"

She nodded. "After I saw Hazelton drive away, I returned to wait for Dr. Bayless, but he never showed. I was about to leave when Kim peered into the office. She asked if Hazelton was still here, and I said no. I asked if she was all right, and she nodded, but I knew she wasn't. She looked as though she didn't know what to do, so I told her I would back her up if she wanted to report anything."

"What did she say?"

"Her eyes melted with kindness, and she said 'Thank you, Larkin.' I didn't even know she knew my name."

"But she never reported it?" He urged her on. He had to know everything.

"No. I told this to the police after she disappeared, though."

John took a deep breath. The police knew Hazelton had assaulted Kim in his office the day before she disappeared, but did nothing about it. Or maybe they did. It never came up in the lives he relived. Even if it had, it wouldn't have been exactly as in real life.

Hazelton attacked Larkin, and Kim saw it. Not real. The opposite occurred, in fact. What else wouldn't be real? What would be? How could he sort it out?

Larkin crossed her legs. "I still think about Kim sometimes."

John still had a few questions. "So Hazelton never did anything to you?"

"No. I didn't know him."

"Can I ask you about a few other people we may both have known?"

"Sure."

"Do you know Dennis Vance?"

"No."

The reply left John speechless for a moment. She never dated him, never slept with him? Never had his baby? Why had she experienced that in his pastor life? It didn't make any sense.

John gathered himself. "Okay. What about Renee Templin?"

"Your wife?" Larkin's eyes scrunched shut and then burst open in recognition. "Renee. I haven't seen her in years. We went to church together when we were kids."

"You didn't know her in college?"

"No. I didn't."

"Larkin, I want to thank you for helping me out. It looks like you have a great life." She hadn't led a tragic life after all. Or if tragedy had struck, she'd coped and moved on. She seemed genuinely happy. They talked for a few more minutes about their kids. She promised to come by the Beast sometime, and he promised her some free coffee.

He drove back to the Beast with the radio off. He had to think. What was he missing?

CHAPTER 41

"Hey, boss. Why the long lunch? We were busy today." Gina opened the door for him.

John mumbled his thanks and returned to the corner he'd occupied earlier.

"We're running low on turkey and rye bread, so I ordered more. Oh, and your wife called."

"Thanks." John booted up his laptop. Then he stretched his arms over his head and arched his back. Fatigue had caught up with him. He'd seen the clock on the nightstand every hour last night. Not exactly a good night's sleep.

The black screen turned to blue, and his desktop background collage of family studio portraits appeared, followed by program icons.

"What's up?"

John jumped. Gina had dropped into the seat next to him. She smelled of coffee and sweet perfume. As hard as he tried, he couldn't help but stare at the tiny stud in her nose. That had to hurt.

"Nothing." He lowered the laptop lid and turned toward her.

"Is everything all right?" she asked.

"Sure."

"I don't know, boss. Are you upset about something?"

His insides froze. Renee might go to jail. There. He'd admitted it. He could lose his wife. His castle was crumbling. But he brushed Gina's concern off with an insincere chuckle. "I'm fine. And, please, call me John."

She stared straight at him, her green eyes seemed to transform into translucent oracles. "You're lying, *John*. You might as well wear a sign saying 'I'm dying inside.'"

He sat up straighter. "Are you serious? Is it that obvious?"

"Maybe I'm exaggerating, but you're spending a lot of time on the computer, and you're not chatting with the customers."

He glanced around the empty dining area. No customers meant no money. Could the Beast really be in such bad financial condition? Had Renee kept the business afloat by stealing? He'd trusted her accounting ability too much. He hadn't done more than glance at the books during tax season for years. "It's trouble at home." A small burden crumbled away from the load on his soul.

Gina arched her eyebrows.

"Not marriage trouble. Business. Renee's having trouble at work. Pretty serious. I'm worried about how it's going to affect our family."

Gina put her hands on his. She was the touchy-feely type. It wasn't awkward.

"I'll be praying for you."

In spite of the piercings, unruly hair, and occasional swear word, Gina was a good person. She attended a progressive church near the center of Oklahoma City in an old Homeland storefront.

"Thanks."

Gina patted his hand and returned to her kitchen duties.

John worked the register for a while after Gina left for the day. He found himself watching each car entering the parking lot, hoping it would be full of customers ready for a hot cup of expensive-but-worth-it coffee. He'd never done that before.

He greeted the late crew, Jamal, Brooke, and Jamie, before leaving. He might have to let one of them go and start working nights too.

* * *

Home felt normal. The kids ran around outside, and Renee pulled a steaming hot enchilada casserole out of the oven. They ate as a family and went for a bike ride. But a tension settled between him and Renee. It became thicker as the night wore on.

After the kids' baths, he burst the thin layer of normalcy. "Renee, we need to talk."

Her sunken gaze pleaded for him to a throw her a rope. "Sure."

They stood in the hallway, surrounded by pictures of the kids on one wall and family wedding pictures on the other. A shrine to their lives.

"Did you find a lawyer?" he asked.

"Is that all you want to know?" She avoided eye contact and scowled. "Not 'how was your day' or 'how are you holding up?'"

John's shoulders slumped, and his will deflated. This was the wife he had loved, adored, and feared he'd never see again. She made a mistake, a big mistake.

He should wrap his arms around her and whisper in her ear that he'd stand by her, but now he could hardly stand to look at her.

But he couldn't just sidestep his anger. He couldn't just ignore the questions. Why had she done it? She'd risked everything he'd worked for. And for what? Two nice cars and a nice house? He cleared his throat and managed to say, "I'm sorry. How *are* you doing?"

She snorted and rolled her eyes. After a moment, she said, "I made some calls to people at church and got several names. There are a few we could go with. Chester McCann said he could talk with us, go over our options, but he's more of a corporate attorney."

"That's what this is, isn't it?"

"I guess. But he defends million-dollar corporations, not small businesses. Also, I didn't feel comfortable explaining our situation to someone we know."

Another blow to his perfect life. Everyone would know what Renee had done. How could he face his friends? His family?

Renee continued. "I talked to Buzz Baker, too. You trust him, don't you?"

He had been staring at the portraits of Sara and Mark as one-year-olds. The pictures formed the centerpiece, and pictures from the following years orbited them. He looked directly at Renee. "I trust Buzz."

"I told him we might be facing a lawsuit and needed someone to represent us, that we couldn't afford much but would pay what we could."

"Did he give you a name?"

"He did. A guy he went to seminary with. A good guy, he said. He dropped out of seminary and became a lawyer. He has his own practice in Norman."

John closed his eyes. His stomach clenched, anticipating the answer before he asked the question. "What's his name?"

"Chad Bailey."

Chapter 42

Shrill peals of laughter came from one of the kids' rooms, while John and Renee sat on the couch a few feet apart. The muted television showed a DVR'd episode of *Survivor*.

"I'll set an appointment with Bailey as soon as possible. Would you like to go?" Renee asked.

"Do I need to?" He stared at the television instead of looking at her, but out of the corner of his eye, he saw her shoulders sag.

"I'd like you to."

"I can. Let me know when, and I'll juggle around my work schedule." His voice sounded deadpan, even to himself.

"Okay."

Silence lingered in the air like an ever-present fog.

He glanced at his watch. Eight thirty. "Could you put the kids to bed? I'm going to talk with Dennis."

"Dennis?" Her voice rose in pitch. "Why?"

"It's about Kim."

Before he walked to the bathrooms to tell the kids bye, he glanced back at Renee. The look on her face told him she didn't have the courage to ask why he needed to talk to Dennis about his missing ex-girlfriend.

* * *

John climbed into the Explorer and turned on the air conditioner to push back the sultry July heat that didn't want to go away. He pulled into the nice suburban neighborhood Dennis lived in north of the Kilpatrick. It was mostly occupied by young professionals with little kids and middle-aged parents enjoying their last years with teenagers at home.

Except Dennis had never married, never had children, and seemed to enjoy it. Ten years ago, Dennis got in on the ground level selling vitamins in an Amwaylike multi-level marketing scheme. Not Nutridyne, but something similar, and did very well with it.

John parked at the curb and stared jealously at the golf-green lawn as he strode to the front door.

As soon as the doorbell rang, Dennis called for him to come in.

John stepped inside and found Dennis sitting on the couch. He still had a full head of brown hair, although some gray had begun to pop up near the temples. He took an inordinate amount of pride in his hair, always experimenting with new styles or perms. And he wasn't too pompous to take a little ribbing about it, either.

His outstretched arm held a remote, and the screen flickered as he flipped through channels. He claimed no one on earth had access to more channels than he did. If DirecTV offered it, he subscribed. Even the Spanish channels. John plopped down on the leather love seat that matched the couch and melted into its softness.

"Long day?" Dennis said.

"Not for me."

"I hear you." Dennis raised his beer in acknowledgement. "If you want something, help yourself."

He knew Dennis meant it and would be offended if he didn't join him, so he got a Mountain Dew out of the fridge and returned to the living room.

Dennis continued to flip through the channels, each one gloriously represented on his seventy-inch Sony. Channels went by at mind-numbing speed.

The flashes of light gave John a headache, so he looked away.

"This was supposed to be an easy job," Dennis said.

"What?"

Dennis pressed a button, and the television silenced. "Renee got me hired, you know. Convinced me that Country Springs would be a great place to work. Told me that even though Ron Stout was a bitter old man, he paid for results." He took a drink and then placed his bottle on a coaster on the coffee table.

"Now, this mess. Our sales meeting yesterday was nothing but Ron spewing his venom. He threatened to shut the place down if he didn't find out who stole the money. He yelled at us for two hours, and then told us he was going to Lake Eufaula for the weekend and stormed out, cursing."

"Who does Ron think took the money?" John asked.

"No idea, man. But I know I don't want to stay there. With the economy these days, there's no point in selling cars or RVs." He stroked his clean-shaven jaw. "Maybe I could sell credit counseling. I read an article about that the other day. Some guy named Dave Ramsey."

So Dennis had no idea who stole the money. But that wasn't why he came over. "Why did you stay so late with Renee last night?"

Dennis's must have noticed the tightness in John's voice. He studied John for a moment before answering. "The stress really got to her. You know how she is. Walks around at ninety miles per hour. Doesn't take breaks. Talks in short, clipped sentences. She said she had to stay late. I knew she'd stay all night if she had to, so I thought I'd help her out."

"You're not an accountant."

"No, but I know my way around financial statements. If it relates to money, I understand it."

At least Renee didn't ask Dennis to stay late with her, he volunteered. Maybe if she'd been alone, she would have hidden her theft. Kept doing it. Made it worse.

"Will she be at work tomorrow?" Dennis grabbed an open can of honey-roasted peanuts off the counter and held it out.

John took a handful. "I don't know. Probably not."

"Ron would go nuts if he knew she wasn't coming in. He expects her to run the place. He trusts her."

"Yeah, I know." He had trusted her too. What a mistake. Being away from Renee for so long had already created distance in their relationship. With her crime hanging over their life, it would be easier to be apart from her.

"Look, Dennis. I didn't come over to talk about the money at Country Springs."

"Oh, really." Alarm flashed across Dennis's face. They were guys. They never talked about emotions or problems or girl stuff.

"Yeah. I wanted to talk about Kim."

Dennis retrieved another beer before answering. "So, buddy, why talk about Kim, and why now?"

He couldn't tell Dennis about the last six months with a teenage Kim, a college student Kim, and a wife Kim, so he told him another truth. "I don't remember much about my life after Kim died."

"You were a zombie."

"I buried a lot of pain. I rebuilt my life and never looked back." He tossed some peanuts in his mouth.

"You did, and I'm proud of you." Dennis raised his glass again.

"I want to find out what happened to her. Who killed her."

Dennis exhaled heavily and put his bottle down. "That's the question lingering silently in the background for years, isn't it? What happened to Kim?"

"We owe it to her to find out."

Dennis's face tightened. "I don't know about this, John."

"What do you mean?"

"What can anyone accomplish that the police didn't? They looked into everything and found nothing."

John studied Dennis for non-verbal cues that might give away another reason why he didn't want anyone looking into what happened to Kim. But if he saw a cue, he'd have no idea what it meant, so he plodded ahead. "I knew Kim best, Dennis. But when she disappeared, everything I knew about her also disappeared. I answered every question the police asked. But I didn't elaborate; I didn't give them any insight. What if I knew something beyond their questions and didn't tell them?"

"Are you going to try to get them to reopen the case?"

"I haven't thought that far ahead. I really want to talk to you about her."

"Me?"

"I've already talked to one of her friends from college. I'm not singling you out."

"I'm not worried about that." Dennis folded his arms across his chest.

"I know you had a close relationship." But would he be willing to open up about it?

Dennis didn't say anything, but John felt himself being studied. His motive, his heart, were they pure?

Apparently Dennis thought so. "Okay. Let's talk."

"Thanks. How *close* were you and Kim?"

A broad smile formed. "John, John, John. What are you looking for here?" Dennis could pull the wool over anyone's eyes or be brutally honest, and you'd never know the difference.

"The truth, Dennis." John's sharp words hung in the air.

Dennis's lips tightened. "John, this is ridiculous. This was twenty years ago and I . . ."

"You and Kim were friends. I know that. I'm not going to judge you or be angry at anything you tell me. I just want to know."

"So you think I might say something that could hurt you?"

We all have secrets.

In his fantasy lives, he hadn't learned anything concrete, but he'd witnessed enough pain. Something might be lurking under the surface.

"Nothing you say can hurt me. Don't worry about offending me."

Dennis shook his head. "I'm not worried about that. I hope you don't expect me to reveal a horrible secret about Kim. There's nothing there, man."

"But there's more to your relationship than I know."

Dennis studied John, and John met his gaze. Dennis rubbed his chin and shifted his chin right to left, as if stretching his jaw. He seemed conflicted, but finally said, "You're right. There is more."

"Okay. When did you first meet Kim?"

"College."

"Are you sure?"

"Why does it matter?"

"Why *does* it matter?" John countered.

"Okay. It doesn't. We met in high school. At a church party."

"So you were friends?"

"No, actually. I met her, but never really talked to her. You know me, I have a casual relationship with the church. I go when it suits me, I admit it. So I went to church a few times, and I saw her. Talked to her. Got to know her."

"Dated her?"

"Yeah, we did." Dennis smiled. "She was a good girl. She had a wild side, but she was a good girl."

John frowned. He didn't ask what her wild side entailed, and didn't want to know how Dennis found out about it. "Did she ever get into any trouble I didn't know about?"

"Not at college." Dennis smiled. He seemed to enjoy making it as difficult as possible for John.

"What about before?" John finished off his now-lukewarm Mountain Dew.

Dennis hesitated, his eyes studying the clutter on the coffee table. "No. No trouble that I know of."

"What about Larkin Connor? Did you know her?"

"Never heard of her."

That coincided with what Larkin said. "What about Professor Hazelton? Did something happen between him and Kim?"

Dennis snorted in disgust. "She never told you about him?"

"No."

Dennis shook his head. "I hated that man. Mainly because Kim hated him."

"What did she tell you?" He should have punched Hazelton in the face when he relived college the second time, or even when he saw him in church or at Dennis's funeral. Wouldn't that have caused a stir?

"He sexually harassed anything with a skirt. That was the bottom line. He abused his position and slept with students."

"Did he sleep with Kim?"

"I hope not," Dennis said in measured tones. "She never said he did, and I never asked."

"One of us would have known if she did," John said, more in hope than knowledge.

"You'd think so." Dennis took a swig from his beer bottle and stared off into the distance.

John quickly pushed the idea of Kim sleeping with Hazelton out of his mind. She was too good a person for that. Too smart. Too spiritual. She wouldn't have done it willingly. But what about unwillingly?

"Did she tell you anything specific?"

"Nope. Not that I can remember."

John leaned back into the soft leather. He hadn't learned anything that could help him. Had he relived his past only to languish with the uncertainty of what happened to Kim?

Suddenly he felt the urge to pray. *Come on, God. I trust you. I need you. I need peace. Kim needs justice. Please help.* "One more thing," John said to Dennis.

"Sure."

"You knew Renee in college, didn't you?"

"Yes. Why? You didn't know that?"

Why hadn't she told him? He racked his brain, trying to recall the first time he introduced the Renee to Dennis and if they gave any indication they knew each other. "I don't think I did, Dennis."

"Maybe you should ask her."

"Why? What is she hiding?"

"I didn't say she was hiding anything."

Something clicked. "She didn't want me to know you knew her. Renee asked you to keep it quiet."

"Something like that." He stared at the television remote as though wishing he could turn the TV back on and end the conversation.

"Why?"

"Ask your wife."

"It's been over twenty years, Dennis. Whatever it is, it's our problem now, not yours. Tell me. I know you want to."

Dennis shrugged. "What can it hurt?" After glancing up at the whirling ceiling fan, he continued. "Renee didn't finish her first semester at OU."

"I knew that," John said. "She dropped out of school to work, and then started taking classes at Rose State in the spring."

"But do you know why she dropped out?"

"She didn't have the money." John said this with authority, because that was what Renee had told him, and he believed her.

"Not exactly," Dennis said. "She was sort of forced out."

John's heart turned icy cold.

"A grade cheating scandal. They caught a bunch of freshman cheating on a paper, Kicked out the entire bunch of them. No second chance."

John felt the color drain from his face. He'd seen the headline in the campus newspaper in Kim's office. That's why Renee had been talking to Dennis so seriously at the party.

"Hey, don't take it so hard. That was a long time ago. I'm sure she's moved on. She didn't want you to know about it, I guess. It was embarrassing."

Renee lied to him. And she obviously hadn't changed. Cheat on a paper, steal from a company. Same thing. Same person. "I need to go." John jumped to his feet.

"Are you all right?"

John brushed him off with a wave. He threw his can away in the kitchen and walked to the front door.

"Hey, I won't tell Renee we talked. She'll never hear it from me," Dennis pleaded, as if he'd given the wrong answer and wanted to make up for it.

"She probably won't be at work tomorrow."

"Okay. Is she sick?"

"Not exactly." John found the need to relieve his burden both sudden and overwhelming, like stepping out of a cave into the rushing waves of a waterfall.

"Kids?" Dennis tried again.

"No." He needed to go. Dennis would guess eventually.

"It's the missing money, isn't it?"

Bingo.

"She's that stressed out about it?" Dennis's face softened.

"She didn't sleep at all last night."

Dennis didn't say anything for a moment. "She took the money, didn't she?"

John found it hard to speak. He just nodded.

"Oh, man." Dennis shook his head in sympathy. "I'm sorry. Is there anything I can do?"

"I don't think so. We have a lawyer and . . ." John's voice cracked. He'd internalized the pain and anger and let it turn into a bitter stew of resentment. Verbalizing that anger was an entirely different story. He couldn't put his feelings into words. Not to Dennis. Not right now. He took a deep breath and regained his composure. "We'll talk later."

* * *

On the drive home, uneasiness formed in John's gut. He searched for the source, a place to put his anger, and settled on Renee. But that left him empty. Sure, she'd made a huge mistake—a potentially life-destroying mistake—but he couldn't find a part of her to latch his hate onto that made him feel better.

Was it Kim? He'd spent half of a year in a dream, or a fantasy, or an alternate reality, and all of it focused on Kim. He returned to his own life, ready to find out who killed her. Yet so far, answers weren't coming easily. But that wasn't her fault.

He parked in the garage and glanced at the toys strewn about. The bikes, the big wheels, the fishing gear, the batting tee. He'd promised Mark and Sara he'd ride bikes with them tonight. When he entered through the kitchen door, the smell of soapy flowers hit him. Renee must have spent the day doing the laundry. The rest of the house appeared as if it had also gotten her full attention.

He peered in on the kids. They were both asleep. He found Renee in their room. She'd cleared everything off the top of the dresser and held an old rag in one hand and furniture polish in the other.

She saw him in the dresser mirror and flashed him a tired smile that disappeared before she turned around to face him. "How'd it go?"

"Fine." He didn't want to linger on the subject. Thankfully, the phone rang.

Renee picked up the receiver and studied the Caller ID. "I don't recognize the number,"

"I'll answer it."

She tossed him the phone, and he caught it with one hand. Walking down the hall—away from Renee—he looked at the number. He didn't recognize it either.

"Is this John Michaels?" The gravelly voice spoke in quick, clipped tones.

"It is."

"It's about time someone answered the phone. I've called several times tonight. I wasn't about to leave a message, and this was the last time I was going to call before I gave up."

John held the phone to his ear, speechless. "Who did you say you were?"

"I didn't say yet. I'm Murphy Hazelton. Buzz Baker told me to call you."

John hurried into the kitchen, grabbed a pen and notepad, and sat at the table. In his quest to locate Hazelton, he'd called Buzz, who promised to get a message to his college friend.

"Okay, yeah, great."

"What do you want?" Hazelton barked.

John dropped his pen. "Sorry to bother you so late . . ."

"Bother me? I'm calling you. But it *is* bothering me, so get on with it." The gruff man on the other end of the line didn't mesh with the Hazelton John knew. But years and a reputation for sexual assault could probably change a man.

"Okay, sure. Do you remember Kim Addison?"

"What the . . ." Hazelton went off on a crude tirade. ". . . of course I remember her. She worked in my office. And it's a tragic shame no one ever found out what happened to her. But as I told the police, and I'll tell you, I had nothing to do with it."

He had to tread carefully here. "Listen Professor . . ."

Hazelton interrupted with a few more swear words. "I don't teach any more. Haven't for years. Call me Murphy."

"Murphy, I was in love with Kim and was planning to ask her to marry me."

"I see." The bluster dropped away.

"I've buried the pain long enough. I want to know what happened to her."

"Well, I can't help you there."

If Hazelton had something to do with Kim's disappearance, or death, of course he'd say that. Still, John had to ask. "You were close to Kim?"

"No, not really."

"I'm realizing there were a few things I didn't know about her. We were best friends, but she didn't tell me everything. Did she ever confide in you?"

"Confide? What is that supposed to mean? I told you, we weren't close."

Enough with being congenial. "Listen, Murphy. I know how you assaulted her and how she resisted. I know you were accused of rape but acquitted. You're a scumbag. But you know what, I don't care. Unless you killed Kim—and you wouldn't tell me if you did—then I don't care what you did. You dated college girls? You tried to make a move on Kim? It doesn't matter anymore. All I want to know is if you can tell me anything that might help me find out what happened to her. If you can't, then this call is over."

Another grunt, and then a pause. "Let me think."

John tapped his pen on the pad.

"Okay, this is all I know. Kim never talked to me about it, but I heard it from another professor in the Quad."

"The Quad?"

"Our suite of offices. Dr. Hamilton asked my opinion on something. She told me Kim came to her with a problem. One of Kim's friends was dealing drugs to the frats and sorority houses, and she didn't know what to do. She wanted to stop him from doing it, but didn't want her friend to get in trouble."

A slow chill crept through John.

"I didn't care what she did," Murphy continued. "If she turned in this friend, someone else would take his place. Dr. Hamilton told Kim she should turn him in. I think she was going to, but I never heard what happened."

No doubt Dennis had been the drug dealer. If Dr. Hamilton recommended that Kim turn him in, she may have been leaning that way. What if she confronted Dennis and asked him to stop? What if she told him she was going to turn him in to the police? Would that be enough motive for him to kill her? Maybe.

"That's all I know," Hazelton said. "Maybe that drug dealer killed her. Did you ever think of that?"

"I just did," John said.

Hazelton grunted. "I've got to go now. I told you everything."

John didn't reply.

"And one more thing."

"What?"

"I didn't kill her." The line went dead.

CHAPTER 43

John put the phone down on the table and wrote "Kim" and "Dennis" on the note pad with an arrow connecting the two. They were friends. They dated. They had some kind of special bond. Kim had a wild side he didn't know about. Dennis hesitated when asked about Kim getting in trouble in high school. Why? Was he hiding something concerning himself, or about Kim? Why protect her now? She'd been gone far too long.

Maybe she confronted Dennis after she reported him to the campus police. To someone like Ray Pope. How far would he go to shut her up? Would he plan to kill her? What if it was an accident? An argument out of control? Dennis had a temper in both real life and in John's high school fantasy. John jotted some notes on the paper.

The first time he woke up back in college, he made it to Dennis's house, and Kim called Dennis. There's no way she would have known John would be there. Did she call Dennis in real life? If so, did he meet her at the Baileys'? Maybe he killed her.

Dennis left at the same time he did, but he didn't know where Kim was. So who attacked them at the Baileys'? Kim had seen someone peering through the trees *before* she called him. No way it could have been Dennis . . . at least in that life. The Baileys weren't home, so probably not Chad either. What about Hazelton? He'd been accused of rape and consistently treated women as objects. A pedophile stalking the Baileys' kids? Teenagers wandering around, getting high or drinking beer?

John got a glass of water and two iced oatmeal cookies. Looking out the window into the darkness of the backyard, he finished the snack without really tasting it.

Neither a pedophile or teenagers looking to get high would have had a reason to attack. If reliving his life were to make any sense, he had to assume the same person who hit him in the head also killed Kim. But the attacker wouldn't have a motive to hurt them both. Kim was the target. The second time, John was only in the way.

It came back to Dennis. Did he go to the Baileys' after Kim called?

Who else? What were the common threads among the lives he relived? Dennis was present throughout. So was Larkin Connor, a woman he never knew until his pastor fantasy. She could still tie in, although he couldn't see how.

He felt so close. He returned to his notes and nibbled on the end of the pen. In his relived high school months, Chad Bailey died in Vegas. In his pastor fantasy, a killer murdered Dennis, massacred Chad and his wife, and would have killed John and Larkin if they hadn't gotten away. What linked them?

Wait a minute. He was missing something: Renee. Dennis knew where a body was buried, and the body turned out to be Renee. Was Larkin the key?

"Who was that the call from?"

He jumped, and his knee hit the underside of the table.

Renee stood behind him in the shadows of the dining room, half of her body obscured by the door frame. "I didn't mean to scare you again."

"No, it's all right," he stammered.

"You were talking about Kim?"

The name sounded strange coming from his wife. Renee knew about Kim, of course, but had not uttered her name once since they'd been married.

"Yeah," John hesitated and then spoke decisively. "Yes, I was."

"Why?"

"I've been looking into what actually happened to her."

"Why now?" She stepped out of the shadows. Her long, navy-blue night gown swished around her bare feet. Her hair was still damp from the shower.

"Why not? Don't you think it's been long enough?" John started to storm. His bare feet smacked against the cool tile floor. Then he stopped. She hadn't been challenging him. He turned around.

Renee remained still.

"I know it's not a good time, for you or for us. But some things have come up that can't wait." He didn't want to explain any further, and couldn't endure any more questions. "I'm going to take a shower."

With scalding water battering the back of his head and shoulders, he allowed himself to think again about Renee. The body Dennis wrote him a note about.

I know where the body is buried.

They'd found a body buried in the woods. In some ways, the Renee of his fantasy life paralleled the Kim of his real life. Could Kim be buried in those woods?

Tomorrow, he'd find out. But first, he had to get through the night.

Renee had already turned out the lights and crawled under the covers. She may have been asleep, or faking, but just as well. The tension hanging between them stabbed at his heart. It shouldn't be like this. He shouldn't be so angry.

He turned on his bedside fan and set his alarm. Renee lay a few inches away, yet miles from him. He could bridge that gap, but he didn't.

Chapter 44

In the morning, everything seemed less urgent. The family ate a breakfast of cereal and milk together. John engaged Mark and Sara in animated conversation about iCarly, Transformers, and the daycare's field trip to the zoo next week.

Renee said nothing, but he caught her occasional smile. She seemed to want to join in on the fun, the laughter, and the good-natured teasing but couldn't bring herself to do it.

While the kids searched for their backpacks before leaving. Renee followed him into the garage. "I'm meeting with Chad Bailey today."

"Okay." If the meeting went long, it would really mess up his plans.

"I don't want you to come."

"Oh?"

She apparently noticed the shock on his face. "I know you don't want to come."

He looked at his feet.

"I want to find out what my options are and where to go from here. When decisions have to be made, I'll let you know."

* * *

He dropped the kids off at daycare, keeping the same routine. No point in upsetting them. They didn't seem to notice Mom and Dad weren't talking much the last few days.

The drive to Norman went smoothly until he reached Moore and the never-ending construction on I-35. The traffic didn't improve his mood. He needed to be at the Beast by lunch. That left him only an hour at most. When he finally reached the south side of Norman, he exited on Highway 9.

As he drove, he realized two things. First, he'd gone too far and missed his exit. Second, ten years ago the York Recreational Center was an abandoned baseball ghost town, but now all evidence of the fields was completely gone. He turned around, drove back, and decided he'd passed it again. He, turned around again, and then pulled off onto the shoulder. *Think, John!* He'd been in the area with Brad and Larkin, so he could figure this out.

Ahead, he spotted the faded pine-green sign indicating 108th Street. The turn-off for the Baileys. This was it. The baseball fields used to be nearby. John rolled the car forward, tires crunching on loose gravel. He turned on his flashers and pulled into the remnants of an entryway. Parts of the old parking lot remained, but weeds and grass had completely overtaken other parts of the recreational center. John drove onto the old fields at the York Recreational Center.

Today would be a scorcher, but right now it was probably only in the upper eighties. He popped the trunk and grabbed the shovel.

Other than a still-standing set of rusty, metal bleachers, he could see no visible proof that kids used to run around on these fields, trying to hit home runs or tag each other out. Beyond them stood the storage shed.

Navigating the old baseball fields proved challenging. He waded through waist–high weeds, using the shovel like a cane to steady himself on the uneven surface. Could he remember where to go after he reached the shed? Would he recognize the landmarks? Would he find a body? Bones?

Dennis's note had said to look for an abandoned truck. Operating in daylight made everything much easier, even once he entered the deep shade of the woods. He didn't have to go far to find the same rusted out pickup in a tiny clearing. He headed south, turning around every few steps to ensure the truck was directly behind him.

The heavy trees blocked the sun, and he swatted bugs away from his face. He brushed low-hanging leafy branches out of his way as he marched forward.

He recognized the tree immediately. Its base rested just above the dried-out creek bed. Thick trunks branched out in two directions, forming two large trees. The same place they'd been the other night. John walked around to the other side of the tree.

Thick weeds and grass covered the ground, offering no signs of a long-lost grave. He studied the ground for signs of a hole or a depression and then stopped. That was ten years ago and a fantasy world. This was real, and this time he wasn't looking for Renee.

Could Kim be buried under this tree? That question summed up all the problems associated with his fantasies. Did all the parallels and inconsistencies mean anything?

He chose to believe they meant everything.

Every single event might not relate to the present, but certain events had a purpose. And that purpose was to find out who killed Kim. He came out here to find a buried body with Larkin and Brad. The body was Renee. This time he'd find Kim. Could he handle it?

John prodded the ground with the shovel before taking out his digital camera and snapping several pictures of the area. Sweat had formed under his arms and on his forehead, and he hadn't even started digging. With the camera back in his pocket, he pounded the shovel into the dirt, looking for soft spots that would be easier to dig.

Sweat trickled into his eye. He could find reasons all day why he shouldn't dig. Thick roots from the surrounding trees created an impenetrable underground maze. Where was the spot Brad found the other night, a smooth surface with no visible roots?

He ran the bottom of his Adidas cross-trainers over the ground between two large roots, brushing away leaves and twigs and revealing a smooth spot of ground. A flash of sunlight broke through the canopy of branches and leaves. It illuminated the location as if God had sent a sign.

With his first thrust, John buried the shovel's blade halfway into the ground. He scooped away the dirt. Then again. And again. He developed a pattern, not stopping even as the sweat ran down his face.

He finally paused thirty minutes later to assess the hole and guzzled from a thermos he'd brought. He'd created a hole about eighteen inches deep. No sign of bones. He moved a little to his left and started again.

Fifteen minutes later, the shovel's blade struck something solid. A root? A rock? He scraped the dirt away with the shovel, dropped to his knees, and brushed more dirt away with his hands. When he cleared enough dirt to see what he'd hit, he jerked his hands back.

A bone.

His heart jolted in his chest as though it wanted to explode. Should he be elated? Devastated? Terrified? Without thinking, he dug his hands around the bone. He grabbed handfuls of dirt and flung them to the side.

He couldn't budge the large gray bone, so he continued scraping away dirt from around it. His fingers brushed across an item with different texture.

John rubbed the mostly buried item with a couple of fingers. Cloth! Time and decay had robbed it of color, but it must be clothing. John stood, stretched, and took a deep breath. Then he grabbed the shovel and began digging again. The shovel handle had rubbed the skin between his thumb and pointer finger raw, but he kept at it until his cell rang.

"Hey buddy, what's up?" asked Brad Mullins, his pastor and friend.

"Just working."

"Really? Okay, cool. Listen, I know you didn't want to play softball this year, but you're still on the roster, and we could really use you tonight. We're short a few guys."

"Tonight?" He had played the last few years, but his age had caught up with him. Fumbling fly balls in the outfield didn't exactly equate with the thrill of victory.

"Yeah, out at the Boomer Complex on 240. Game is at eight. Can you make it?"

John started to say no, but stopped. As of a few months ago, he was a high school baseball star. Did he still have that skill? "Sure, I'll play."

"Great."

"Who's there?" called a voice in the forest.

John dropped the phone.

"Is anyone there?" The man's voice called again, closer.

John grabbed the phone, disconnected the call, and scrambled for his thermos and shovel. Why was someone else out here?

More rustling came from the east. "Hello."

John took a final look at the hole and took off. He tried to maintain a straight path back to the abandoned pickup and the storage shed. He forced himself not to sprint. No one was chasing him.

Adrenaline pumped through his veins, but he had no reason to run. He didn't do anything wrong, except maybe trespassing. But if Kim really was in that grave, he didn't have anything to worry about. He should have stayed.

Too late now. He stumbled upon the abandoned truck, circled it, and then peered over the hood back the way he'd come.

He spotted movement in the trees. He tried to slow his breathing, but that just made the pounding in his chest louder.

The figure moved closer. John pictured a man in overalls, a straw hat, and skin baked by the sun stepping into a clearing with a shot gun leveled directly at him.

Before he could decide to leave, the figure came around a tree. He wasn't armed, and he wore blue jeans and a faded Oklahoma Sooners T-shirt.

Chad Bailey.

Of course. Bailey lived close by. He had every right to be out here.

John started to step out, to identify himself and explain what was going on. But a thread of doubt held him in place. What was Bailey's role in Kim's death?

If it was her body he'd discovered—and it had to be—then he'd found her right next to Bailey's property. She had gone to their house to ask about the nanny position, and John had gone there with her when he'd relived her last day.

When Bailey turned the other way, John scooted along the path he'd taken into the woods and soon saw the storage shed ahead. Within minutes, he was back in his car. He turned the air conditioning to high and headed home for a shower before returning to the Beast.

What were his options? Report the body to the police. Tell Dennis or Renee or Brad. Or do nothing. He chose nothing. He drove back to the city in silence, occasionally wiping stray tears from his cheek.

He'd found Kim.

CHAPTER 45

Arriving home a little before six, John found the kids spread out on the couch watching television. Sara held a baggie of pretzels, most likely a leftover from her lunch. No sign of Renee.

"Hey, guys." he plopped down between his kids and gave them both a squeeze. Their gaze never wavered from DVR'd *Duck Dynasty* reruns. He missed the days when they greeted him with unabashed glee when he came home from work.

Renee came from the hallway. "What are we going to do for supper? The kids are hungry."

"Brad called and asked me to play softball tonight. I told him I would."

"Okay." She remained in the marble-tiled entryway.

"I was thinking the kids could come."

Her nose wrinkled in disapproval.

He sighed. The kids were too young to be allowed to roam free. "You, too."

"Okay." Her face brightened as much as it could without actually smiling.

"The game is at eight. We can grab dinner on the way."

* * *

With Radio Disney tuned in and McNuggets in hand, the ride across town remained peaceful. John exited on Sunnylane and pulled into the nearly full parking lot. The Boomer Softball complex looked a lot like the York Recreational Center must have before it closed, with four fields, bleachers, and scoreboards. Advertisements for local businesses lined the outfield fences, and a large building at the center housed bathrooms, concession stands, and offices.

John wore gym shorts and an old church jersey from a few years ago. He grabbed his glove and led the family through the maze of cars. The evening air was crisp and hot, with the smells of hot dogs and beer floating on the wind.

A tingle of excitement tickled his muscles. In his alternate high school life, he could easily crush a baseball out of the park. Could he do the same tonight, or would he be what he'd always been, a hack?

"I'm hungry," Sara said as they approached the concession stand.

"You can have a snack during the game." Renee gripped each of the kids' hands, guiding them past beer-bellied men and other moms trying to keep an eye on their children.

John caught sight of Brad's wife. "I think we're over here." He led his family to Field 4. Renee began talking with some of the wives she knew, and the kids found a few friends playing in the dirt behind the bleachers. They would be fine.

He chatted with Brad and a few of the other guys and then joined the team in their warm-up behind the dugout while they waited for the first game to conclude. Twelve men either played catch, stretched, or swung a bat to loosen up.

The first game ended with shouts from members of the winning team and a spattering of applause from the stands. After backslapping, high-fiving, and congratulations from the other team, the players gathered their equipment and headed to their cars.

John's team filed into the dugout. "Michaels, you're in right field," said the bald, angular, fifty-year-old patriarch of the team.

"Sure, Lee." John rushed out to his position, ready to get under the first towering fly ball or sprint after a line drive.

The opposing team, a Baptist church from Edmond, scored two runs in the first inning but hit no balls to right field. That was the idea, put your worst fielder in right where no one would hit the ball.

He hustled back to the dugout and checked the batting line-up. Last, of course. He swallowed his dismay, took a seat on the bench, and shouted encouragement to each of his teammates when they came up to bat. They scored three, but the inning ended with John on deck.

He set the bat he'd chosen back against the fence, grabbed his glove, trotted out to right field, and watched two more batters get on base. He perked up when a left-handed hitter approached the plate. Maybe this guy would pull the ball.

On the first pitch, the batter laced a line drive to John's right. He raced to cut it off and caught it after one bounce

The second baseman yelled, "Throw it to third! Throw it to third!"

No. He was going to try and get the runner scoring from second. He planted his right foot and unleashed a throw that would never have been able possible before his time traveling.

The ball exploded from his arm and flew in a line straight to the catcher. The surprised runner didn't bother to slide. The catcher easily tagged him out.

A few fans clapped, not knowing they'd just seen an amazing throw.

"Great throw, John!" Lee called from the pitcher's mound, followed by shouts from a few other teammates.

Evidently, the baseball skills had stayed with him. He punched his glove. Batting should be fun.

No more balls came his way. He jogged back to the infield at the end of the inning, ready to bat. He tossed his glove into the dugout and grabbed a bat. Before stepping to the plate, he glanced at the bleachers. No Renee. He took a quick look behind the umpire and spotted her in line at the concession stand with the kids. He stepped into the batter's box and took his stance.

To get used to the trajectory of the ball, he let the first pitch sail by. Previous years of softball futility flashed through his mind. He'd never hit a home run before. Ever. He'd given up trying and settled for line drives. Even that had proved difficult.

The bat rested on his shoulder. When the pitcher released the ball, John lifted the bat an inch and tracked the ball's descent. It had almost nestled into the catcher's glove before he uncorked a violent swing. As soon as he made contact, he knew it was out of the park. He began a slow trot to first.

The players in the dugout erupted in irreverent cheers. A few fans clapped in the stands. The second baseman gave him a good natured smile as he trotted by. He crossed home, gave the next batter a high five, and returned to the dugout.

"Wow, where did that power come from?" Brad held out his fist, and John gave it a bump.

"My dreams."

John played right field the rest of the game. He caught two fly balls but didn't throw anyone else out. He hit another home run, and his kids saw this one. Mark cheered wildly, but Sara ran off to play in the dirt before he rounded the bases. Renee gave a melancholy smile. Later, he hit a line drive into the right field alley and legged out a triple.

Even with John's outstanding help, they lost 12-10. After the game, everyone shook hands. "Feel free to come out next week," Lee told him.

"I might."

Brad appeared out of nowhere, a duffle bag slung over his shoulder. "Hey, I need to talk to you. Can I call you later?"

"Sure."

"Thanks, buddy." Brad departed without talking to anyone else.

"Good game," Renee said.

"Thanks."

Someone in the knot of people ready to watch the next game caught his eye. "Renee, could you watch the kids for a second?"

When he approached the woman standing behind the third base bleachers at field three, he stopped. He didn't really know her, not in this life. But like everything else, maybe there was a reason for seeing her tonight.

"Lanie."

His high school crush turned to face him. Though older, she still had vibrant hair, soft skin, and glowing eyes. She started to speak and hesitated.

"I'm sorry, we went to high school together . . ."

"John," she said. "I recognized you. How are you doing?"

"I'm great. How about you?" Half of him wanted to hug her, but he settled on a wide smile.

"Good. I'm watching my husband play. She pointed to the field. "You remember Phil, don't you?"

"Of course. Baseball. State Championship MVP."

Lanie chuckled, and her eyes sparkled. "Don't let him hear you say that. When he gets out here, he still thinks he's in high school."

Relief flooded John. Seeing Lanie getting along so well in this life allowed him to let that part of his fantasy life go. His high school romance faded from his soul like a distant dream.

As he headed back to his family, he spotted Lee next to the south wall of the concession complex talking with a tall man in navy athletic shorts and an UnderArmour gray top. Behind them, a bulletin board displayed schedules, standings, and tournament news.

A blue Texas Rangers cap covered the tall man's head, but the angular cheek bones and sharp nose gave him away. Ray Pope.

Making the assumption he'd seen Pope for a reason, John veered towards the men.

Lee acknowledged him with a nod, but Pope remained motionless, almost as if he were not aware of his surroundings.

Up closer, Pope's trim, athletic body revealed he'd already started losing the battle with age. Wrinkles creased his tanned face, and gray hair billowed beneath his cap. He had to be close to fifty, yet he dressed as if he was ready for a solid workout.

"What's up, John?" Lee asked, as Pope started to walk away.

John stuck out his hand, partially to block Pope, partially as an offer to shake hands. "Hi, I'm John Michaels."

Pope gave firm shake and offered a quick, but engaging smile. "You a friend of Lee's?"

"I go to his church."

"Lee's crazy, you know," Pope said with a gleam in his eyes. "You keep an eye on him."

Lee was anything but crazy, but John had his doubts about Pope.

"I'll see you gentlemen later." Pope took off at a brisk walk and disappeared around the corner of the concession stand before John could say another word.

"You don't remember Ray?" Lee said. "He's been running this place for years."

John racked his brain. "I guess I never noticed him."

He and Lee talked a few more minutes until Renee approached carrying Sara. Their daughter's patience had reached its limits. Time to go.

* * *

Back in the car, the kids bickered over their Happy Meal toys. John shook his head and changed lanes in front of Crossroads Mall.

Seeing Lanie Simpson and Ray Pope in the span of a few minutes brought Kim back to the front of his mind. He hadn't called to report what he'd found out at the York Recreational Center, but he would soon. Maybe, buried with the body, would be evidence that could identify the killer.

Renee stared out the window. Defeat suffused her posture and actions. She seemed to have accepted his attitude towards her, a punishment she deserved, and now didn't even try to talk to him. Why? Was she afraid? Did she think he'd yell at her or be mean? Or did she believe it wasn't worth the effort? The possible answers depressed him.

He had to break the silence. "Did you talk to Chad Bailey today?"

"Yes, I did." She turned away from the window. She squinted, the receding sun shining through the windshield.

"How did it go?"

"He wants to talk to both of us tomorrow."

CHAPTER 46

Brad called when both of John's kids were taking showers under Renee's supervision, Mark in his bathroom, Sara in the guest bathroom. There wouldn't be any hot water left for John.

"It isn't too late, is it?" Brad asked.

"It is." John grinned.

"Oh, well." Brad chuckled. "Are you watching the news?"

"I don't watch the local news."

"You should check this out; I'm on Channel Eight."

John turned on the TV and then thumbed the mute button. The attractive brunette anchor broke for a commercial.

"Commercial," Brad said. "Try Channel Ten."

John switched channels and a wide shot of police cars with flashing lights came up. A police spokesperson. A shot of a forest and trees.

He froze. His skin felt a few sizes too small for his body.

When Chad Bailey appeared on the screen, John turned up the volume. The woods behind the York Recreational Center were Bailey's property. That made sense. His was the only house out there. He must have found the body and called the police.

"It's quite a shock," Chad told the reporter. "I hope the police can figure out who it was, and why they were buried on my property."

If Bailey had something to hide or knew about the body, he would have hidden it or certainly not reported it. So he probably had nothing to do with Kim's disappearance. Or maybe he wanted to be the hero. Maybe he figured since he found someone snooping around, he should report it first.

"Hmm, you think Kim might be buried out there?"

"What?" John had almost forgotten Brad was on the line.

"The one time we talked about it. You told me Kim was going to see a man named Chad Bailey. I always remembered that name because later I met him through Buzz Baker. And now I hear Bailey is helping you guys with some legal issues."

Brad knew about that? John gritted his teeth at the lack of privacy and then shrugged it off. He probably found out when Renee was searching for a lawyer.

"He is. I'll have to keep an eye on this."

"Yeah, well I'll be there for you, no matter what."

John knew he could count on his friend.

"But that's not why I called. Brad's voice grew quiet. "Have you heard from any of the church board members?"

"No." Something twisted in John's gut.

"You will, probably in the morning."

"Why?" John put the television back on mute, and a cold tingle prickled through his veins. But he already knew why. Another tie to his fantasy life. Except John wasn't the pastor this time; Brad was.

"There's going to be an emergency board meeting Sunday afternoon."

"Really?" John leaned forward, pressing the phone hard into his ear.

"Yeah, they're going to talk about me."

That confirmed John's fears. "What did you do, Brad?"

"Don't tell anyone, okay?"

"Tell anyone what?"

"I'm telling you now because you deserve to hear it from me and no one else."

"Let me hear it." John's entire body ached for Brad.

"The board is going to ask me to resign."

"Why?"

Brad let out an exhausted sigh. "I had an affair."

John imagined Brad alone in his living room, wife and kids in the other part of the house, watching the life and dream he'd built crumbling and about to be destroyed.

"It started last year," Brad continued. "I met her . . . well, I don't want to tell you that. She goes to our church, but it's no one's business who it is."

"You're right; I don't need to know."

"Anyway, it's over. It has been over. I ended it before anyone found out about it. Shannon heard about it through the rumor mill. She's furious. Devastated. Angry."

Kim had been angry too. *"It's a little too late for that John. You've ruined our life. You've destroyed everything we've worked for, everything we've dreamed of."*

"I'm sorry I let you down," Brad said with a quiet tone. "I just wanted you to know that."

"What are you going to do now?"

"Get a real job," Brad said through a half-hearted chuckle. "You know Sergio Gomez, right?"

"Isn't he the one who started the Hispanic church on 10th Street?"

"That's right. He needs some help around the church. His wife has been sick, and he needs to spend more time taking care of her."

"What will you be doing?" John asked.

"Odds and ends. The place needs a lot of work. I'm also going to be doing some landscaping."

Loss echoed through the phone line. From head pastor to gardener. John cradled the phone. "Brad, I'm here for you." He breathed a heavy sigh, and resolved to be at Brad's side as he found his way back to God.

They talked for a few more minutes, and then with a heavy heart John said good-bye. A pastor. A man. Broken. John's heart ached for his friend.

Chapter 47

Late Fridays usually meant snuggling on the couch, watching a romantic movie or a TV show they'd recorded during the week. But not tonight.

John rested on the bed watching SportsCenter when Renee emerged from the bathroom, smelling fresh and clean. "What time do we go to Chad Bailey's tomorrow?"

"Ten."

"That may have to change."

"Why?"

He'd tell her everything some day. Well, not everything. Could he ever tell Renee everything he'd seen and done? He'd relived high school and could name most of the elements on the periodic table because he'd learned them for a test. He could still see the weed-covered outfield grass at the high school practice field. He could conduct a funeral service. He could recall the softness of Lanie's hand in his as he found a new high school sweetheart.

His heart jumped with guilt. Why had his thoughts gone there?

When he didn't respond to her question, she said, "I'm going to check on the kids," and disappeared down the hall.

While she'd foolishly and ignorantly stole funds from her employer, he'd acted naively, but deliberately, and sought out a girl he'd always thought unattainable. He felt no guilt at the time, because that Lanie wasn't real. He'd been alone and angry. Now that he was back in his real life, he could honestly say that relationship didn't exist because it hadn't happened in his real life.

But it was real. It was in his heart . . . and it always would be. The truth socked him in the gut. He'd been given a second chance, but not to cheat on his wife or to soil his marriage. He could say he never physically cheated, but that wasn't true either. A single kiss, a single thought, meant he'd betrayed Renee.

So ugly.

He couldn't stand himself. He rolled over onto his stomach and closed his eyes. "Lord, forgive me." He held his breath.

Peace flooded his soul, and he breathed deep. He needed to change his ways, and he'd start with talking to Renee.

"Why can't we meet with Mr. Bailey tomorrow?"

"Did you catch the news after you put the kids to bed?"

She shook her head. Fatigue etched her face.

"Brad called and told me to turn it on. The lead story was about a body being found in Norman. It might be Kim."

That got her attention. "Why do you say that?"

He sat up and numbered the reasons with his fingers. "First, the body was found on property next to Chad Bailey's. Second, a reporter interviewed him because he found the body. Third, Kim had plans to work for the Baileys as a nanny around the time she disappeared. Fourth, Kim was last seen at the Bailey's house."

Renee turned off the light and crawled into bed. "I didn't know she knew the Baileys."

"Tomorrow you should call Chad and tell him we'd still like to meet with him. We can move it back if he is too busy."

Now he wanted to meet with Bailey. Not just to resolve Renee's legal issues, but to see if Chad might have murdered Kim. While nice on the surface, could Chad have a hidden, violent heart? Kim was last seen at Chad's house. Chad reported the body to the police. Had he finally been discovered and wanted to get on top of the situation?

No, wait. John mentally smacked his forehead. How could he ever forget the violent, dark night when he and Larkin barely escaped from a deranged killer? Why had that man murdered Chad and his wife? And had the same man murdered Dennis because he'd discovered where the body was buried? Renee's body.

If real life paralleled his fantasy life, it couldn't be Chad. Yet it all centered around his property. John had surely relived his life so he could bury the past once and for all. Yet it wasn't making sense.

Renee wiggled a little bit and finally settled into sleep. John remained awake. He stared at the ceiling fan, watching it go round and round.

* * *

John had made the drive to Norman a lot lately, but this trek felt like the final time. Whether or not Chad killed Kim, he had to be at the center of it somehow. And with the body found, the truth would be out soon.

As they drove past Robinson, John asked Renee, "What are we exactly talking about today?"

"I don't know for sure. Mr. Bailey said he'd like to meet with us to go over our options."

They exited on Highway 9.

The number of vehicles, police, press, and onlookers gathered in the crumbling parking lot of the York Recreational Center surprised him. He slowed and stared as they drove by. "They probably haven't identified the body yet. I have no idea how long that takes. But my gut instinct tells me it's probably Kim."

Renee nodded. She looked straight ahead.

As he drove the last half mile, he mentally ran through the questions he planned to ask Bailey. By the time he turned onto the dirt road that led to the Baileys' house, he'd worked out a tentative plan.

An overhanging tree branch scraped the roof of the Explorer as he turned the SUV into the winding driveway. The house looked remarkably similar to the versions he'd seen in 1992 and 1999. The trees were much bigger, the cars in the driveway were different, but the flowers in front were vibrant and the yard trimmed. He half expected to toys strewn across the backyard, but that was twenty years ago. This time, there was nothing but green grass.

Renee rang the bell, and after a brief wait the door popped open. Chad Bailey still had a thick head of hair, except this time it was the color of slate. He'd put a little weight on, but based on the twinkle in his eye, he still appeared to be a charmer.

"Welcome, come on in." He greeted them with a smile and a hearty handshake. "It's great to finally meet you, John. Please follow me, and ignore the mess. We're in the process of moving."

John didn't see a mess, just boxes stacked in orderly fashion. They walked through the tiny living room, where the clearly-labeled boxes were stacked four and five high in the corners. They passed more boxes stacked on the kitchen countertops and on the table.

John searched for visual clues to tell him more about Chad, but the house mocked him, refusing to give anything away. If there had ever been any pictures on the wall, they'd been removed and boxed away.

"Here, this is my office. It used to be a Derek's room, but when he left for college, I took it over." He gave conspiratorial chuckle. "It's all mine, now."

The room was what he envisioned when he pictured a lawyer's office. Hardwood floors polished to a dark brown. Bookcases filled with titles that gave him a headache just glancing at them. Framed Oklahoma Sooners paintings on the wall. An autographed football. But nothing personal. No family photos.

Chad sat at his desk, and John and Renee took seats across from him. A single folder with two pens on top sat on an uncluttered wood desk. A laptop with its screen raised sat to the side. Chad pulled a set of papers from the file and set it in front of them. "Would you like to go over the deal first?" He pressed his hands together in a steeple.

"Deal?" John's eyes widened and his pulse quickened. What was going on?

"You didn't tell him?" Chad's bemused smile gave nothing away.

Renee flashed John a smile of shame and embarrassment. "I didn't want to get his hopes up." She may have wanted to talk to him, but he'd been too busy to listen. Too caught up in Kim, in his own life, in what mattered to him.

"Okay, I'll start at the beginning." Chad looked at John.

John leaned forward, his fingers gripping the edge of the seat. Like a kernel of corn set over heat, hope began to form.

"I talked extensively with Renee yesterday, and she told me everything. We went over the options and what would be possible considering your financial situation. Afterwards, I contacted Mr. Stout, and we had a long meeting. Then I called Renee to tell her the results."

John turned to Renee, to Bailey, and back. In his heart, he'd prepared for the repercussions of the embezzlement to last months before changing their lives for the worse. He'd lose the coffee shop. They'd have to move. He'd be disgraced, and Renee humiliated. Possibly jail time for Renee. And their marriage? Would it last? Finally, he asked, "What did he say?"

"After he finished cursing?" Bailey's attempt at humor almost pulled a smile from John. "He first threatened to press charges," Chad explained, "but I talked him out of that. Did you know embezzlement cases are almost never prosecuted? The victims are embarrassed that someone they trusted stole from them, or they don't mess with it because it won't help them get the money back. He's decided to let it go. He's not going to press charges."

"What?" John looked at Renee. The weight of the world slowly slipped off his shoulders.

She smiled and bit her bottom lip. Tears formed at the corner of her eyes.

John looked away. His own throat tightened, and if he closed his eyes, tears would run down his cheeks.

Thankfully, Chad moved on. "The terms are negotiable, but basically you'll be required to make payments every month. Mr. Stout will also require that you volunteer for the March of Dimes, his favorite charity."

No problem. He could march. He could serve. He could volunteer. He could do anything, *would* do anything. Relief rushed through John's veins like a cleansing rain. All the pent-up fear of a trial, jail, bankruptcy, or a broken family washed away with Chad's words.

He stole a glance at Renee, and the image of a manipulative, dishonest marriage-wrecker melted into the girl he fell in love with. A girl who promised for better or worse and would battle to the end of the world for him. She'd done that—although in an illegal way—and he'd hated her for it.

Chad smiled expectantly. "I expected this, but you never know. Some people get really mad, but Mr. Stout was quite gracious in the end."

John didn't know if he could speak without choking up, but one of them should say something. "I don't know how we can ever repay you or thank you. I don't think we ever envisioned an ending like this." He hadn't, at least.

Chad waived a hand. "Don't worry about it. I'm just glad to see a happy ending." He took the time to go over each page.

John listened but also used the time to check out the room. Nothing in here to provide some answers. He'd need to use his plan to check out the rest of the house. He didn't know what to look for and wouldn't have much time to search, but he had faith he'd find answers.

Chad offered each of them a pen.

Renee signed first and slid the papers to John. A part of him felt like he was signing his life away, but the rest of him rejoiced that everything had worked out so easily.

"I'm sorry to bother you," John asked as he handed the papers back to Chad, "but I really need to use the restroom."

"There's one right in the hall, but it's a mess. I'm in the middle of a remodel before selling. Let me show you." Chad walked to the door.

Behind Chad's back, John mouthed to Renee, "Keep him busy."

Renee gave a slow blink and nodded.

John gave her a quick wink, and the corners of her mouth may have actually gone upward. Progress.

Chad put one hand on John's shoulder, pointed with the other, and gave him the directions.

As John walked away, Renee asked, "So, your new house is ready?"

John passed through the kitchen and then skirted around a large dining room table and through the family room to the bathroom. He stepped quickly to the master bedroom instead.

Finally, a room that looked lived in. Clothes were scattered about—both men's and women's. The first evidence of Bailey's wife Debbie.

Since he had no idea what to look for, he opened the drawers of the dresser. Cleaned out.

He moved to the closet. Only enough items for a few days. He wiped his forehead, and his hand came away damp.

The bathroom counter contained nothing of interest. "Come on, God, help me out," he muttered. Not the most reverent, but a prayer nonetheless.

He returned to the master bedroom. Where else could he look? Under the bed? Behind the dresser? Behind the toilet, like in *The Godfather?* His gaze drifted across the room.

The nightstand.

The bottom drawer held nothing but socks. The middle drawer, men's underwear. The top drawer contained golf tees, a commemorative poker chip, a deck of cards, several travel brochures, and a small, battered, gift box, the size that held jewelry.

Inside he found a single hoop earring.

It probably belonged to Chad's wife, but— No, he recognized it.

The adult Lanie reached into her purse and pulled out an earring. It looked familiar. It was a double-hoop gold ring, with tiny diamonds cut into the surface. "Is it yours?"

"No. Dennis was seeing someone." Scorn drenched Lanie's tone.

A wave of relief flooded over him. Everything would end today. He'd find Kim's killer. And that started now.

Chad had the earring in this life. Only one. Lanie had presented an identical earring as evidence of Dennis's infidelity in John's pastor fantasy. It looked familiar then too.

But whose was it, and was it evidence of an affair, or murder? He turned it over in his hand. Didn't Renee have a pair of earrings like this? Maybe he could somehow pull her away from Chad and show her the earring.

In the pastor fantasy, it belonged to Renee. Lanie got it from Dennis, but Dennis got it from where? A girlfriend? A dead body? As a souvenir?

If he was right, it was Kim's. Had Bailey taken the earring after he killed Kim? But why would he keep it so long, and in such a prominent place?

Another idea hit John. Maybe Bailey found the earring when he discovered the body John unearthed.

That was the connection! Renee was the murder victim in the pastor fantasy. Kim was murdered in real life.

The doorbell rang.

John crammed the case into his pocket and slipped into the bathroom just as Chad approached the front door. After flushing the toilet, he washed and dried his hands. At the end of the hall, he stopped. From the corner, he could see into the family room. He couldn't see the front door, but heard muffled talking.

When he returned to the office, Renee sat staring out the window. She jumped when he touched her shoulder. "Who's at the door?"

"I don't know, but I found this." He flipped open the box and showed her the earring. "Don't you have a pair like this?"

She picked it up and studied it. "I do, but I haven't worn them in years."

"Kim had a pair, too." His heart pounded in the thrill of discovery.

Her eyes brightened at what that meant. "How do you know?"

"I just do."

Understanding brightened her face. "He has one earring. Where's the other?"

"Buried with Kim," John said. It had to be. "That's the proof we need."

"But he found the body. Maybe he found the earring." Renee looked over John's shoulder to the door.

"Why would he keep it? Why would he put it in a box?"

The voices came their way. John quickly slid the box back in a pocket.

Bailey entered first, and his guest stopped at the door.

John's heart fell in his chest. He should have expected him.

"John and Renee, I take it you both know Dennis Vance."

Chapter 48

Renee jumped up from her seat. "Hi, Dennis."

Dennis's eyebrows arched, as though he was just as surprised to see them. He looked at Chad, then back to John, then down.

Bailey grinned. "He's a little early. Sorry."

John smiled. "I expected to see you today, Dennis." The pieces jumbled in his brain. He needed a bit more time to put them all into place, but Dennis had been involved in every segment of his fantasy life. Of course, he'd be present now. John tried to read evil in his face, but saw only a solemn sadness. If Dennis hadn't come to silence John, or even Chad, why was he here? But what role had he played ? Killer? Friend? Lover? He needed the last piece to make it all fit.

A booming echo shattered the silence.

Dennis fell to the ground in a heap.

Renee screamed.

A dark red stain spread across the back of Dennis's white T-shirt.

Chad cursed, ducked, and stumbled over Dennis. He rushed into the hallway."NO!" he screamed as he slammed the door behind him.

John's heart beat double time. It was just like in his fantasy life. But this time it was real. He could die. Renee could die. And what would happen to Mark and Sara? What did Chad and Debbie know that made someone want to kill them?

A thud against the wall rattled the framed painting next to the door.

A grunt. A muffled curse.

Renee stared at Dennis. "Is he alive?" she whispered.

Dennis groaned and rolled over. "Barely." He clutched his chest, just under his shoulder.

In the hallway, a thud was followed by scuffling and a bang against the wall.

Every muscle tensed and on edge, John waited for another gunshot to signal the end of Chad Bailey's life. How close would real life follow the fantasy?

Instead, someone crashed against the wall again. Quick footsteps followed. The voices trailed down the hallway as the fight moved toward the living room.

John sprang to the window, unlocked it, and shoved it up. He held out a hand to Renee. "We need to get out of here."

"What about Dennis?"

Dennis squeezed his eyes shut. "I'll live," he said through clenched teeth." He reached into a pocket.

John grabbed Renee's hand and pulled her to him. What was Dennis grabbing for? He stepped in front of her.

Dennis pulled out his phone. "I'll call 911." He let out a moan. "You guys get out of here."

John nodded. Dennis would make it . . . if the killer didn't return. He drew Renee to the window. "We've got to go."

She gave a slight nod, put her feet on the windowsill, and slid to the ground.

John clambered through the window behind her. He took her hand and they ran to the edge of the trees. He took her hands in his and looked into her eyes. "Stay here and call the police. I'm going back in."

"Why?" she pleaded. Her wide eyes held unshed tears.

"Dennis and Chad are still in there."

"But you could be . . ."

The thought of death robbed him of breath for a moment, but a soft spirit nudged him and whispered into his ear. He had to go back. That's where the last piece of the puzzle was. It had to be.

He crept back in through the sliding door into the dining room. He peeked around the corner into the empty front room.

Glass crashed from the end of the house with the bedrooms.

John pulled back. He gulped in a deep breath. Chad needed his help. And if he wanted to know who killed Kim, he needed to see the attacker. He darted into the front room.

Once-perfectly-stacked moving boxes were torn and dumped. Their contents were strewn across the floor like candy from a piñata.

He picked his way across the litter-strewn floor. He stepped over a cluster of pictures, photo albums, and wooden frames and stopped.

A rustic-style frame held an enlarged snapshot of the Baileys. With a sparkling beach for a background, they stood next to a man with close cropped hair and a goofy smile. Chad Bailey, Debbie Bailey, and Ray Pope.

Another connection, but not the right one. How could he have known Kim?

He reached for the picture, but a glint of metal several feet away caught his eye, something not shaped like a picture frame. He brushed aside the photos concealing most of it and stared at a gun. His fingers closed around the handle, and he picked it up.

A loud grunt came from the direction of the bedrooms.

Gun in hand, John rushed toward the fight.

Chapter 49

Figuring he now had the only gun in the house, John sprinted into the master bedroom, gun arm extended. "Step back!"

Bailey stood in the corner. Blood dripped from his nose, but he was coiled and ready to fight.

The attacker faced Bailey, but John recognized the navy athletic shorts and gray shirt. Finally, he knew who killed Kim.

"I have your gun! Turn around!"

The man turned slowly, and raised his hands. Ray Pope.

John cleared his throat. "The police are coming."

Ray stared at him, breathing hard, eyes glittering.

The sirens grew louder. Moments later, three patrol cars roared to a stop in the drive outside the bedroom window. They'd probably come from the York Fields next to the Baileys' property.

Pope glanced at the police cars. He was trapped and he knew it.

John continued to stand his ground, but the building tension eased. They'd won. He'd finally see justice served.

Ray darted forward.

John cocked his finger but didn't pull the trigger.

Ray barreled into John and ran past him into the hallway.

John's bottom hit the floor hard. His arms flew up, and the gun clattered somewhere behind him.

Ray veered to the right, but John grabbed one of his feet. As Ray fell forward, Chad landed on him in a leaping tackle. John rolled over and grasped Pope's thrashing legs while Bailey held his upper body.

His skin flushed, Ray thrashed and hurled curses at them.

"John? John?" Renee called from the hallway.

"In here!" he yelled.

"Ma'am, don't." The footsteps sounded like a herd of cattle thundering across a field, even on the carpet.

Renee burst into the room, an officer still grasping at her. Renee glowed, her skin flushed, strands of hair stuck to her forehead, but she'd never looked so beautiful to him.

More police poured into the room. It was over.

* * *

The next few hours blurred together into a mess. The police used Bailey's office to question each person in private. When his turn came, John answered the questions and tried to make sense of what happened.

When the police ran out of questions, John breathed a heavy sigh of relief as he left the room. Kim had been found. Formal identification would have to take place, but he knew it was her. He'd finally completed the journey started months ago. Now he could move on. He'd always miss Kim and regret all the pain her death had caused, but he had Renee and two kids. He had a life to rebuild.

He found Renee sitting on the hood of their Explorer in the front yard. He sat next to her, with his shoulder touching hers.

She stuck out her bottom lip and blew air up across her face.

John shook his head. Other than the police cars, everything looked so normal: a cultivated flower bed, a trim lawn, a nice house, decent cars. Yet inside, vicious violence had almost claimed their lives. You could dress up life all you wanted, but evil couldn't be contained. It existed, and it had found them today.

John reached for Renee's hand. She eagerly grasped it, and they shared a look of relief and contentment.

"I'm sorry," John said.

"For what?" She looked at him, as if she'd expected him to talk, but not to say that.

"I don't know. For everything."

"I'm the one who should be sorry. I was so stupid."

"It's over. We can move on."

"But we still have to pay the money back." Renee looked down at the crisp, green grass. "I feel like I need to do more than just say 'I'm sorry.'"

He knew what she meant. Not only would Renee have to deal with what she did, she'd have to come to terms with what kind of person she really was.

"We'll figure it out," he said.

She shook her head. "I'm so sorry."

"I know you are. You've apologized, and you're killing yourself inside over it." He took a deep breath. "And I've let you do it. I thought you deserved all the pain and guilt. So I didn't forgive you at first. And then, I haven't told you . . ." Why were the words still so hard to say? "So, here it is. I forgive you."

"Thank you." Eyes watering, she put her arms around him and gave him a tight, strong hug. They stayed in each other's arms for several minutes.

* * *

John leaned against the wall in Dennis's hospital room, thankful to be away from the crime scene and done with the questioning. Every muscle, every fiber ached from the events of the day. He needed a month off of life to recover. He glanced at his watch. Renee should be home by now to relieve his sister Becky of her babysitting duty.

Dennis groaned as he reached for the small carton of milk on the tray of food before him. He fingered his wrapped left shoulder, where the bullet had done painful, but ultimately minor, damage.

Chad Bailey leaned against the sink, next to his wife Debbie, who had joined them after dealing with the police and media. Debbie had silky red hair and sharp green eyes. She'd been busy furnishing their new house when all the violence took place.

"Who is Ray Pope?" John asked. "The police wouldn't tell me anything."

"My brother," Debbie said. She didn't meet anyone's eyes.

After seeing the framed photo on the floor, John figured they'd been related. It killed him to know the connection had been right there in front of him. "How did this happen? When did you find out?"

"If we had known it was Ray, we—"

"Let me explain, dear." Chad took one of his wife's hands. "We didn't know. We never imagined Ray would do anything like this. He has a hot temper and can be unpredictable, but . . ." He shook his head. "I didn't realize he might have been Kim's killer until last night." He paused, as if expecting a reaction.

When he got nothing but stares from John and Dennis, he continued. "Ray's always been an up-front, in-your-face guy. He boasts about his personal life, his girlfriends, his money, and his athletic accomplishments, even when most of his supposed feats are way in the past.

"One night, ten or fifteen years ago, Ray told me about the beautiful blonde girl who got away. He gave me a name, April or Angie or something. I don't remember. He told me an elaborate tale of seduction and a weekend romance. This supposed dream girl disappeared, and he had no idea where she went. He spoke of her as if she were a siren in a myth. I didn't believe him, but he showed me a single earring. Gold, double hoops, inlaid with diamonds. I thought it was strange, but dismissed it because Ray is kind of strange.

"Yesterday, I was out on my property when I heard a noise. Probably just kids, I thought, but I checked it out."

John coughed to cover any reaction that might have shown on his face.

"I was shocked to find a big hole and bones. Human bones," Chad continued. "I thought, 'Hey, I found a body. I'll be on the news. I'll get my fifteen minutes of fame.' I sifted around in the dirt with a stick, seeing if I could see anything else. I didn't. Just clothing fragments.

"Then the sun flashed on a small object. I knelt down to examine it. It was a single earring. Gold, double hoops, inlaid with diamonds. Overwhelming fear washed over me. I knew who had the matching earring. And I knew we'd finally found Kim.

"Without the other earring, I was afraid there wouldn't be enough evidence for the police to connect Ray to the murder. So I took the earring and planned to confront Ray with it, try to convince him to turn himself in."

John cleared his throat. The heartache with which Bailey delivered that last line brought a new thought. "How exactly did you know Kim?"

"You don't know?" Bailey asked, a laugh almost escaping.

"No." John looked from Dennis to Chad and Debbie. What were they not telling him?

Bailey turned to Dennis. "You never told him?"

Dennis shrugged his good shoulder and then winced.

"What, Dennis?"

"I always loved Kim," his friend said.

John couldn't help but smile. "You were insanely jealous." But his lips tightened, and a lump developed in his throat. Kim was *his* girl.

"I was. But by the time you came into the picture, we were just great friends. You have to believe me."

"You said Kim and Dennis have been friends for years?"

Leslee nodded.

"They met at college?"

Leslee looked away and then looked back. "No, John. They've known each other since she was in the ninth grade."

The pleading in Dennis's voice told John many things. Dennis never had intruded on his relationship with Kim, and he really was a good guy. "I believe you." John nodded.

"I'm glad. Because this next part is hard." Dennis shifted in his bed, and he looked John straight in the eyes. "Kim had a baby when she was in high school. I was the father."

John broke out in a cold sweat. A huge vacuum seemed to suck all the air out of the room. Kim? A baby? Why didn't Dennis reveal this the other night? What had he waiting for?

The Baileys looked at him with compassion, but Dennis seemed calm and relieved.

Kim's words from his final fantasy life—his second time returning to college—came back to him. *"I am not afraid to die. I've made peace with God and know that when I die I will go to heaven."*

A peace enveloped John.

"I'm sorry, John." Dennis said. "I know we should have told you. But we agreed not to tell anyone. Ever. Especially our friends. The baby was put up for adoption."

"It's all right," John managed.

"But Kim had changed, and I didn't want to get in the way of that change."

"It's a secret, John. We all have secrets." Kim and Dennis had a baby together? Unbelievable. "What about that professor in college. Hazelton?"

"A real jerk," Dennis said. "But that was after us. She told me about it because she needed a witness and thought I could do something about it, if necessary. If the professor needed to be roughed up a bit, she wanted me to do it. She didn't want you involved with that part of her life."

A sharp pang of sadness twisted inside John. Why couldn't Kim tell him everything? "What happened to the baby?"

"It was a coincidence that I got involved," Bailey said. "I'd been doing volunteer work for Choose Life. Kim and her parents were referred to me because they wanted to give the baby up for adoption. Debbie and I helped Kim and her family through the process."

"That doesn't seem like Kim." John looked at Dennis. "I can't see Kim giving up a baby, no matter how inconvenient."

"She didn't abandon the baby, John. Chad and Debbie adopted her."

"Whoa," John muttered. "She was at your house the day she disappeared. She was applying for a job as a nanny."

"Sort of," Chad said. "She had the job. She was going to watch our daughter, her daughter."

The room turned colder. Adoptive parents usually didn't let birth mothers become so close to their children. Why were the Baileys different? "Then what happened that day?" John asked.

"I've wondered that for years. We should have been there. It was a misunderstanding. Kim wasn't supposed to be out there until the evening.

"Now that we know Ray murdered her, it all fits together. Ray had told me earlier that week he'd stop by after he returned the lawn mower he borrowed from the York Recreational Fields. He was going to put it in the shed at the field along the edge of my property. He left a message on our machine, telling me he'd come out on Friday and stay for dinner. He loved Debbie's good cooking.

"But he never showed up. At least that's what we thought. He called Tuesday, said he'd been sick, and would bring the mower by on Wednesday. I never thought anything about it again . . . until now.

"It is so easy now to see that Ray must have been here when Kim showed up. He saw Kim. Something happened." Chad shook his head. "Ray always was an impulsive guy. Maybe he was quick to take advantage of a beautiful woman in a lonely place."

John nodded. "And maybe quick to kill her when she resisted." He remembered the scratch on Hazleton's neck. That answered all of his questions but one. "Her car had been at the Baileys' and wouldn't start. But it had never been found. What could have happened to it?"

Chad shrugged. "There are ways to get rid of a car. Drive it into a lake. Take it to the desert and torch it. Whatever."

John shook his head.

Chad let out a long sigh. "Hopefully, it will all come out during Ray's trial."

The darkness and horror of it shuddered John's soul. "Why did Dennis come to your house today?"

"I wanted to tell him what I discovered, to discuss our options. Should we go to the police? Should we tell our daughter?"

John shook his head. Maybe the months he spent reliving his past weren't supposed to tell him everything. But it told him enough. In the pastor fantasy, Dennis was murdered because Chad told Dennis he'd discovered who killed Renee, and then Chad gave Dennis the earring. In that life, Dennis had loved Renee in high school, and they had a child.

In real life, Dennis was nearly murdered because Bailey was about to do the same thing—tell Dennis he'd discovered the killer. Ray must have seen the TV coverage and figured out that Bailey knew now.

"But Ray acted before you had time to meet." John spoke more to himself than the others. "He had to silence anyone who could tie him to Kim. So he came after you, Chad. Dennis, you just showed up at a bad time."

Both men nodded.

"So let me get this straight, Chad," John said. "You raised Kim and Dennis's daughter as your own. You adopted her?"

"We did."

"You were going to allow Kim to be an active part of her daughter's life?"

"Dennis too," Chad said.

Dennis buttered a hard, crusty roll. "But I was too selfish to be around much. I was a kid. I didn't understand what I was missing until it was too late. Just a few years ago in fact, when I met her."

"You'd never met her?"

"I saw her some when she was little, but she didn't remember."

John found it strangely exciting to discover Kim had a daughter. If life had been different, it might have been his daughter. And then . . . No, no, no! He wiped that from his mind. He had a wife. He had two kids. That was his life, and nothing could change it. "I'd like to meet her daughter."

Dennis wiped his mouth with a napkin. "You already have."

Chapter 50

John returned home and told Renee everything he'd learned. Someday he could tell her everything that led up to the events of the day, but not now. Then he could confess to being an idiot. He'd dated a high school Lanie and felt the repercussions of some other self having an affair with her as an adult. Why had he lived these alternate lives, or whatever they were? Maybe to tell him he had everything he needed right here.

The kids were at the neighbors playing, and so they ate a nice, quiet dinner to celebrate the surprising grace they received from Mr. Stout. Renee talked about plans for a new job, maybe two, where she could begin paying back Mr. Stout. John went over some ideas he had for the Beast: some new marketing plans and menu items.

They considered selling the house and downsizing. They didn't need a house this big and never would. They could trade in cars and lower their monthly payments. It felt good to work with Renee and try to find solutions to their problems instead of the silence and placing blame.

John dried the dishes and then offered to get the kids.

"No, I'll get them. You go to work. I'll wait up."

"Thanks."

They hugged tightly and looked each other in the eye. Renee started to speak, but John stopped her with a hard, passionate kiss. She pulled away and laughed.

"What?" he said.

"I didn't see that coming." The happiness in her eyes made John glad he'd followed his impulse.

"I know." A little romance could cure a lot of marital issues. Or, at least, John planned on seeing if it could.

*　*　*

The Coffee Beast stayed open until two in the morning on Saturday nights. It was one of his busiest nights, and he usually had four or five people working, even at eleven o'clock.

Gina wasn't scheduled to work that night, but she sat at a corner table and waved him over. As he meandered through the crowd, he locked in on Gina's pierced appendages, high cheekbones, and striking eyes. He didn't see Kim or Dennis in that face, and certainly didn't see Kim in the dark hair.

"Surprise," she said as John sat across from her.

He couldn't help but snicker. Okay, he could definitely see Kim in Gina's personality. She was sweet, sincere, honest, fun-loving, and in spite of her rebellious appearance, the type of Christian he could only aspire to be. "I take it this isn't a coincidence you work here?"

"Oh, I don't know. I'm an experienced barista, so that's a coincidence."

John raised his eyebrows.

"But I did seek you out."

"Why."

"Because I knew all about you. And I wanted to meet the man my mom was going to marry."

"Whoa."

"I found out about you when Kim's mom gave me her diary. She said she'd only recently gone through a box of Kim's things, and she found the diary." She pulled a faded, cloth-bound journal from her big purse. The denim cover was dotted with tiny red and yellow flowers.

John's heart lodged in his throat. He sat on his hand to keep from grabbing it.

"She really loved you." Gina's eyes dimmed. She set the diary on the table and pushed it across to John. "I want you to read it. Take your time, read it, copy it, whatever. Then give it back to me. Okay?"

"Sure." He picked up the frayed journal and rubbed his fingers across the stitched-on flowers. Unshed tears clouded his vision. "Thanks, Gina."

John's phone buzzed in his pocket. After a quick look at the number he said, "I'm sorry, but I need to take this."

Gina nodded and gave him a quick hug before returning to the counter.

"What's up, Brad? You're calling awfully late."

"Sergio called. He took his wife to the hospital." Brad's voice sounded strained. "He asked me to find someone tonight to preach on Sunday. I've made half a dozen phone calls already, and I thought of you. You know lots of people. Any ideas?"

A chill rushed through John's body. Would he get an opportunity to preach?

His words to a fourteen-year-old Kim came back to him. *"You might think I'm crazy, but being a pastor always appealed to me."* Then he became a pastor in his thirty-year-old fantasy life. Maybe a failed pastor, yet the knowledge he gained from it remained. He still knew how to perform a funeral and a wedding. Spanish was still fresh in his mind. Most of all, he knew now that he strayed from the straight and narrow path and needed God's grace just like everyone else.

Could he effectively counsel others? Perhaps so. And something told him that buried in with his knowledge of how to put together a sermon he would find a wealth of biblical information.

John smiled to himself. Maybe he'd lived his fantasy lives for more than just to put to rest a twenty-year-old mystery. If he liked preaching at the mission church, maybe he'd take an on-line class or two at a Christian university and see how it went. The possibilities swirled through his mind as he told Brad, "Tell Sergio I might know somebody."

* * *

John waved goodbye to the last of the employees to leave and locked the door behind them. His head still swam from everything that happened today. He needed some time to sort it all out. He slid into a seat at a tall, round table, set Kim's diary out in front of him, and savored the silence.

He did a quick review of the amazing events of the last several months, but all the highlights fell flat. So what if he got to relive a high school dream, be an athletic prodigy, and date the cutest girl? So what if he was given the opportunity to lead and minister to a congregation? In each of those fantasies, other lives had been destroyed.

On the other side, he'd had the opportunity to see Kim again. An opportunity as real as his son's thick head of hair. Reliving his life had allowed Ray Pope to be caught, and it had rejuvenated John.

He rubbed a hand across the cover of Kim's diary. He had a piece of Kim to treasure. No, two pieces. He smiled at the memory of Gina saying "Surprise."

John let his gaze wander around The Coffee Beast. He loved The Beast. He'd poured everything into it. Maybe too much. It was his career and his job, but it shouldn't be his life. He had a beautiful wife and two precious children who needed him. And now he'd be helping out at the Spanish mission.

It came to him suddenly that he no longer had any regrets. His life might not be perfect— and it never would be—but life never turns out the way you expect it. You couldn't change the past, you shouldn't hope for the past. He'd gotten a glimpse of his, and hindsight wasn't 20/20. Different choices created different problems.

For the first time since Kim disappeared, John looked squarely ahead to the future instead of living with one foot in the past. And he liked what he saw.

Epilogue

October 4, 1992
Dear Diary,

I'm scared. John is going to ask me to marry him. And I'm going to say yes. No, I don't know when, but I know he will. I want to spend the rest of my life with him. I guess I'm afraid he's going to ask me to marry him before I can tell him the truth. I don't think it'll change his mind. In fact, I think he'll love me even more. He's that kind of person.

When you become pregnant at the age of fifteen, it changes you. My parents supported me every step of the way, and so did my church. For me, I never considered keeping the baby. It just didn't make sense; I wasn't ready for that responsibility. I carried the baby to term, delivered, and surrendered her to the Baileys. Then I lost track of them. Everyone told me it should be that way. If you give your baby up for adoption, it's best to let go.

My romantic relationship with Dennis lasted about as long as it took to get me pregnant. Amazingly, we've sort of remained friends, even though our lives have gone in opposite directions. He's been hosting keg parties for college kids, and I've been, I guess you could say, on the straight and narrow.

I now spend all my morning devotional time asking God what I should do about the baby. When should I tell John? Wait, she's not a baby any more. She's seven years old.

And I now have an incredible opportunity, an incredible answer to prayer, a chance to spend time with her.

The Baileys have always been nice to me. I'm still shocked that they've asked me if I'd consider being a babysitter for Gina. It's a big decision. I'll have to quit my job on campus.

And I'll have to tell John.

God's grace has served me well, and I'll have to count on it again. John and I have followed God's path for our lives, and that is going to be tested now.

I think I'll tell him after he goes to the OU-Texas football game. I want him to have fun, and I don't want to burden him with the fact that I'm a mother until he comes back.

Ten years from now, I'll look back on this and laugh. John and I will have kids of our own. We'll have a small house with a beagle in the backyard and a cat in the house. We'll both be so happy.

Dear reader,

I hope you enjoyed my story as much as I enjoyed writing it. If you want to help spread the word about it, please leave a review at Amazon, ChristianBook.com, or Goodreads (or all of them) and be sure to recommend it to your friends!

Want to hear when my next book comes out? Be sure to sign up for my newsletter at BillGarrisonAuthor.com.

Until the next one!

Bill Garrison

Made in the USA
Charleston, SC
07 October 2014